Harvest Moon

LISA
KESSLER

Entangled Publishing, LLC
2614 South Timberline Road
Suite 109
Fort Collins, CO 80525
Visit our website at www.entangledpublishing.com.

Select Otherworld is an imprint of Entangled Publishing, LLC.

Edited by Liz Pelletier
Cover design by Heather Howland
Cover art from iStock

Manufactured in the United States of America

First Edition September 2015

For Amber —
I'm so lucky to have you as my best friend for over thirty years.
Through everything, we've still got the Eye of the Tiger!
This one is for you, Amb!

Chapter One

"Night, Dr. Ayers."

I glanced up from my computer.

My office manager, Therese, gave me a wink. "You've been the last one out for a couple weeks now. Everything all right?"

Damn, "all right" seemed like a pipe dream. "Yeah, I'm fine. Have a great night."

"Anything I can help with?"

I leaned back in my leather executive chair. "I wish you could, but I've got it under control."

"Okay." She nodded, but her eyebrow rose like a natural lie detector. "I don't mind staying."

"Nah, I'm almost done anyway." I forced a smile. "See you in the morning."

She nodded and stepped back as the door closed,

swaddling me in the silence. I flexed my bruised right hand and then fisted it, working out the stiffness in my joints. Tiger, my opponent last night, had an iron jaw, and I'd slammed too many jabs into it.

The welcomed pain kept me anchored in the present. Reminded me I was alive. Lately, I needed all the reminders I could get.

My cell phone alarm beeped. I had to take another bag of fluids and liquid nutrition over to my parents' place for my dad. A knock sounded at the door.

I got up and opened it. At first I stared right over the top of her head, before I shifted my focus lower. A nurse dressed in jungle-themed scrubs narrowed her dark eyes, tipping her chin up in my direction. Her arms were crossed over her chest, and one hip jutted out to the side. Her black hair sat on top of her head in a loose bun, and her flawless tan skin glowed with life.

Although she stood barely over five feet tall, her stance made it clear she expected my respect.

She also looked vaguely familiar. "Can I help you?"

"I hope so. Two weeks ago I assisted you in reviving a man who'd been injected with potassium chloride. I was just informed the patient was never checked into the medical center. I'd like to know why."

Damn it. This was the nurse who'd helped me save my father's life. Or at least get his heart beating again. Whether or not he actually had a "life" anymore was up for debate.

"I'd give you an answer if I could, but my hands are tied. Patient privacy regulations." I could almost smell the bullshit coming out of my mouth. "I can tell you he's feeling much better thanks to your help."

"Enough with the elitist doctor double-talk." She swiped her hand in the air and placed a fist on her shapely hip. "I've got to record the medications we used on your patient. If he's not admitted, I can't do that. I could get fired over the missing medicine, and I *need* this job. So save your privacy line for someone who gives a crap. Now what the hell happened to that man?"

Elitist doctor double-talk? I almost laughed.

"I'm sorry if you're in hot water over the insulin and glucose." What was her name? My brain replayed that evening. She had told me, but I'd been so wrapped up in trying to save my dad I couldn't recall it now. "I'll come by tomorrow and talk to the head nurse for you. I'm sure I can get it straightened out."

"And you'll tell them you're there on behalf of..." She waited. I didn't attempt to guess her name. She rolled her eyes. "You don't even remember my name, do you?" I opened my mouth to apologize, but she went on before I could get a word in. "Typical. I'm Kilani."

Kilani. Beautiful name. Polynesian, maybe?

"Are you listening to me?"

Shit. "Yeah, I'm listening."

She shook her head, her gaze holding mine. "You know what, never mind. I'll handle this on my own. The last thing I need is a guy who can't even remember my name to be poking around the hospital to 'help' me."

Spinning on her heel, she walked away. I went out the door after her. "Kilani, wait."

She stopped but didn't turn in my direction.

"I'm not usually such an ass."

Her shoulders relaxed a little and she faced me again.

"Most doctors don't apologize."

The doctor jibes were starting to get to me. "That *patient* is my father."

"I remember." She nodded. "That's why I was so surprised you didn't admit him. I don't know what your relationship with your dad is like, but you of all people should understand he needs twenty-four-hour care. He could have brain damage or…"

"God damn it. You don't think I know that?" I yelled, and I didn't give a shit. If anyone on earth understood how dire my dad's situation was, it was me. And if I could, I'd have him in the hospital, but my dad was also a werewolf, and one blood sample in the wrong hands could expose our race to humans.

I might be the Pack doctor, but I couldn't offer them the best treatment because it always came back to exposure. What good was my medical degree when my hands were tied? The medical center's equipment could help my father—but it could also prove to the human world that werewolves existed.

We couldn't risk it, even if it meant I might lose my dad.

"I'm giving him better care than he would get in a hospital, so spare me your judgment." I forced in a slow breath and lowered my voice a couple of notches. "I'm sorry if you're in trouble over the missing medication. I meant what I said about talking to the head nurse for you to smooth it over."

"No thanks." She put her hands up. "Nothing *you* could give me would be of help. I hope, for your father's sake, he has a full recovery."

She walked back toward the atrium that connected the

medical office building with the hospital next door. Her hips swayed in a natural motion. Her job was at risk now. My fault.

"Kilani, wait."

She didn't slow and she didn't answer. In another minute, she was gone.

I'd been an asshole to the one person who'd helped me keep my dad's heart beating. And the hits just kept coming.

The sour scent of sweat and blood stung my nostrils as I taped my knuckles. In the center of the makeshift boxing ring, the two titans clobbered each other in a bid to face me next. As reigning champ of the underground fight club, they all wanted a shot at my title.

Boxing had started as a fitness regimen. I enjoyed training and sparring, but after Adam's father, our Alpha, died because I couldn't get him into an operating room to stop his internal bleeding, an unfamiliar fire smoldered in my gut and sparring didn't relieve the pressure.

In a sick way, I wanted to be pummeled—punished for the blood on my hands. I also wanted to beat the shit out of something. A stupid risk for a doctor to batter his hands in a gladiator's sport, but ever since one of the guys in the locker room of the club whispered a veiled invitation to me, I couldn't seem to quit.

"Hey Wolf, need help with your gloves?"

We didn't have names down here. Not the names on our birth certificates anyway. In the underground fight club world, I was just Wolf. And I liked it.

I glanced up at Marv and nodded. "Sure. Thanks, buddy."

Marv was a big guy, about my age, but his mild autism always made him seem younger. His older brother, Todd, ran the fight club, and Marv tagged along, helping as much as he could.

I held my hand out while he tugged the gloves on. I had taped it tight, but in spite of the added support, my joints still ached as he pulled the glove over them. I probably should've taken some X-rays, but I was too far gone for that. Just forcing myself to sit out a night or two to heal was getting tough.

Even if I found broken bones, I wouldn't stop fighting. I couldn't.

This ring was my sanity now. Without it, I'd go crazy with the guilt and frustration that festered inside of me. Here, reality narrowed into a bloodstained twelve-foot-by-twelve-foot boxing ring. Facing opponents, landing punches, and taking them were all actions I controlled. In the ring, I was the master of my own fate. I couldn't save Malcolm, our Alpha, and now my father's life hung in the balance. I'd had my fill of feeling useless.

Here, my destiny rested in my own hands, mine to direct. This ring and these fighters gave me that.

"Those tight enough, Wolf?"

I punched my hands together, testing the support around my wrists. "Feels great, Marv." I rubbed his head with a gloved hand. "Thanks, buddy."

He grinned, sheepish about the praise. "Good luck tonight. I know you'll win."

"That's the plan." I started warming up, jogging in place and windmilling my arms to loosen up my sore shoulders.

After Malcolm's death, I'd been fighting once a month, but since Nero attacked my father, I'd been accepting as many matches as I had challengers. The beatings were catching up with me, but sore muscles and joints weren't going to keep me from my sanctuary in the ring.

The big guy who went by the moniker "Pirate" tumbled to the ground. Roddy, our ref, started the count while Shark backed away, his cold stare on my face. Hunger burned in his eyes. Every fighter here had demons. God only knew what powered this hulk of a man. In spite of fighting an earlier match and now besting Pirate, this big Hispanic guy still had some fire left.

That was good. He'd need a goddamned inferno to best me.

Since the altercation with Kilani, my frustration levels had skyrocketed. I'd been a dick to her, and her only crime had been to help save my father. I hadn't even remembered her name.

If that wasn't enough, my father's vitals revealed his temperature was slightly elevated. I'd need to bring him some intravenous antibiotics and hope for the best. A bad bladder infection or bed sores were both common ways to cause organs to shut down in bedridden comatose patients.

Foreboding, and an all too familiar lack of control, roiled in my gut. My opponent might be hungry for a win, but I was famished. Something in my life would be a victory.

Sorry Shark, I wasn't going down tonight. No chance.

Roddy grabbed his glove, raising it over his head. "Winner! Shark in the fifth round."

Cheers and the hum of activity filled the space. The tiny crowd of spectators consisted of other fighters and a few regulars who were once fighters and now turned to small-time wagering. Cash changed hands, notes were scribbled on pages, and Shark paraded around the ring, high on adrenaline.

I watched him as I shadow-boxed, warming my muscles. We were both about six foot two inches, so our reach would be well matched. He looked like he outweighed me by maybe twenty pounds, so on paper he'd have more power behind his punches.

On paper.

No one in the club knew werewolves existed, let alone that I was one.

But my wolf wasn't the power behind these punches. Rage, pure and undiluted, fueled my inner fire. And nothing released the pressure like a good fight.

Shark narrowed his eyes, his jaw jutting forward as he paced the ring. I'd only seen the last couple of rounds of his fight with Pirate, but it had been enough. Shark was a southpaw. I'd have to keep protecting my eye while I went in with my right. A good southpaw could clock you with a left hand if you gave him that opening.

I rolled my head, then my shoulders, while I danced on the balls of my feet. My gaze never strayed from Shark's face. Even when he turned away, the first thing he saw when he faced me again was my stare. No fear. Only hunger.

Without breaking eye contact, I climbed in the ring. My wolf clawed to the surface, sensing a battle for dominance. The full moon was still a few weeks away. No threat of shifting into a wolf with an audience, but I welcomed his predatory instincts.

We met in the center of the ring, face-to-face, while

Roddy barked out his usual reminders. No low blows, no head butts, and once a fighter was down, you waited for the count over in your corner. We knocked gloves and went to our corners. There weren't any stools, no trainers to sponge you down, only a fresh towel to wipe away blood and a fresh rubber mouth guard. I popped mine in, grinding my teeth while I awaited the bell.

The *ding* set us moving toward the center of the ring. Shark came in like a freight train. He jabbed my ribs with his right, nudging me toward the ropes. I countered with an uppercut to his jaw, knocking him back a couple of steps. He shook his head, snarling around his yellow mouthpiece, and came back at me, landing a combination to my midsection that knocked the air from my lungs.

Strong opponent. Good.

I blinked, stoking the fire inside of me. This was no longer a man in the gym. This wasn't a man at all. This was a fight with fate and destiny. I landed a right and a left to his body for my father's fever. He stumbled back toward the ropes and I pursued, landing a jab to his chin for my mother's heartbreak over caring for her husband who might never speak to her again.

Left, right, to the body, to the head. He put his hands up to block my attack to his face, so I concentrated on his body; each punch became a retribution for my inability to save Malcolm, my inability to wake my father. Every bad choice I had made in the last year, I pummeled into Shark's body.

His big hands shoved at my shoulders and I lost my balance, jogging back a few steps to steady myself. Shark heaved for breath while I waved him forward, inviting his attack. I wasn't ready for the fight to end. Not yet. His punches, the pain they brought, were a penance for my failures, a reminder to keep fighting.

The bell rang. I wiped my face and waited for round two, watching Shark struggle to catch his breath. Marv came by with a water bottle and a bucket. I took the water and winked at him. "Thanks."

He grinned. "You're doing good, Wolf."

I swished the water around and spit into the bucket as the bell rang again. Shark came on the attack before I got out of my corner. His right hand was relentless, pummeling my abs until my entire body ached. I lowered my elbows to block his attack, and his left hand clocked me in the eye.

Stars lit around the edge of my vision. I bit down on my mouthpiece, forcing myself to stay upright. I landed a couple of unfocused blows, trying to break out of the corner where he had me pinned. Shark's knee slammed into my balls. Hard. It was all I could do to stay on my feet and not curl into the fetal position on the floor.

Shark backed away with a glint in his eyes.

"No low blows, Shark!" Roddy yelled. "Next time you're out."

Oh, there wasn't going to be a goddamned next time.

I rushed him, slamming him back into the ropes. He couldn't escape my attack, trapped by a flurry of punches. My attack to his ribs had him breathless, and when he started to stumble sideways, I caught him, pinning him upright in the corner so I could hit his face. Again and again. Right, left, right.

"Okay, Wolf. Enough." Roddy forced his way between my prey and me. "Damn it, Wolf, I'm callin' the fight. Back off."

I stumbled backward and Shark timbered onto the floor.

Oh shit. I'd lost myself to this dark pit eating away at my sanity. What the hell was I doing? Regardless of the beating this guy gave me or the kick to the balls, I had to help him.

His pulse thumped in a steady rhythm I had no trouble hearing with my heightened senses, but blood ran from a cut over his eye, and his nose and lip bled onto the mat. There was also a better than average chance he had a nasty concussion. I rushed over, tearing at the ties on my gloves with my teeth as Roddy counted down.

Ripping the glove off my right hand, I called to Marv. "Get me some ice and a clean towel."

Roddy declared my victory while I pressed ice to the back of Shark's neck. He groaned. Conscious.

Marv took over holding the ice pack on Shark's skull, and I got up and out of the ring. Alone in my locker room, I rested my head in my hands. Every fight, it took more blood and more pain to quench the fire. I could've killed that man. Where was the line in the sand? Aggression and anger were changing me into someone I didn't recognize. I'd taken an oath to preserve life. This…this club, these nameless fighters…I was far from my calling.

Tremors racked my usually steady hands.

I was spiraling out of control, and I didn't have a fucking clue how to stop it.

Chapter Two

It had been hours since my run-in with Dr. Ayers. Why couldn't I let it go?

I stuffed my scrubs into the overloaded hamper by the door, kicked off my sandals, and dropped my keys into the hollowed-out coconut shell on the table. Exhaustion weighed on me, but my stomach's demands for food kept me from collapsing on the easy chair. I scanned the fridge for something that was both simple to prepare and not spoiled.

Neither existed.

I slammed the refrigerator closed and snatched a banana from the fruit basket on the counter. Drawing the peel down, I wandered back into the main room of my studio apartment. My first bite drew a groan of delight. Either I was starving or this was the all-time best banana ever consumed on the planet.

Mid-bite, I sank into the chair and reached for the remote, ignoring the looming laundry basket. The trip to the Laundromat around the corner was imminent, but I could relax for a little bit first. The washing machines would be busy right now anyway. If I waited a couple of hours, the families should be gone. The last thing I needed was awkward conversations while folding my underwear. After all, I was supposed to be laying low in this town, not building a new network of friends.

But I couldn't put it off another day or my hamper was going to have a blowout.

The channels flipped by as I clicked the remote. Habit, I guess. I didn't even want to watch anything, not really. What I wanted was to be distracted from replaying my conversation with Dr. Ayers.

The guy had a chiseled jaw and light hazel eyes that demanded your attention. Not to mention his loose-fitting doctor's smock couldn't begin to hide the well-built body underneath. But his gorgeous exterior wasn't what haunted me.

I'd been at his side while his father lay on the ground without a pulse. I'd witnessed him working with no regard for himself or anyone else, his only concern, his full attention, resting solely on saving his dad's life. Moments like that revealed true character, true self, and although he never surrendered to panic, he'd radiated guilt, worry, and a quiet confidence.

Acceptance of his position, his responsibility.

But in spite of all that, Dr. Ayers didn't admit his father to the hospital for treatment. It didn't make sense.

None of my business. But if the head nurse traced the missing meds back to me, I'd be out on my ass. I should've been focused on keeping my job, not pondering what might be going on in Dr. Ayers's mind.

My cell phone rang. I glanced over at my bag on the table while my tired body whined about letting the call go to voicemail. My aching muscles shut the hell up when my extrasensory abilities realized who was on the other end of the line.

My psychic ability to see into the future sounded like a handy tool, but it came with a huge catch. I could only see a couple of minutes ahead, and they were sporadic. Pretty useless, unless you were a nurse. Being able to know and anticipate what a patient needed before the doctor asked for it made me a commodity in hospitals.

It had also been my ticket to freedom, to getting off the island.

I scrambled up and grabbed my phone without wasting a second to check the caller ID. "Sebastian?"

"Kilani. We don't have much time."

The banana in my stomach turned to rock. "They're here, aren't they?"

"Your name came up on the weekly target list."

"That sounds bad." I stared at the ceiling, blinking back tears. "I don't even know what Nero really is. I'm no threat. It's not like I'm going to say anything. Not that I'd have any proof anyway."

"You found Grace's body. You're a loose end now." The phone rattled and his voice dropped in volume. "They have an entire country to search, Kilani. You should be safe for now. The last place they'd look is in Reno."

"How can you be so sure?"

He cleared his throat. "Nero has enemies in Reno. That's

why I sent you there. You remember where to go if you sense trouble?"

"Yeah." I nodded. "I still don't understand why a horse ranch would be safer than going to the police, but I trust you."

Silence. Did he hang up? I checked my phone. It said connected.

"Trust is what got Grace killed. Trust no one, least of all me."

My pulse thrummed, my mind tumbling toward panic. "You're not inspiring confidence."

"Good. Be aware and watch. I do not want your blood on my hands, too."

Blood. Everywhere. All over the bathroom mirror, the sink, the floor. And still I'd checked her for a pulse, nurse until the end. I clamped my eyes shut, tight, struggling to wipe from my thoughts the memory of discovering Grace's body.

"You said Reno would be the last place. Where will they look first?" I didn't want to hear the answer, but I had to.

"Hawaii. A team left last night."

"Grandma Nani." My legs wobbled.

"She doesn't know where you are."

"What if they hurt her?" My throat closed on a silent sob.

Sebastian paused. I'd found my roommate, his girlfriend, disemboweled in our bathroom. If anyone knew what Nero was capable of, it was me.

"They were ordered to kill Grace. Their orders are to gather information this time."

It didn't sneak by me that he didn't deny they might hurt my grandmother. "I've got to warn her."

"If you make contact, they'll find you. I've done all I can. Don't render my efforts useless."

The line went dead. I swiped the screen to call history, but Sebastian's number was blocked. Damn it. My grandmother wasn't defenseless. She'd been a respected Kahuna on the islands for most of her adult life, quietly passing the ancient island traditions and beliefs to the families who came to her.

I'd been too hardheaded to listen. Young and certain I had all the answers. Too late now.

She'd have no warning if I didn't think of something soon. I got up, pacing the room like a caged animal while my mind whirled. There had to be some way to alert her about the potential danger. I glanced at my bare feet and stopped, staring at the turtle tattoo on my ankle. The *honu*, sea turtle, was the *aumakua* for our family, our protector. They were also messengers through dreams and visions.

Not that I truly believed it, but I was desperate. At this point, I'd be willing to give just about anything a shot.

I dug my iPod out of my bag and spun the dial until I found my stash of Neil Diamond songs. Grandma Nani was his number-one fan on the island. I used to roll my eyes while she belted out "Song Sung Blue" or "Sweet Caroline," but as the distance and years grew between us, I started buying his songs and discovering fond memories of home.

Now I hoped it would help me connect with our *honu*. My grandmother used to get visions and prophetic dreams often. Maybe I could send her one.

Suddenly, I wished I'd paid more attention when she tried to teach me, instead of fighting every step of the way like a stubborn mule.

With my ear buds in place, I laid on my futon and closed

my eyes. In the darkness, "Play Me" started. In my mind, Grandma Nani sang. I concentrated on every angle of her face, her long silver hair, and the deep lines from years of smiles that framed her dark eyes. A single tear leaked down my cheek as I made her image as clear as possible. My chest tightened, my heart clenching.

God, I missed her.

I pulled in a deep, slow breath, silently calling to our *honu*. The tattoo on my ankle glided through the inky depths of my thoughts. I coaxed it closer, wrapping my fear and worry for my grandmother around his flippers. Gradually, Nero's logo of the proud lion head with an *N* emblazoned in the center, the same emblem I'd seen on the cornerstone of my school and on the inside of Sebastian's wrist, glowed in our *honu*'s giant shell.

Nero is coming. They will lie. Kilani is safe.

The massive turtle turned so his wise eyes met mine. While he didn't speak, his mind touched mine. He would find her, warn her.

And he loved me.

I sat up, tears streaming down my face as a sob choked my throat. I didn't deserve his love. I'd dishonored my family and run as far from them as I could get. How could our ancestors feel anything other than disappointment in me?

I rubbed the tattoo on my ankle and whispered, "Please keep her safe. Tell her I'm sorry. For everything."

The glass doors of the hospital rolled open as I approached. Before I made it across the lobby to the elevators, a familiar cheery voice called, "Mornin', Kelly."

I stopped. Hearing my alias still took me a second to process. I sucked at being undercover. I'd already dropped my real name with Dr. Ayers, too. *Shit.* Slowly, I turned around to find Stan, our volunteer greeter. He grinned, somehow coaxing a smile out of me. After last night, I thought I'd forgotten how.

"You feelin' okay, lass? Look a bit under the weather."

Stan was a widower, my first friend when I started here a few weeks ago. Although he was from Ireland, his wife had been a Nevada native, and after he lost her, he decided to stay.

"I'm okay, just didn't get much sleep." *Any* was more like it, but I didn't want him to worry.

"This place workin' you too hard?" He winked, and I nearly laughed in spite of the funk that had its claws buried in me.

"No rest for the wicked."

"Bah." He swiped at the air. "Not a wicked bone in your body."

I stepped into the elevator and waved. "See you later, Stan."

On the fourth floor, I walked out and froze. Dr. Ayers and my head nurse both turned in unison. He glanced at me and back to my boss. "That's Kilani right there. Remember her now?"

Candace, the head nurse, raised a brow. "You mean Kelly Jones?"

"Kelly?" He almost flinched at the force of my *I'm-pissed-at-you* frown. Taking the hint, he faced Candace again. "Oh, Kelly. I must've misheard. My mistake."

"And she's the one who assisted you with a non-hospital patient?"

Oh shit, he was making it monumentally worse. I hustled over. "It wasn't like that."

Candace crossed her arms over her chest. "How *exactly* did you give him a full dose of glucose and insulin for a patient we don't have admitted here?"

I opened my mouth, but Dr. Ayers beat me to it. "I take full responsibility. I had a patient in the medical office building who suffered from a potassium-induced arrhythmia. It was an urgent situation, and without Kelly's prompt assistance, I probably would've lost him. I'm happy to sign off on the medication. My office can pay the hospital for it."

She relaxed a little, but my pulse rate did not. "That's a serious life-threatening event. Why wasn't he admitted?"

"His health insurance," he replied without hesitation. "He's not covered in this facility."

She cocked a brow. And I tried not to stare at Dr. Ayers. He hadn't mentioned health insurance or a hospital yesterday. He also didn't tell Candace that the "patient" was his father. Apparently I wasn't the only one in this hallway with secrets.

"Fine." She sighed. "You pay for the meds and sign off for their use and we should be covered." She turned toward me, her lips tightening. "You're new here, Kelly, so I'll chalk this one up to not knowing better. If you ever pull a stunt like this again, you'll be out. Are we clear?"

"Crystal."

She nodded and walked away. I glanced up at him and frowned. I'd been so angry when I saw him talking to my boss, I hadn't noticed the cut over his eye. Now that I was closer, I could see the discolored skin around the wound.

"What happened to you?"

He reached up but stopped short from touching his eyebrow. "Hit my head. I'm fine."

"Or someone else hit it for you. More than once." I lowered my voice. "You didn't tell me your father was at another hospital."

"Yeah, well, you didn't tell me you have a different name on this side of the building, either." He slid a hand into his pocket.

I rolled my eyes. "Fine. We're even. Thanks for paying for the meds."

"Thanks for helping me save my dad." He turned to go and stopped. "I'm taking my lunch at noon. Will you let me buy you some food? It's the least I can do."

A red alert screeched in my head. Doctors and I didn't mix. Two doctors had already stomped all over my heart leading to my pact to never trust another one. Besides, we were both already bending the truth.

There was no point in pretending we weren't both liars.

"Sorry. My lunch hour isn't until one o'clock."

"Oh." He nodded. "I understand. Maybe next time."

"Maybe."

He walked away, and I released a breath. Whatever he was hiding, I shouldn't get involved. And more importantly, I shouldn't want to.

Chapter Three

I stretched out my fingers. Typing prescriptions on my iPad didn't used to be painful. "Used to be" was a dangerous road to travel. My dad didn't used to be in a coma, my brother and I used to be close, and I used to heal people with these hands, not beat the crap out of them.

The fight club had to stop. At least for a while. Until the joints in my hands quit throbbing. Damn it. What was happening to me? I couldn't keep abusing my body like this. Eventually permanent damage would set in.

But in the end, what would it matter? I got up and crossed to the mirror hanging on my closed office door. The cut over my eyebrow was beginning to discolor around the edges. I'd need to ice it again tonight. Werewolves healed a little faster than humans, but we weren't Superman. I could get a nasty shiner just as easily as the next guy.

Resting my forearms on either side of the mirror, I stared into my own eyes. I didn't recognize the man staring back at me. The man in the reflection wore his pain in the cut over his eye, the swelling in his hands, the bruises lurking under his shirt, lining his rib cage. As his doctor, I'd recommend a counseling session with a therapist right away.

But therapy only worked if you were honest with your therapist. I couldn't sit on a couch and admit werewolves existed, any more than I could explain my father was attacked because I was so desperate to save a woman's life that I got into bed with the enemy.

Even after my dad warned me of the danger from Dr. Granger, I thought I could handle it. Maybe I did suffer from a god complex like Kilani claimed plagued every doctor.

Kilani. But the hospital thought her name was Kelly Jones. I would bet Jones was no more legitimate than Kelly. So what was she hiding?

Not my problem.

Being a part of the fight club was a mistake, but out of all the aspects of my life right now, boxing provided the only release from the worry and regret swirling inside my soul like a tempest. I couldn't give it up completely. Not right now.

A knock came from the other side of the door, jolting me back into reality. I straightened up, paused a second, and opened the door.

"Dr. Ayers? Everything all right?" Therese's stare pinned me down, concern lining her forehead.

"Why wouldn't it be?"

She shrugged, but her intensity didn't waver. "It doesn't usually take you two hours to give me the prescriptions to call in; you normally go out and eat during your lunch hour;

and don't even get me started on that shiner."

"This?" I touched the wound over my eye a little harder than I intended and fought to keep from wincing. "I just hit my head on the corner of a cabinet. I'm fine."

She crossed her arms, her hip tilting out slightly. "I know a black eye when I see one. The cabinet must've hit you more than once."

I walked over and leaned against the edge of my desk, taking a second to pull my thoughts together. "I've got a lot on my mind right now, but I'll be all right."

She softened her stance, allowing her arms to drop to her sides. "You've got broad shoulders and a big heart, but you don't need to pile all the weight up there alone. We can all help carry the burden, whatever it is."

Now there was a wishful thought. "I appreciate your concern, Therese. My dad is having some health issues, and I can't figure out how to heal him. I'm a doctor. I should be able to cure him."

"Being a doctor doesn't mean you can fix everything. Sometimes you just need a little faith. If your daddy is half as strong as the boy he raised, he'll come through this. Be patient and believe in him. Maybe I can help with—"

"No." I pushed up from the desk and walked behind it to grab my tablet. "Thanks, but we've got him plenty of care." I scrolled through the new prescriptions and hit send. "You should have the 'scrips now."

She took my hint and turned to go. "My offer still stands. Better to talk to a friend than get yourself beat in a bar brawl."

The door closed behind her. A bar fight would be easier to explain than my membership in an underground fight club.

I glanced out the window as I rounded the corner of my desk. A few floors down, a woman crossed the parking lot wearing scrubs with a mound of untamable long black hair on top of her head. Kilani. I stepped closer to the glass as she tugged a stick out of her hair and it fell down in one silky wave. She shook her head and ran her fingers through her hair before lifting the hatchback of a silver economy car. She hopped in the back and sat cross-legged, popping off her shoes and opening a mini cooler.

Forcing myself away from the window, I sank into my chair. Voyeurism wasn't usually my thing. But something about the tiny woman with a fake name eating a picnic lunch barefoot in the back of her economy car fascinated me. Her disinterest in me made me even more curious to discover what made her tick.

So far I'd done a great job pissing her off, but what would make her smile?

This was insane. Maybe it was because she turned me down. Classic case of wanting what you can't have. Basic psychology.

Unable to resist the temptation any longer, I got up and leaned against the side of my office window, studying her. She bit into an apple, reading a paperback in the other hand. From this distance, even with my heightened werewolf senses, I couldn't make out the title, but the mystery made her even more of a beautiful distraction from the darkness that was currently bleeding into my life.

Suddenly she lowered the book and her dark eyes met mine. My heart stuttered, but I couldn't move my damned feet. Like some kind of creepy Peeping Tom, I remained anchored at the window. Her head tilted slightly before she shook her head and broke eye contact. I spun around and headed for the door. Maybe I could run down there and explain myself. I had no clue what I'd say. *I know I lied to you before, but I really wasn't spying on you.*

Yeah, she'd love that. *Shit.*

"Dr. Ayers, are you going someplace?"

Therese busted into my mental smackdown, stopping me in my tracks. I frowned. "I was going to run down and grab a sandwich or something."

She sat in front of her computer screen and shook her head. "Your lunch was over a half hour ago. Mr. Norton is waiting for you in room three with an elevated temp and possible ear infection."

I glanced at the clock on the wall. She was right. I wasn't going anywhere. "Any cancelations this afternoon?"

She clicked her mouse a few times and sighed. "Not at this point. You're full until four o'clock."

And then I needed to get to my parents' place to check on my dad. Apparently I wouldn't be explaining myself to Kilani today. But really, what the hell could I say? Besides, she made it pretty clear she didn't have any interest in me.

Maybe if I hadn't taken so many punches to the head recently I would've realized the best course of action was to walk away from this one.

Mr. Norton did have an infection in both ears, but nothing a heavy round of antibiotics couldn't clear up. The rest of my day passed in a blur with a case of bronchitis, an annual physical, a crushed finger from a car door, and one sprained wrist. I didn't mind. For a few hours, I had a respite from thinking about the nurse who ate lunch barefoot in the parking lot.

I stretched my aching fingers and grabbed my tablet and keys before leaving my office. The late afternoon sun lit the empty patient waiting room in spite of the lights being off. The computer was off, and the magazines on the table were freshly stacked. Therese had left a few minutes before. After a last look around, I entered the alarm code and exited the building.

Walking through the parking lot, I noticed Kilani's car even though I was trying not to look for it. Obviously, I was way overdue for a date. I hadn't been out with a woman since Nadya.

Shit, this was *not* a path on memory lane I wanted to wander down again.

I pulled into my folks' driveway, parked, and stared at the house. I didn't want to go inside. It had been weeks since his heart stopped. And although I got it beating again, every day that my father remained unconscious brought me one step closer to a conversation I never wanted to have with my mom and my brother. If Dad was brain dead, there was no point in continuing his care. He and my mom had been together for decades. How in the hell was I going to look her in the eyes and tell her he was already gone?

The front door opened as I finally got out. I expected my mom, not my twin brother, Jared. I ground my teeth together, mentally preparing myself for whatever he might throw my way. Until recently, we'd been best friends, twin brothers, and pack mates.

We were still twins and pack mates, but that was it.

"Hey Jared."

"Jason." He nodded and headed for his truck, but he

glanced my way and stopped in his tracks. "What the hell happened to your face?"

"I hit my head. Nothing serious."

He stared at his pickup, his fists clenched at his sides. "Bullshit." His eyes cut to me, his lips tight. "Enough with all the bullshit lies."

When I'd brought the scientist from Nero into Reno to help save Nadya, I hadn't told anyone, not even Jared. My dad had found out on accident and ended up paying the price.

"I've been doing some boxing in my off hours. Happy now?"

"Ever heard of wearing protective headgear?" He crossed his arms, studying me. "Not wise for a doctor to fight. Even if you win, you beat your hands all to hell, right? And if you lose, you end up with head trauma."

Jared was older than me by less than three minutes, but ever since we were little he'd always tried to protect me as if he were years my senior. As the distance between us expanded, I'd almost forgotten.

"I'm fine. And in case you're curious, I won."

He chuckled but didn't smile. "Winning and losing won't matter if you can't use your hands or remember your name."

I groaned, struggling to keep my emotions in check. This was the most my brother had said to me in weeks. "I can take care of myself. I'm careful."

"Your eye says otherwise. Corner of your mouth is swollen, too. Bet you're also nursing some bruised ribs."

"I didn't come here for counseling, I came to treat Dad. How's he doing?"

"His heart's beating."

I nodded, pain twisting in my chest. My mistake with Nero tore my entire family apart. Cost me everything. I cleared my throat, but my voice was still softer than I intended. "I want to make things right."

Jared set his jaw and took a couple steps toward his truck. "Not sure that's possible."

"I never meant for him to get hurt."

"You think that's what this is about?" He stopped and turned around, eyes narrowed. "You're my brother. You'd lay down your life for your family. But you fucked up, Jason. Hell, we all do it. What pisses me off is this goddamned lying. I could've helped you or protected Dad. But I didn't get the chance. Shit, I didn't even know you brought Nero back into Reno. You kept me in the dark." He let his words die away before pulling in a slow breath. "I could never cut you out of my life, and I don't know how to handle knowing you did it to me."

Until now, I hadn't realized I could feel even shittier. I stared at my brother. Our features were the same, but his outdoor carpentry work left his skin a deeper tan and he wore his hair a little longer. He stood, stoic, waiting for me to answer.

What the hell could I say?

"I'm an asshole." Not what I'd planned to start with, but it was the truth. "I wanted to tell you, but I was so worried about Nadya…"

"She's Gareth's mate. Not yours."

"Oh, please." Rage bled into the well of guilt, brewing up a pint of bitterness in my gut. "You don't believe in those old Pack legends. There is no physically possible way you could touch someone's skin one time and know you're mates for life. It's a pathetic myth to get young Pack members to settle down and reproduce so the Pack doesn't die out."

"If we believed everything in those medical textbooks, then werewolves couldn't exist either, but here we are."

"That's a physiological condition that can be mapped in our DNA. Relationships aren't part of our physical makeup."

He shrugged. "I've seen what it did to Adam and Aren when they found their mates. And look at Gareth… I'm not ready to write it off as fiction." He came a little closer. "None of this explains your lies and secrets."

"I couldn't tell anyone. If Adam realized…"

"Adam would've sent Dr. Granger packing. You didn't want that to happen, so you cut everyone out. Even me."

"Nadya was dying and I didn't have the time or resources to stop it on my own."

"And in the end, it took her mate to save her anyway."

"Why the hell are you shoving this down my throat? I screwed up. I get it, believe me."

He walked to me, standing eye to eye. "You still won't admit it."

"Admit what?"

"You wanted Nadya for yourself. You wanted her to be yours so badly you were willing to give up all of us."

"Enough." I ran a hand back through my hair, my gut twisting as I rubbed my brow. Regret strangled me, and my breath caught for a second. "What is it you want me to say?"

"I don't want you to *say* anything." I met his eyes and he added, "I want you to look in the mirror and be honest with yourself. You may not believe in mates, but you wanted one. You wanted one enough to risk everyone you cared about." His expression softened a little. "You're a good guy, Jason, but deep down, you're lonely, and until you're ready to admit it, things aren't going to change."

I shook it off, looking at the door. "It wasn't like that. Nadya is intelligent and beautiful inside and out. Until she touched Gareth and started believing werewolf mates could actually be real, I thought we could be together. I was happy when I was with her."

"Did you love her?"

I sighed, closing my eyes for a second while we ripped off another barely healed emotional scab. "Not yet. But I think I could have. I wanted to."

"But you didn't. Face it, Jason, you've had girlfriends over the years, but have you ever really *loved* any of them?" He pointed at the house. "You're surrounded by strong unions, our folks, and now three of our Pack brothers have found their mates. We've got new children in the Pack. Things are changing around us. It's natural to want what they have."

"You're one to talk. You've never been in love, either."

"True." He nodded. "But I'm not afraid to have a little faith. Maybe my mate is out there, too. I just need to find her."

I raised my eyebrows at his admission. "Since when do you believe in the old Pack legends? Finding your one true mate and recognizing her the second you touch is an impossible dream. It's magic, not reality."

Jared crossed to me, staring into my eyes. "I don't know if you've noticed, but reality sucks ass at the moment. I've got no problem giving magic a shot. What's your excuse?"

I ignored his question. Truth was...I had no idea how to answer, but I'd been told to have faith enough for one day. I clasped my brother's forearms in the traditional Pack greeting and he pulled me in for a tight hug. We stepped back, and a smile tugged at the corner of my mouth.

"Are we good now?"

Jared pressed his lips together for a second. "No more lying?"

"No more."

"Good." He smiled and hooked an arm around my shoulders. "So how about telling me who messed up your face so I can go kick his ass?"

I laughed. I'd forgotten what it sounded like. "I already kicked it, but thanks for the offer."

"I've got your back. Don't forget it." He went to his truck and waved before he started the engine.

He pulled out of the driveway, but my feet stayed planted. When I'd brought Nero in to Reno without telling anyone, it had been to cure Nadya. I didn't think I could heal her, and I couldn't lose her.

My faith in my own abilities was shaken after I couldn't save our Pack Alpha and…and…I was lonely.

I did want a mate.

Holy shit. When did my brother get so damned smart?

Chapter Four

My shift was over, but I had no desire to walk to my car. Anxiety's talons had gripped me ever since the premonition flashed in my mind of Dr. Ayers watching me. It didn't help when I glanced up toward his floor of the medical office building and found him staring back, confirming the precognitive vision.

His earlier lunch proposal didn't seem freaky until I caught him spying on me. Sebastian's words echoed to trust no one. Nero was searching for me. Hospitals would be the first place to look for a nurse. It wouldn't be a long jump in logic to assume they'd pay doctors to spy for them.

And like an idiot, I'd blurted out my real name the day his father's heart stopped. Kilani wasn't a common name, and now that he'd talked to my head nurse, he knew I was using an alias. I scoured my memory for a glimpse of Dr.

Ayers's wrists. If he worked for Nero, he'd have the lion head tattoo with the *N* in the center of the lion's forehead.

Maybe he didn't actually work for them, though. He could just be a watcher, a spy emailing them tips for money. How long until the men who killed Grace showed up for me?

They were probably already on their way.

But I hadn't sensed them yet.

"Everything okay, Kelly?"

I gasped and did my best not to jump. "Hey Todd, are you off for the night, too?"

"Sure am. Want to split a pizza before we pass out?" Todd worked as a nurse on the stroke floor just above mine, but we'd bumped into each other in the cafeteria a few times since I started working here. He seemed nice enough, in a goofy boy-next-door kind of way. Not really my type, if I had a type, but I wasn't really excited to be alone at the moment, either.

I should've been keeping my distance from everyone, but between Sebastian's warning and catching Dr. Ayers spying, my nerves were shot. I'd be careful. It wasn't like Todd and I needed to become best friends, I just needed to get to my car in one piece.

"Sounds great. Where?" I waited. He grinned and his eyes got that she-likes-me-too twinkle. Whoops. I shifted my backpack to the other shoulder. "Just friends, though, right? I'm not looking to date or anything."

His shoulders sagged a little, but he nodded, doing his best to force a smile. "Yeah, that's fine. Just friends works."

I walked with him to the parking area, chastising my-self for being such a coward. If Dr. Ayers was really a Nero informant, they could show up at any time and poor Todd wouldn't be able to protect me. In fact, I was putting him in danger without even warning him.

"This one's mine." I stopped in front of the silver Ford Fiesta hatchback. He gave me directions to Mona Lisa Pizza just in case we got separated and then headed over a couple of rows to his little pickup.

I peered through my windows as I unlocked the door. Empty. I let out a sigh of relief as I settled behind the wheel. I plugged my phone into the car jack, fired up my playlist, and watched for Todd's truck.

We munched on pizza, talked shop about doctors and demanding patients, and gradually my muscles relaxed. "Do you know Dr. Ayers over in the medical offices next door?"

Todd took a swig of his Coke and lifted a shoulder. "I know *of* him. He's supposed to be a good general practitioner. I've heard through the grapevine that he's had a couple of his patients on my floor in the past, and he came by to check on them even though they were under the hospital's care. That's pretty cool considering most HMOs won't pay for the extra doctor visit, so he checked on them on his own dime. Lots of the docs won't follow up without being able to bill someone."

Maybe Jason wasn't as self-centered as most of the doctors I'd worked with. I lifted another piece of pizza onto my plate. "Has he had his practice here for long?"

"Few years, I think. Why?" He took a bite.

"Just curious." Having an office in the same building for a while didn't mean Nero hadn't contacted Dr. Ayers to be on the lookout for new nurses from New York.

Todd rested back into the booth. "I get that he's good looking and he's a doctor. His bank account is healthier than mine, but he's got demons hiding in the shadows just like the rest of us. He's not that special."

"I didn't say he was." I popped a piece of pepperoni in my mouth, wondering if he'd elaborate on the demons, but Todd didn't say anything. Sipping my drink, I met his eyes. "I'm not interested in Dr. Ayers. I swore off doctors a long time ago."

This seemed to perk Todd up even though I'd already told him I wasn't interested in dating him, either. Guys were a strange breed.

"Good thing." He took a drink of his Coke. "You'd have plenty of competition."

I had no doubt. A doctor made good money, add being well built with rugged features that resembled Hugh Jackman, and it sweetened the pot considerably for single women looking to marry up. He could have his pick of blond bombshells.

This should not bother me. Jason was a potential spy for a company who wanted to silence me forever. Not really dating material.

Plus he was a doctor.

I shouldn't have to remind myself of this. I wasn't attracted to him anyway.

Not really. But I was still human.

"So he dates a lot, then?" Why did I ask? I didn't want to know.

"I heard he used to. Nurses talk."

I nodded. Nurses definitely talked. Maybe that's why Dr. Ayers no longer dated people at the hospital. Spies needed to lay low. But what did I know? For all I knew Todd could be the spy. He licked the grease off of every finger and grinned at me.

Definitely not James Bond material.

"Are you from around here?"

"No." My pulse raced. I hadn't thought of a cover story. "I moved here from New York." I groaned inwardly. At least it was a giant state. Still pretty vague. I hoped.

"New York?" His eyebrows almost reached his hairline, like I was an alien instead of an east coaster. "Why'd you move all the way to Reno?"

Questions like that were why I shouldn't try to make friends here. I needed to put more thought into my fictional life. "Bad breakup. I needed a fresh start and Reno sounded...fresh."

God, even I didn't buy that story. I held my breath.

"Was he a doctor?"

"Who?"

"The bad breakup."

"It's that obvious, huh?"

He nodded and grabbed another piece of pizza.

I hadn't technically lied. My last relationship breakup was with a doctor. That split was how I landed on Grace's couch. We ended up finding an apartment together, and I swore off doctors. But technically, it wasn't my ex-boyfriend who brought me to Reno.

"Thanks for the company, Todd." I put my pizza down. "I better head home."

"Sorry. I didn't mean to dredge up bad memories."

"Nah, it's not that." I stood up and hooked my bag over my shoulder. "Just tired from my shift."

"Okay. See you around, then."

I got in my car and rested my forehead against the wheel, forcing the painful memories of the night I found Grace back into a mental box. At least the crippling fear weighing me down at the end of my shift receded a little. I started the car and drove to my apartment. A pair of headlights in my rearview mirror followed me all the way, but they zoomed past when I pulled into the parking lot.

Maybe I was just being paranoid.

I jogged to my apartment when the vision hit, just a flash of a text message. In front of my door, I dug my cell out of my purse. Nothing yet. Once I was inside, my phone buzzed.

Beware the Jabberwock – S

"Shit." His number was blocked, but the meaning was clear. Time to head to the horse ranch. I didn't know Sebastian very well, but in spite of being employed by a company that had no qualms about killing, he had a fondness for poetry. Grace loved that about him.

This line was his code, a warning. The only one I'd get.

Nero was closing in.

I hurried around my studio apartment, grabbing all my essentials and electronics. Had they found Nani? If they hurt my grandmother I'd… I couldn't think about it. She wouldn't have known where I was anyway. If they were heading to Reno, Dr. Ayers must've tipped them off.

But if he was working for them, why talk to the head

nurse and pay for the medication I used for his father? Maybe it was all part of being a good spy. Seem like a nice caring guy and no one ever suspects you're a wolf in sheep's clothing.

Damned doctors. I should've picked another line of work. They were pompous, cocky, and always hell-bent on screwing up my life. At least it seemed that way lately.

Satisfied I had all I needed, I set my bag by the door and made one last walk through to be sure I didn't leave anything behind they could use to track me. No loose credit card slips, business cards, or junk mail with my alias.

The place was clean.

I hurried out, putting the address into my phone. According to my GPS, the ranch was thirty minutes away. Then the fun would really begin. I had no idea who these people were or if they'd really help me, a total stranger, but I didn't have any other options. After everything that had happened, I wasn't about to be stupid.

This wasn't a game.

I pulled down the drive toward the barn. The lights were on, and I figured it'd be a better place to hide my car if Nero was already searching for it. I turned off the engine as a man walked toward me. With the lights behind him, his face was hidden by shadows. I couldn't make out his expression, but I hadn't gotten a flash that I was in danger. Yet.

By the time I got out, I could see him better. His brown hair was tied back, revealing a strong chin and determined eyes. Very light blue eyes. "Can I help you?"

"Hope so. I'm looking for Adam."

His shoulders tensed. "Is he expecting you? Little late if you're here to look at a horse. I've already fed them. Maybe tomorrow."

"It's not about a horse." *This isn't weird. Nope.* I sighed. "Look, it's late, I get it, but I need Adam's help."

His eyes narrowed. "So he's *not* expecting you."

"Sebastian sent me."

He encroached into my personal space, backing me up against my car. Confusion and fear comingled into a sick feeling in my stomach.

"Get back in your car and tell Sebastian whatever it is, we're not interested."

What the hell had Sebastian been thinking sending me here? I reached for the door handle, but with my butt pressed against the car, the door wouldn't budge. A wave of inappropriate laughter escaped my lips. The more I tried to hold them in, the worse they became.

The imposing would-be guard dog grit his teeth, his voice dropping an octave. "What part of this do you find funny?"

I shook my head, trying to speak coherently through the unwanted laughter. "I can't get my car door open. You're pressing me against it."

"Is there a problem here, Luke?"

The enforcer spun around. "I've got everything under control."

The other guy was a little broader across the chest, maybe a few years older, too. He hooked his thumb in the pocket of his faded jeans and glanced my way. "Who is this?"

"Sebastian sent her, so I was just showing her out."

The other man raised a brow, his hands tensing at his

sides, his green eyes locked on my face. "Who are you?"

And as suddenly as they appeared, the inappropriate giggles were gone. I cleared my throat. "I'm Ki...Kelly. Kelly Jones. I need help."

He came up next to the one he called Luke. "And Sebastian sent you to *us*? Why?"

"He said you'd help me. I have no idea why he thought going to a horse ranch would keep me safe." I pushed away from the car. "I'm sorry. This is all a mistake."

The older one crossed his arms over his chest. "Sorry, Kelly. I can't let you go without knowing what Sebastian is planning."

"Can't let me go?" I shifted my gaze between the two handsome yet impassive faces. "What the hell is going on here?"

My cell phone was safely in my purse inside the car. *Shit.* My pulse kicked up a notch, while I struggled to remain calm.

"I'm asking you that same question."

I rolled my eyes, hoping I masked the wariness and animalistic urge to run. "I came to Reno to hide from some bad people. Sebastian gave me this address and said if I noticed them getting close, I should come here and ask for Adam, so I did. He said you would be able to protect me from Nero. That's all I know."

The older guy looked at the younger one and tipped his head toward the house. "I've got this. Can you tell the others to be alert?"

Luke nodded. "I'm on it."

Once we were alone, he turned my way, his stance relaxing just a little. "I'm Adam."

My tongue dried up in my mouth. "I'm sorry. I shouldn't

have come."

"If it's Nero who is after you, then Sebastian was right. We're the only ones who can protect you." He paused, his tone darkening. "But my family comes first. If you can't be straight with me, then I can't help you."

"I've told you everything I know."

He didn't look convinced. "Why are they after you?" He took a step closer. "And how about your real name?"

I gaped a little. "I told you I'm Kelly Jones."

"You started to say something else." He shook his head and backed off. "Never mind. You're wasting my time. I can't help you."

He walked a few paces toward the house while my mind whirled. Where would I go?

"Wait."

He stopped.

"My name is Kilani Akamu."

Adam turned. I took a slow breath and met his eyes. "My roommate was Sebastian's girlfriend. Nero killed her a few weeks ago." Saying the words out loud brought all the memories back. My voice wobbled. "I'm a loose end, and they're coming to clean it up."

"You're a loose end, how?"

I blinked hard, forbidding a tear from sliding down my cheek. "I found her body, and I know she was seeing Sebastian. His father owns—"

He put his hand up, silencing me. "I know who he is." A muscle in his cheek jumped. "So Nero is back in my territory. Again."

"Probably. I noticed a doctor spying on me at lunch, and then tonight I got a text from Sebastian warning me they're coming. The spy must've tipped them off."

"A doctor?" He looked less than convinced.

"I'm a nurse. I work at St. Mary's Hospital."

"If there's a doctor working for Nero over there, we'll find him. I have a friend who has a practice in the medical offices. I'll have him ask around."

My tense muscles relaxed slightly. He believed me. "That would be great. His name is Dr. Ayers."

Adam frowned. "Jason?" He chuckled, shaking his head. "You think Dr. Jason Ayers is working for Nero?"

It was my turn to frown. "He was spying on me today, and tonight Sebastian texted me to run. It's not tough to connect the dots."

"If Jason was watching you, it definitely wasn't for Nero."

"How can you be so sure?"

His features sobered. "Because he hates Nero almost as much as I do."

Chapter Five

Adam wouldn't say why, only that I needed to get my ass over to the ranch. Now. I envisioned one of the twins fell down the stairs or someone got kicked by a horse, the list went on in my head. Either way, I was lucky the highway patrol wasn't nearby. My foot rode the gas pedal, hard.

I made the usually twenty-minute drive in just under fifteen minutes. Adam met me outside before I could get to the door with my med kit.

"What happened?" I tried to keep moving, but Adam blocked my path. "Who's hurt?"

"No one."

"What the hell?" Something snapped inside of me. "This is bullshit, Adam. I've got enough stress in my life right now without a late-night call from my Alpha to get my ass to the ranch. I don't need this." I turned to go back to the car, but he grabbed my elbow. I stopped, but I didn't turn around.

"Sorry about that." He let go of my arm. "I should've told you it wasn't a medical emergency, but it's still urgent and it involves you…and Nero."

I huffed out a little frustration and shifted to face him. "I swear; I've had no contact with Nero. None. Not since Granger."

He nodded. "I've got a woman in my house claiming Sebastian told her to come to me for protection, and the one she wants protecting from is you."

"What?" He was speaking English, but his words didn't make any sense.

"I was just as confused as you, so rather than try to explain it, I thought you should hear it straight from her."

"Fine." I didn't bother putting my kit back in the car and followed him inside.

Her scent hit me before we stepped over the threshold. I smelled fresh flowers and the sea. Kilani. The fog of confusion thickened.

She popped up from her spot on the couch the second I came in. Before she could say anything, I frowned. "What are you doing here? And how do you know Sebastian?"

"No." She shook her head, pointing in my direction. "You don't get to ask the questions first."

The determination in her eyes sparked something inside me. She was the smallest person in the room, but her spirit was ready to take us both on. You had to be tough and mentally strong for nursing, and, safe to say, she was probably awesome at her job.

"Fine." I shrugged and set my kit on the floor by my feet. "Ladies first."

"Why were you spying on me earlier today?"

Adam shifted his focus, reminding me we weren't alone.

"I wasn't spying."

"I was eating lunch and looked up to see you at your window watching me."

"*Watching*, not spying."

She rolled her eyes. "I don't have time to debate semantics, *Doctor*." She walked toward Adam. "Hate to break it to you, but this guy you call a friend also called Nero and told them I was in Reno."

"You are miles off base." I turned to Adam. "Will someone please tell me what the hell is going on here?"

She wheeled around, glaring up at me. "Nero murdered my roommate, and I found her body. I know they did it. Now, because of you, they're coming to tie up a loose end. Me."

Adrenaline shot through my veins like wildfire, hot and furious at the thought of Nero touching her.

"I tried to tell her she had it wrong, but she didn't believe me." Adam glanced from my face to hers and back again. "If Nero really is on the way, then you two better get your heads on straight. I won't put my…family at risk."

I caught the hesitation in Adam's voice. Whatever Sebastian had told Kilani, Adam didn't think she knew we were werewolves. In front of guests we weren't his Pack, we were family. I gave a subtle nod of my head.

"Work this out." Adam walked away toward the stairs, leaving me with a very angry Kilani.

"There's nothing to discuss. I'll take care of myself." She went toward the door and I almost reached out to stop her, but given her current frame of mind, I stopped. If she thought I was a Nero spy, manhandling her wasn't going to help my cause.

"I watched you today because you're beautiful. It had nothing to do with Nero or spying." She froze and turned slowly. The sudden spurt of honesty rattled me, but she didn't run out of the house screaming, so I went a little further. "It was a fluke when I saw you leave the building for the parking lot. I thought you'd get in your car and drive away. When you didn't, I was curious…"

She came one step closer, staring up at me. Studying me? She had beautiful dark, almond-shaped eyes. Wise. And her sun-kissed skin looked soft, tempting. I closed my hands to keep from reaching out to touch her.

"If you didn't call Nero, then who did?" A crease marred her smooth brow. "I've been here for almost two months and everything was quiet, then I catch you…watching me, and I get a text from Sebastian that they're coming. Pretty huge coincidence."

I nodded. Her conclusion was logical. Wrong, too, but now I understood why she believed it. "Can we sit down and start over?"

"No." She pressed her lips together for a moment. "I bet caring for your father is expensive."

The pivot in conversation stunned me for a moment. "What does that have to do with anything?"

"That was the only missing piece. Spying goes against everything anyone has told me about you, but paying for in-home staff for your father has got to be pricey, even for a doctor. You might need extra cash. Making a phone call about a nurse named Kilani could be a huge payday."

"Wow." I raked my fingers back through my hair. "You think you've got this all figured out." My hands were tied. I couldn't tell her the real reason my dad wasn't in a hospital or why we couldn't risk in-home nursing. I was running out of bullshit. I met her eyes. "It was a doctor from Nero who shot my father up with potassium chloride that day. I discovered he'd been poisoning a friend of mine and he attacked my dad to slow me down while he got away. I had to choose, catch the bastard or save my father. I chose family."

She watched me for a second and slowly let out a breath she'd been holding. "That's why Adam said you hated Nero…"

"I wasn't fond of them before they stopped my dad's heart, but I'm even more anxious to take them down now." I raised my hands slightly. "Are we good now?"

She lifted a shoulder. "I might've been wrong about you being the spy, but I'm not sure that makes us good…" Her words faded as she came closer to me. I followed her stare to my hands. "Are those bruises?"

I started to drop them, but she caught one, studying it. Something inside me came unhinged. The wolf howled in my mind, deafening my ears for a second, my pupils dilated, nostrils flared, and my lungs filled with her scent as I struggled for breath.

"Gobsmacked" didn't begin to describe the insanity. What the hell was happening to me?

"Dr. Ayers?" She released my hand and I stumbled backward, blinking hard. Gradually the world came back into focus. She came closer, reaching out to steady me. "Whoa. You should sit down before you fall down. We need to get to the hospital for a CAT scan. You're probably nursing a concussion. You've got all the symptoms, Dr. Ayers."

"Jason." I shook my head. This couldn't be real. There had to be an explanation. "Call me Jason."

"Fine." She came closer, reaching up to inspect the cut on my brow, her breasts so close to my chest, the heat of her body warmed me right through our clothes. "Jason, we need to get you to a hospital. Your brain could be swelling."

Oh, something was swelling for sure, but it was nowhere near my brain.

"I'm okay."

Her gaze shifted from my cut to my eyes. "You're saying that lack of balance and coordination, coupled with your rapid pupil dilation, was normal?"

"No." I shook my head. "But it's not a concussion."

Her hands rested on her hips. "All right, then what was it?"

"You wouldn't believe me if I told you." Hell, I didn't believe it, either.

"How's it going out here?"

We both turned to find Adam in the hallway. Kilani glanced up at me for a second before sighing. "You're right. I don't think Jason called Nero."

Adam nodded and came over to my side. "I need to talk to you. Alone."

"I'll go. I'm sorry Sebastian sent me here. I never would've come if I had known you weren't expecting me."

"No." I spun around faster than I intended. She flinched a little. "If Nero is after you, you're not going anywhere on your own."

Her shoulders squared. "I admitted to being wrong about you spying. I did *not* agree to you being in charge of my life. I don't know you and you don't know me. If Adam can help, great, but if not, I'll figure something out."

The wolf's agitation grew. It paced inside of me until I

wanted to scream. "This is no time to go off headstrong and half-cocked. Sebastian sent you here because we're the only ones who can stand up to Nero."

"We?" She shook her head and pointed to my Alpha. "He told me to go find *Adam*, not you."

Hearing Adam's name on her lips made me want to punch something. My hands flinched at my sides. "Just don't go anywhere."

Adam clapped a hand on my shoulder. "Sorry. Our doctor sometimes forgets he can't order folks around outside the hospital. Can you give me a few minutes before you go?"

Her gaze swept across the floor, but finally she sighed. "Fine."

"Thanks." Adam nodded toward her. "We'll be right back."

I took a chair in his office as Adam closed the door. He crossed to the desk, leaning against the edge with his arms over his chest. "We can't get involved here."

"What?" I got to my feet. "We can't just look the other way while Nero kills someone on our territory."

He opened his hands. "We don't even know if her story about the roommate is true. Sebastian could be counting on us to feel sorry for the pretty little thing, and then he'll swoop in with a mercenary team to grab Lana and the twins. It's too risky and we can't be sure of the facts. Why would Sebastian send this woman to us?"

"So we're just going to tell her good luck and pretend we don't see her blood on our hands." My pulse galloped faster than a thoroughbred, and my urge to punch something swelled. "When did our Pack start being afraid of Nero?"

"Are you questioning my motives?" Adam straightened

up, his tone dropping to a menacing growl. "What the hell is wrong with you? There is no reason for Sebastian, heir to the Nero machine, to help us or need our help. This makes no sense."

"Yeah, it doesn't make sense." I went to the door. "But I can't stand by and pretend she's not in danger."

"Jason, she's not our problem."

I shook my head, my knuckles aching as I balled my fingers into tight fists. "She's my mate."

His eyes widened. "What?"

"It's crazy, but she just touched my hand and…"

"And the earth tilted on its axis?"

I nodded, staring at my knuckles. "Something like that. It's not possible, but…" I met his eyes. "But my wolf recognized her. I heard him howling."

The corner of Adam's mouth quirked up. "No shit." He clasped my forearms and chuckled. "You've got your work cut out for you."

"Why, because she hates doctors, or because she thinks I'm a Peeping Tom spy, or maybe because Nero wants her dead…" I let go of him, rubbing my hands down my face. "I'm screwed. Why is everything in my life turning to shit right now?"

He took his place against his desk again. "We still don't know if we can trust her. Mate or not, you need to find out whatever you can about her roommate. I can't believe Sebastian cared about anyone other than himself, let alone felt responsible for saving her friend. None of this adds up."

"She doesn't think she can trust me, either."

"Until I understand what Sebastian's endgame is, I can't get the Pack involved, mate or not."

"Shit." I groaned and reached for the door. "I can't let anything happen to her, Adam."

"I know." He nodded. "Keep me in the loop. If her story turns out to be true, the Pack will stand with you."

I had to get *her* to stand with me first.

Goddamn fate could stop fucking with me any time now.

Chapter Six

KILANI

Jason disappeared down the hall with Adam, leaving me alone to get a grip on reality. A vision assaulted me the moment I touched his hand and he stumbled away. And it wasn't a vision of him betraying me to Nero.

I was naked in his arms.

And instead of being repulsed, a flush of heat fanned out through my body. I needed a cold shower. Now. Not only was Jason a doctor, but I'd already caught him lying to me, and I still had all my clothes on at the time.

Not to mention catching him watching me while I ate lunch.

But my visions of the future usually came to me right before they occurred. Ending up in bed with him in a few minutes wasn't going to happen. No way. Maybe it was a mistake? Just a jolt of lust. He was intelligent and good looking, if you could overlook the god complex and the secrets.

Until now, all my visions came true unless I chose to do something to change the outcome. This vision made no sense.

I got up and went to the window. The barn was still lit, and the horses in the pasture grazed in the moonlight. Peaceful. But their peace couldn't distract me or get Jason out of my head. I kept seeing his eyes when he admitted he thought I was beautiful. He'd bared himself, even though he was well aware of my distrust and less-than-friendly attitude toward him.

My thick emotional shields faltered. He was sexy when he told the truth.

Too bad he didn't do it often.

"Hey."

His voice brought me back to the present. I glanced back over my shoulder. "Where's Adam?"

"He's got some things to take care of."

I turned to face him, my mouth going dry. "He's not going to help me?" When Jason didn't answer, I nodded, hoping I looked braver than I felt. "That's okay. I'm sorry Sebastian was mistaken."

I walked to the couch to grab my bag.

"I'm going to help you."

"Excuse me?" I slid my bag over my shoulder.

"Just for now. Adam can't get our family involved until he's sure of Sebastian's motives. I'll protect you while we get a clearer picture of why Sebastian sent you here."

He stood tall—of course everyone was tall to me, but his broad shoulders were rolled back, his bruised face raised in defiance, and his banged-up hands balled into loose fists. I'd never met such a rugged doctor. He almost looked like he could protect me from anything.

Anything but himself.

I sighed and shook my head. "I appreciate the offer, but I can handle this. If I see anyone out of the ordinary, I have the police on speed dial. I'll be ready."

He tensed but pulled in a slow breath before he spoke. "I get that you don't trust me, or doctors in general, but this is serious. There's a detective in Reno who might be able to help us contact Sebastian and get some answers."

"Give me his name and I'll call him."

"Her name." He shook his head with a humorless chuckle. "And there's no way she'd get involved if you called her."

I walked over to him, trying not to let the vision of us naked into my consciousness. Too late. "Tell me something… Be *honest,* if possible. Why are you offering to help me? What's in it for you?"

This close, his light hazel eyes were almost golden, hypnotic. His gaze never strayed from mine. "Let's get something straight." His voice was deep and rough, intimate. "I wish I could tell you everything you want to know, but there are parts of my life I can't share. The truth could hurt those I love, so I protect it. I don't know what kind of asshole, lying doctors you've known, but I am *not* one of them."

Ignoring the annoying flutters in my belly, I shook my head slowly. "You still didn't answer my question."

He didn't miss a beat. "You helped save my father's life. I want to return the favor."

I swallowed the lump in my throat. This was no lie, no agenda. "Thank you."

His shoulders relaxed and he pulled his keys out of his pocket. "Let's grab your things and get out of here."

I bristled. "I'll just follow you. I've got all I need in my car."

"Nero could already be looking for your car."

"Fine." I sighed, glaring down at my shoes to keep from seeing his face. "But I want to be sure we're clear. We're not sleeping together."

He chuckled and I couldn't help but peer up at him. Damn, he had a great smile.

"I was thinking more along the lines of taking you to see the detective who might be able to contact Sebastian." He raised a brow. "But I'm flattered."

"Flattery wasn't my intention." The image of our naked limbs entwined together on a king-size bed flashed through my head again as I brushed past him toward the door. I needed to get a little self-control. I wasn't about to let this vision become a self-fulfilling prophecy. Jason had baggage and secrets.

And I had enough of those on my own.

J ason made a call on his cell and then started the engine. "She's at her sister's place, but I told her this wouldn't take long."

"She couldn't just give you Sebastian's number?"

He glanced my way. "Contacting him isn't something you pass along over the phone. Nero has ears everywhere." He stared out the windshield at the dark road ahead. "Plus Sasha will want to hear this directly from you, or she won't get involved."

A few silent minutes later, we pulled into a parking lot for a garage. "Takoda Harley Restorations?"

Jason nodded, focused on the sign over the door as he turned off the car. "Yeah, Sasha's sister moved in with her..." He hesitated for a second. "Her boyfriend. He owns the place and has a studio apartment in the back."

I got out and followed a pace or two behind Jason to the door. He rang the bell and a willowy raven-haired woman with familiar green eyes opened the door.

"Nadya?"

Her eyes narrowed slightly. "Oh my God, Kilani?"

She and I closed the distance between us and embraced. I held her at arm's length, taking in her grown features. "How long has it been?"

"More than fifteen years."

Jason cleared his throat, reminding me we weren't alone. "You two...know each other?"

Nadya grinned. "We went to Brightwood Academy together. Kilani was a few years older than me. She used to help me with my homework."

Jason opened his mouth but closed it again without speaking. Instead he shook his head and smiled, but it looked forced. "Small world."

"Sure is." Nadya took my hand and pulled me inside. "I can't wait for you to meet Sasha."

"She's your older sister. The one studying to be a police officer, right?"

"That was a long time ago. She's a detective now."

When we rounded the corner, another woman with the same fine Russian features as Nadya got up from the couch, and two dark-haired men stood at the bar of a modest kitchen.

I reached out to shake her hand. "You must be Sasha."

She nodded with a firm grip. "And you are?"

Nadya answered for me. "This is Kilani. My friend from Brightwood Academy."

Brightwood was a small boarding school for girls with psychic abilities. What were the chances we'd find each other in Reno of all places? Had Sebastian sent her here, too?

The other two men tensed at the mention of Brightwood, a similar reaction to Jason's outside. And one of the men was...Adam? No, this guy had shorter hair. A twin brother?

I let my hand drop to my side. "Is there something wrong?"

Jason came around the corner and stopped behind me. The heat of his body teased me through the back of my shirt. Apparently he was very close but not quite touching. I forced myself to remain still. The air sucked out of the room for a moment until he came up beside me.

"Nero owns Brightwood Academy."

I frowned, turning to Jason. "What? How could you possibly know anything about Brightwood?"

"Have a seat and we'll fill you in." Jason led me to the sofa.

Sasha remained standing. "She's the one you called about? Sebastian sent her here?"

A big guy with his black hair pulled back in a ponytail and a tattoo around his chiseled biceps came around the corner. We stared at each other while I tried to place why he looked so familiar. Maybe he was doing the same thing. He took Nadya's hand, his questioning gaze focused on Jason, and that's when I figured it out.

"You're the guy from the hospital that day. You came and found me to get the insulin and glucose."

His dark eyes moved from me to Jason and back again before he nodded. "Yeah. That was me."

Man of few words. He took Nadya's hand and I realized he must be the boyfriend Jason mentioned. Wow. She coaxed a smile out of the big guy and I almost followed suit. I couldn't get over seeing her all grown up. Seemed like just yesterday that we'd been kids at Brightwood.

And never in a million years would I have pictured her moving in with a biker. If what they were saying about Nero owning Brightwood was true, my vision all those years ago about Nadya's parents may have saved me.

Nadya's boyfriend tipped his head toward Jason. "What happened to your face?"

"I'm fine." Jason gestured toward him. "Kilani, I don't think you got properly introduced before. This is Gareth."

He didn't make a move to shake my hand. "How do you know Sebastian?"

Okay, so we'd skip the flowery *nice to meet you*. Worked for me. "My roommate was dating him."

Sasha took up a spot beside her sister. "Jason told me a little. Why don't you fill in the blanks?"

I told her about Grace and the night I discovered her body. My voice only cracked a few times. "I called the police and then Sebastian. He told me through clenched teeth that he wished I'd contacted him first. I didn't understand why at the time." I crossed my arms, wishing I could insulate myself from the fear. "Apparently his employer, Nero, put out a hit on Grace and didn't realize she had a roommate. They'd wanted Sebastian to discover her body. Since I found her and then got the police involved, I became a loose end they want to tie up."

Sasha frowned. "And Sebastian told you to come to Reno?"

"He said I should go to Reno and find a new nursing position. When I got here, he had new IDs waiting for me. I got a job at the hospital, and he told me if I noticed anyone following me or asking questions, I should go to Whispering Pines and ask for Adam."

Sasha looked at Jason. "And Adam thinks this is a set-up."

Jason shrugged. "He wants us to make contact with Sebastian to determine his motives. That's why I wanted to talk to you."

Sasha turned my way. "What made you go look for Adam?"

"I got a text from Sebastian." I pulled out my phone and clicked on the text. "Beware the Jabberwock."

Sasha took my phone, staring at the message for a second. She handed it back to me, her gaze moving around the room. "That's Sebastian's signal not to contact him. His cell and email might be compromised, and Nero is on the way."

"We need to find him." Jason's words were clipped, injected with urgency. "Adam won't get the…family involved. Not until he knows Kilani isn't a plant for Nero."

"If she was a tool for Nero, Sebastian wouldn't mention the Jabberwock. If they found out he's used it before, to help me…" She shook her head. "It'd be deadly for him to make that kind of mistake."

Gareth straightened to his full height. "The night I tangled with him up in Virginia City, he'd been drinking. He said his father killed someone he cared about. That was why he didn't try to take Nadya in for Nero to study. He wanted to punish his father. If he was telling the truth, and he really did feel something for Kilani's roommate, maybe he's protecting her because she was Grace's friend."

Sasha pondered that for a minute before shrugging her shoulders. "That seems like a stretch unless he's experienced huge amounts of personal growth over the past few months, but I guess anything is possible. We'll go talk to Adam. Until we have a plan, you should stay close to Jason."

I nodded, but inside, butterflies tickled my stomach. Maybe I could spend the night with Nadya instead. My attention landed on her boyfriend and I remembered this was a studio apartment. No sale.

I lifted my gaze to find Jason watching me. Did he have to be so freaking good-looking? Even with a cut on his eyebrow and some swelling at the corner of his mouth, he'd turn heads.

"Fine. But I'm working third shift tomorrow at the hospital."

"We'll figure something out." Jason glanced at the others. "Thanks, Sasha. Sorry to intrude."

Nadya wrapped me in another hug. When she stepped back, her smile seemed tentative, worried. She'd always been a strong empath. No doubt, my fear pummeled her mental shields. "We have lots of catching up to do."

"Once this blows over, we'll meet up."

Everyone in the room nodded like this was a certainty, and we said our good-byes without ever acknowledging the huge elephant in the room.

There was a better than average chance, when this blew over, I'd be dead.

The suffocating silence in the car did nothing to ease the knot in my stomach. I pulled my hair back from my forehead and released a pent-up breath. "Are you sorry you offered to help me yet?"

Jason chuckled but kept his eyes on the road, bruised knuckles tight on the wheel. "You probably already know I'm not."

"What?" I turned his way, frowning. "What're you talking about?"

"You went to Brightwood Academy. You're a psychic of some kind."

Now I was connecting the dots. If they knew Nero owned Brightwood, and Nadya was part of their group, they had to know about the criteria you needed to meet in order to get accepted into the school. I shifted in my seat, watching the lights pass by the passenger window.

"I have a little twinkle."

"A twinkle?" He waited, but I didn't turn to look at him. "What's that supposed to mean?"

"Look, I appreciate you helping me, but I hardly know you and I'm not ready to spill my guts to a total stranger. You have secrets, and I have a few, too."

He groaned, guttural, almost like a growl. "Fine. Let's get to know each other, then."

"I just want Nero out of my life and then I'll be out of yours. We don't need to pretend we're friends."

He wound up a pine-tree-lined private road and finally into the driveway of a slate-gray single-story home with a stone entranceway. The garage door opened and he drove inside, closing the door behind him. He turned off the key before he looked my way.

"What is it with you? Are you always this stubborn, or is it just that I repulse you?"

His jaw tightened, clenching his teeth to keep from saying more. He still gripped the steering wheel with one hand, his muscles in his arm tight and distracting.

Yeah, he didn't repulse me at all. That was part of the problem.

"What's so hard to understand?" I popped my door open, dispersing the fresh, almost wild scent I was starting to associate with him. "From the day we met, you lied to me, just like every other doctor I've dated. Forgive me for learning from my past mistakes and protecting myself."

"Okay, ask me something that doesn't have anything to do with my family."

"I won't know if you're lying."

"I think you will." His bright hazel eyes sparkled in the dim light of the garage.

"All right." I had no clue what to ask, and then a vision flashed through my head. Jason in a ring. A boxing ring. Blood trickling from his nose. And then it was gone. My confidence in my visions was wavering. First our naked entwined bodies, and now a boxing ring? The last thing a doctor would get involved in was boxing. They made their living off their brains and their hands, and both took a beating in a boxing ring. Jason was smarter than that. I thought.

His bruised knuckles twisted on top of the steering wheel as he awaited my question. I swallowed the disbelief and opened my mouth. "How did you really get that cut on your face and the bruises on your hands?"

He hesitated and rubbed a palm down his face before meeting my eyes. "I've been boxing."

My jaw threatened to drop wide open. "Why?"

He shook his head. "There's not enough time to answer that now."

He got out of the car and I followed him inside. His house wasn't what I expected. There wasn't opulence or a sense of supremacy in a bookcase lined with leather-bound first-edition books or polished ancient fossils. The décor embraced the grays of the stone fireplace in the center of the room. All the wood was natural pine, not some kind of rare walnut or cherry wood, and his walls weren't covered in awards and accolades; instead there were black-framed charcoal sketches of wolves.

I wandered closer to the wall. The drawings were intricate. Each wolf had character, his spirit shining in his eyes. I turned to find Jason behind the bar in the kitchen. "These are amazing. Who's the artist?"

He glanced my way as he brought two glasses out of the cupboard. "I used to sketch. It helped me focus my thoughts."

"*You* drew these?" I leaned in closer to the frame like I might find his signature hidden inside. "You missed your calling."

He let out a wry laugh as he dropped ice cubes into the glasses. "My family needed a doctor not an artist."

Family. He'd given up on a dream for his, and I'd run out on mine. I didn't even know if Grandma Nani had gotten my warning.

Who was I to judge this guy? Another brick in my emotional barrier wobbled.

Chapter Seven

JASON

She perused my wall, examining my artwork while I filled two glasses with ice water. I couldn't take my eyes off of her, wondering what was going on in her head. Usually I had an easy rapport with women, but there was no pinning her down.

It didn't help that since she'd touched my hand, the wolf inside of me was wide awake and eager to be near her. Coherent thought threatened to slip right through my bruised fingers.

Just like every other facet of my damned life, I had no control.

While she was distracted with the wall of wolves, my gaze wandered over her features, memorizing every curve of her face. Exotic and beautiful. And a complete mystery. Her blatant dismissal of doctors made it clear, she'd had her heart broken before, and as irrational and stupid as it was, I wanted to kick his ass for hurting her, for forcing my mate to build this impenetrable emotional barrier.

My mate. Insanity.

I came out from the kitchen. "Water?"

She took it with a hint of a smile. "Thank you."

I took a swallow from my glass and noticed her bare feet. Her sandals sat next to the front door. Not that I was married to shoes, but unless I was in the shower, I usually had them on. Seeing her tanned feet and ruby red toenails seemed intimate in a way. And incredibly foreign to me.

"Does the turtle symbolize something?" The sound of my own voice shocked me. Jesus, I'd blurted the question out loud. What was it about this woman that made me lose my shit around her?

She looked puzzled, staring up at me for a second before realization dawned. Looking down at her ankle, she pulled her pant leg up a little higher to expose the entire tattoo. "He's a *honu*. I'm from Hawaii. The sea turtle is my family's *aumakua*, our protector."

She'd shared something personal. Holy shit. I did my best to hide the shock. Playing it cool came naturally to me. Usually. With Kilani I couldn't seem to find my footing.

"Is your family on the mainland now?"

Focusing on the drawing of my brother Jared in his wolf form, she shook her head. "No, I'm the only one who left."

Before I could probe further, she walked her glass over to the counter. "Do we have a game plan to avoid Nero when I go to work tomorrow?"

Apparently we were through talking about her family. I sat in my leather easy chair. "If they know where you work, then you aren't safe there. You should call in sick."

She came to the sofa and sat down with one bare foot tucked up underneath her. "I'm too new to be calling in sick. I'll lose my job."

Every word Nadya and Adam had ever mentioned to me about the pull of our wolf once we found our mate didn't even scratch the surface of this undeniable urge to protect her and keep her safe. The human part of me understood the importance of income, but the animal wanted to lock her in my bedroom where I could guard her properly.

"Losing your job won't matter if Nero finds you."

She crossed her arms. "You know, I'm freaked out enough without you making this into a horror movie. It's not like they can waltz into the well-lit hospital and shoot me."

"No, they'll inject you up with a sedative, put you in a wheelchair, and take you far away from the well-lit hospital to finish the job."

She popped off the couch, mouth tight. "Stop it!"

The want to comfort her and the need to apologize threatened to overwhelm me. I clenched my fists and stayed my course. "Not until you understand that if Nero is coming here, then they know where you work, they probably know where you're staying, and they're well aware of Adam's ranch. They have no idea where I live and no connection between the two of us. Yet. So for now, this is the safest place for you to be."

"You seriously expect me to stay here like your prisoner as I lose my job and my only hope at a fresh start?" Angry tears shined in her eyes, breaking my heart and shaking my will. "Screw you. You have no idea how terrified I was that night. They didn't just kill Grace, they tortured her. When

Sebastian told me to run, I had to box up the fear, grab my things, and disappear into a new life. If I let it, the anxiety could consume me without any help from you."

I reached for her, and she recoiled. Shit. I stepped back, rubbing a hand down my face while the wolf inside of me growled in protest. "Sometimes fear keeps us safe. I just don't want anything to happen to you."

"I don't want that, either, but I barely know you. I don't know who to trust and hiding might be safe, but it sure as hell isn't living."

She spun on her heel and stormed into my bedroom and slammed the door. Apparently I'd be in my guest room tonight. Great.

I was on the porch when Jared's truck drove up. We clasped forearms in the traditional Pack greeting before he pulled me into a tight hug. He stepped back and took the other chair on the porch.

"Bring me up to speed."

I stared at my hands. The ache in my joints did nothing to deaden the hunger in my heart. I'd hurt her tonight. I hurt her to save her. Didn't make it any easier, or me any less of an asshole. It was fucking unfair, and I needed to lash out before the club closed.

"The nurse who helped me with Dad is here. Locked in my bedroom."

Jared raised an eyebrow, the corner of his mouth curving into a crooked smile. "Pretty kinky, bro."

I shook my head with a disgusted chuckle. "I wish." I

met his eyes. "She's my mate."

His grin spread, but I put my hand up to silence him before he could congratulate me. "She also hates my guts and thinks I'm a liar."

"So my brother finally believes in mates and she isn't interested?"

"Fate is fucking hilarious, right?"

He rubbed the back of his neck. "Sorry, man. Anything I can do?"

"Yeah. Stay here and make sure she's safe. I need to go take care of something." I closed my fist, rubbing my knuckles with my other hand. "It won't take long."

"You know beating the shit out of someone isn't going to change anything."

"Can't make it any worse," I growled, my tone a little louder than I intended. I sucked in a slow breath through my teeth and met his eyes. "I need to blow off some steam. Can you stay or not?"

He stood up, arms crossed over his chest. "I guess I'm wasting my time reminding you that you haven't healed up from your last *stress relief*."

"Just be sure she stays here. Nero is looking for her. I won't be gone long."

"Yoga hardly ever punches back."

"That's why it won't help." I went to my car and turned back. "Thanks, Jared."

He shook his head. "Don't thank me for letting you get your ass beat."

The fight club was inside an old furniture warehouse, long forgotten by most. Outside there was no new signage, just a faded, half-broken FOR LEASE sign. Three silent partners had purchased the building, and Todd recruited and managed the fight boards.

They'd be closed in an hour. If I was lucky, I could grab the final spot. Since I still held the club champion title, the other fighters would want to challenge me, but no one would be expecting me back tonight, not after last night's match.

Marv's eyes widened when I came in the door with my gym bag. "Wolf. You come in to watch?"

"No." I narrowed my eyes at the brackets on the far wall. "I'm here to fight."

"B-but you just beat Shark last night." He pointed a timid finger at my eye. "You ain't healed yet."

I shrugged, walking toward the ring. "I'll survive."

Marv tailed after me, but no amount of talking could stop me. I came here for something real. Pain, focus, and maybe a taste of being in control of my own destiny for a little while.

"Wolf!" Todd called from the makeshift grandstand. It was probably an old set of risers from a high school choir, but it served its purpose either way. "Just in time for the final bracket. Want in on it?"

"Who's still standing?"

He checked his clipboard before scanning the club. He poked his thumb toward a big guy working the medicine ball in the corner. "Bruiser."

Bruiser turned, his lips pulling back into an eager sneer. His partially toothless smile reminded me of a hockey player who forgot to wear a mouthpiece. We were similar in height, but he had to outweigh me by at least fifty pounds.

This wasn't going to be pretty.

"I'm in."

"Final bout…" Todd shouted. "Bruiser against our club champion, Wolf!"

I headed for the locker room. Five minutes to the bell. Already adrenaline laced my blood stream, feeding on my festering rage. Yeah, this was going to get ugly.

I stood in the center of the ring, toe to toe with Bruiser while Bob rattled off the fight club rules. Bob had refereed for the amateur boxing circuit through the USA Boxing organization for twenty years before he retired from the ring, but retirement hadn't fulfilled him like boxing did. Now he climbed into our underground ring to keep order between gladiators. His thick accent and thready smoker's voice always reminded me of Mickey from the Rocky movies.

Bruiser exhaled slowly, his halitosis daring me to turn away and break eye contact. I ground my teeth together, allowing a growl to rumble in the back of my throat.

"Get to your corners."

Neither of us wanted to be the first to walk away. Bruiser gave me a shove as he turned and I clocked him in the jaw. He rushed toward me, but Bob boldly slid between us. "Save it for after the bell."

"I'm comin' for you, Wolf."

"Bring it." I went to my corner and bit into my mouthpiece while I loosened my muscles and rolled my shoulders and head without ever taking my gaze off of my opponent.

The wolf paced inside me, hungry for a show of dominance.

The bell sounded, igniting the aggression smoldering in my gut. We both charged toward the center of the ring and I landed jabs to his forehead, backing him toward the corner. Bruiser swung a wild right hand. I dodged the blow, answering with an uppercut to his abdomen. He stumbled back, hitting the ropes, and I pursued.

I had expected more from this guy. *Wanted* more. I took a step back, taunting him to follow. "Thought you were comin' for me."

A fire sparked in his eyes. He lurched forward, landing a solid punch to my chest that knocked the air out of my lungs. That was more like it. I wanted the beating. Deserved it.

He grinned around his mouthpiece, sensing he'd slowed me. The jabs came faster than I could block, pummeling my already battered ribs.

"You got nothin' left, Wolf. You're mine." His putrid breath stung my nostrils just as his glove hit my jaw.

The bell rang and Bob rushed in to point us back to our corners. No trainers waited to offer strategy, no stools to rest our legs, and no ice to clear our heads. I watched him take a swig of his water and wipe his face with his towel. I didn't move. Sweat rolled down my face. I didn't give a shit. The weight of my stare had him trying to focus on anything other than me, jumpy, like a rabbit sensing a wolf nearby.

"I got plenty left," I grumbled as the bell rang.

Bruiser already had his hands up in an effort to block my combinations hitting his face. Once his body was exposed, I shifted my assault to his abdomen, landing heavy blows. Each time my glove connected, my mind filled with a primal howl. This one was for my father. This one was for Nero. And the final blow, an uppercut to his chin, *that* was for my mate, for the danger surrounding her, and my inability to gain her trust.

Bruiser stumbled to the right. I took a few steps back as his legs crumpled to the mat. Bob counted while I pulled in air. Exhaustion calming the beast inside.

Bruiser groaned on the ground and Bob grabbed my wrist, hauling my arm up. "Wolf. Winner by knockout."

The modest group of spectators and fighters shouted my name, but I hardly noticed. Now that the rage had been spent, my entire body ached. I climbed out of the ring, pulling out my mouthpiece so I could loosen the laces on my gloves with my teeth. Inside the dingy locker room, I yanked them off and stared at my hands, opening and closing my fingers. Sometimes I didn't recognize them anymore, the joints swollen and red.

But, damn it all, I felt better. The physical pain gave me something else to focus on, a distraction from all the fear, the emotions that threatened to suck me under.

As I left the warehouse, Marv trailed after me. "Wolf?" I stopped and turned around. "You done good." He stared at my shoes, avoiding eye contact. "You should rest for a week or two."

Even Marv recognized I'd been fighting more often. Too often.

I clasped his shoulder. "Thanks, buddy. I think I will." I glanced around the club. "Where'd your brother go?"

"Todd had to go work."

Apparently Todd worked the night shift someplace. Since all of our true identities never walked through the door of the club, I didn't know his, either. Didn't matter anyway; I just wanted to be sure Marv was taken care of.

"Do you have a ride home?"

"I'm taking the boy home." Bob had a gym bag on his shoulder and a Wolf Pack baseball hat on his head. It usually made me chuckle to see the University of Reno gear, but I was too exhausted to smile. No one had any idea a real Wolf Pack lived here.

"Thanks, Bob."

The lines in his face deepened. "Marv's right about res-tin'. This club is for recreation, not for a guy with a death wish."

I ground my teeth and nodded. "Yeah. I'll take a few days off."

"See that you do." His expression lightened. "Good fight tonight."

"Thanks."

But deep inside, in places I didn't want to examine, I knew there was nothing *good* about what I did tonight.

Chapter Eight

After slamming the door, I turned around to find the king-size bed from my vision. Shit. Really? The first room I storm into is his bedroom? I pulled the elastic band out of my hair with a groan. If I opened that door, Jason would be standing there ready to dose me with more fear.

Did he seriously think I needed more?

I sat on the edge of the bed, trying to resist pulling the comforter back. Part of me wanted to find out if the sheets were the same from my vision, and the rest of me didn't want to know. There was no way I'd allow myself to get naked with that man out there.

Sure, he was gorgeous, and the artwork on the walls proved there was more to him than I ever would have guessed. But I'd sworn off doctors for my own protection, and this one not only already lied to me, he also wanted to make me completely dependent on him, and that was something I'd never do, danger or not.

I noticed a stack of hardback books on the nightstand and wandered over. Stephen King, Dean Koontz, and Richard Matheson. Fiction. I'd expect to find some hardcore nonfiction titles about patient care, or new studies on green diets, or maybe a reference book on investments, or... Well, anything other than fiction.

Somewhere in Time was on top. I opened it carefully, keeping the pages he had tucked inside the book jacket from sliding free and losing his place. I hadn't read the novel in years, but I remembered it fondly. The romantic notion that love could transcend time infatuated me. I'd been young, naive. Life had quickly set me straight. There was nothing mythical or magic about love. It was more of a shell game.

Just when you thought you had it, it already found a new place to hide.

The front door closed. I placed the book back on the stack and moved to the bedroom door. After all the talk of danger, he left without a word? I frowned and cracked it open.

Empty.

I slipped out, embracing the frustration brewing inside. Anything was better than fear. I wandered past the artwork-covered wall into the spacious kitchen. I wasn't really hungry, but a snack would be nice. A welcome focus for my scattered thoughts. I needed to get my head together so I could think straight and plot out my next move. I'd left my car at the ranch. Mistake. And now I was in Jason's house with no way to get away.

Where would I go anyway? Whatever security I thought

I had in the well-lit halls of the medical center, he stole from me.

His fridge was well stocked, bringing about a whole new set of problems while I tried to figure out what to eat. I finally pulled out a slab of Colby jack cheese and laid it on the counter. Now all I needed was crackers. After poking into a couple of cupboards, I found a box of crackers. I plucked the knife from the wooden block when the front door opened.

My grip tightened on the handle, and my breath caught in my throat.

It was Jason. I was about to chew him a new one when I noticed the cut over his eye was healed, no swelling around his lower lip, and his hair was longer.

"I'm Jared, Jason's brother." He put his hands up in mock surrender. "Not here to hurt you."

I glanced at the knife and set it on the counter by the cheese. "What is it with all these twins? Is it in the water here?"

He shrugged with a crooked smile. "We've got a few of them in our family."

"Where's Jason?"

He sobered a little and crossed to take a stool at the bar. "I ask that a lot lately. He called to see if I could watch the place while he…worked out a few things."

I rolled my eyes and opened the box of crackers. "He told me he's boxing." I laid some crackers out on a plate and started cutting cheese. "Why would a doctor take that kind of risk? He knows what that does to your motor function when you take all those blows to your head, not to mention the beating on your hands." I glanced toward Jared. "Sorry. It's not really any of my business anyway. Want some cheese and crackers?"

"I'm never one to turn down food."

I cut a few pieces of cheese and laid them on the crackers before walking it over to the bar. "So did your brother tell you why I'm his prisoner?"

Jared raised a brow as he picked up a cracker from the plate. "He didn't mention anything about a prison, but he did tell me Nero is looking for you. I don't know your connection to them, but they're dangerous. That's why I agreed to hang out here until he got back."

"My connection. Short answer?" I took a bite and tried not to notice the way he studied me. "They killed my roommate. I found her. Now they want to keep me quiet."

He swallowed and shook his head. "I'm sorry you got sucked into their web. How'd you end up in Reno?"

"Sebastian sent me a new ID and told me to come to Reno. If there was trouble, he told me to find Adam. I did that, but Adam doesn't believe me so..." I shrugged.

Jared rested a forearm on the counter. He had the same strong, solid build as Jason, but he wasn't as cut. His muscles weren't from a gym. His tan skin and rough hands told me he worked outside.

"Jason told me you helped save our dad the day he was attacked."

I nodded. "I work in the medical center by his office. Can I ask you something?"

"Sure."

"Why isn't your father in the hospital? Jason told me he'd admit him that day, but he never did. Why did he lie to me?"

"He had to tell you something." Jared got up from the

stool. "You probably wouldn't have accepted the fact that our family can't go to the hospital."

"What do you mean? Is it your religion? He's a doctor. He knows your dad needs professional medical care."

"Yeah, he does." Jared walked to the window, his back to me. "Why do you think he's out there somewhere getting his face beat in?"

"That makes no sense."

"Doesn't have to." He glanced over his shoulder. "He's a doctor. But having the answers doesn't mean you can solve anything. Our family is…" He focused out the window again. "It's complicated."

"Has your dad regained consciousness?"

He stared into the darkness. "No."

My chest tightened. The chances of his father waking up now were extremely slim. The brain damage must have been too severe. Jason would know that. Had he told the rest of his family, or was this a burden he'd been carrying all alone?

I walked out of the kitchen and sat on the couch. "I'm sorry."

"Yeah, I am, too." He came over and sat at the other end of the sofa. "Your family must be worried about you."

I hoped he didn't notice my shoulders tense up. "I don't have a big family like you. What's left of mine is still in Hawaii. I'm on my own."

"Do they know you're in trouble?"

I thought of the message I'd sent Grandma Nani through our family *aumakua*. "I think so. I'm trying to keep them out of it."

"Family is leverage to Nero. They need to be warned."

I got up and went back into the kitchen to clean up.

Sitting still was an unachievable dream at the moment. "If I warn them, Nero will know right where they are."

He paused for a second and then glanced my way. "You probably understand my brother better than you think. He knows what he should do, too, but he can't. Having your hands tied when lives are on the line sucks."

I put the cheese back and slammed the refrigerator door harder than I intended. "I just need to lay low until they lose interest."

"Not likely to happen with Nero."

Okay, Jared wasn't making me feel any better. "I'm really tired. I think I'm going to try to rest."

He nodded and picked up the TV remote. "All right. Jason should be back soon." I started for the bedroom door when he called, "Thanks for helping Jason save our dad."

"No problem." I went inside and closed the bedroom door. Leaning against it, I blinked back a wave of tears. I hadn't helped save his father.

I helped restart his heart, but the irreparable damage to his mind was done.

And Jason must've already known that.

I jerked awake when the bedroom door opened.

"Sorry. Didn't mean to startle you."

Jason's deep voice had never sounded so good as relief flowed through me.

"Just need a shower and…"

"All your clothes and shampoo and everything are in this bathroom."

He nodded. The light blazed behind him, keeping his face shadowed. I clicked the TV off with the remote and got up from bed. Apparently being terrified was more exhausting than I realized.

He didn't move or speak, just watched me. When I stood in front of him, I could see the swelling under both eyes, and the cut over his brow had reopened. I couldn't find my voice as I stared up at him, my gaze meeting his.

"I was an ass earlier." His voice was barely a whisper. "But I can't take losing anyone else. I know you don't understand it, but…"

I took his hand. Carefully. Jesus, his fingers were swollen, too. Shifting my attention back up to his face, I walked him into the bathroom. "Let me help."

"I'm fine."

My eyes welled with tears as I shook my head. "I'm pretty sure we're both *miles* from fine."

He wrapped his arms around me, and instead of pulling away, I clung to him, careful not to hold too tight. I had no doubt his shirt was hiding some nasty bruises, too. He rested his head on top of mine and whispered, "I'm warning you now. I'm a horrible patient."

I smiled in spite of myself and pulled back. "Of course you are. That's why you're a doctor."

I closed the lid on the toilet and had him sit down so I could get a better look at his banged-up face. In the bright lights of the bathroom, it was tough not to cringe. "You have some first-aid supplies, I hope."

He nodded. "In the medicine cabinet."

I opened the cabinet on the wall and chuckled. "Bactine and Band-Aids? You call this a first-aid kit?" I turned around to find him shirtless, and my breath caught. Every muscle was well defined, strong, and discolored. So many bruises. "How many fights have you been in?"

"Too many."

"Understatement of the year." There was no way Bactine and Band-Aids could fix this. I set them on the counter beside him. "Have you had any X-rays? Your ribs are probably cracked in a few places."

"They're bruised, but I don't think I have any breaks."

There was the confident doctor god complex. I sighed, glancing around the marble counter. "Cotton balls?"

He pointed under the sink. I pulled a bag out of the cabinet and soaked one in the antiseptic. Gently, I touched it to the cut over his eye.

"Jesus." He pushed my hand away. "That's making it worse."

"You *are* a bad patient." I raised a brow. "If you get an infection, this could get even uglier. Better to clean it now."

I pressed it back over the cut, ignoring his growls. By the time I finished with the contusions, he'd given up fighting me. He probably recognized in his present state I could take him. Nurses weren't shrinking violets. And I was a damned fine nurse.

"Can I shower now?"

I inspected his face one last time, trying not to allow my gaze to linger on his lips. "I guess so. I'll get some ice packs ready for your face and a bucket for your hands."

He got up as I went to the door. In the reflection of the mirror, he rolled his eyes. "I don't need ice."

"The hell you don't."

Before I got out the door, a vision flashed in my head. Jason collapsing in the shower, his head bouncing off the cold tile, and blood. I spun around as he hooked his thumbs in the waistband of his shorts.

"Wait. Leave them on. I'm going to help you."

He looked back at me, confusion in his swollen eyes. "I'm perfectly capable of showering."

"I'm sure you are, but you probably have a concussion, so we should be careful."

He shook his head and turned on the shower. "I don't have a concussion, but if it'll make you feel better…"

His words drifted off as his eyes rolled back.

"Shit." I rushed to his side, easing his drop to the floor. There was no way I could support his dead weight, but I could keep him from hitting his head. Once he was on the floor, I wet a washcloth with cold water and sat down, lifting his head into my lap. I pressed the cool cloth to his forehead and patted his cheek, wishing I had smelling salts handy. "Jason?"

His eyes moved behind his eyelids and finally they opened. He stared up at me, disoriented at first before he reached up to take my hand from his forehead. "How? How did you know?"

"Know what?"

"About the concussion. You knew I'd fall."

"Just a hunch."

He sat up slowly, almost nose to nose with me. His gaze locked on mine. "You don't have to lie to me."

"That goes both ways." Steam filled the room, masking the electricity zipping between us. His eyes dipped to my lips, and some idiotic part of my heart hoped he'd kiss me. Thankfully a bolt of clear thought jolted me into action. "We should get you in the shower while the water is still hot."

He blinked and sat up, putting some distance between us. His master bath had a spacious glass shower stall and a big Jacuzzi tub in the far corner. He opened the glass door and a wall of steam billowed out. I braced him, my arm firm around his waist as he stepped inside.

"What about your clothes?"

I glanced down at my T-shirt and jeans. My only clothes I had with me. My bag was still outside in Jason's car. But he couldn't be trusted in a shower alone at the moment. If he passed out again...I didn't allow myself to replay the vision of his blood washing down the drain.

"They've been wet before."

"You don't need to come in here. I'm much better now."

"You are not. I'm coming in with you, or you're not showering." I nudged him forward with my hip. "Stop being a baby and get in there."

The warm water soaked through my clothes, but I hardly noticed. All my attention was focused on Jason. He was much taller than me and probably outweighed me by at least seventy-five pounds, but if he lost consciousness again, I could slow the fall and protect his head.

He tipped his head back under the water and closed his eyes. Before I could say anything, his mouth curved into a smile. "Still awake, but my eyes sting enough already without getting shampoo in them."

I chuckled. "They wouldn't sting if you stopped getting them punched."

He lifted his head from the water, all his attention on me. "Thanks for helping me tonight." His gaze wandered lower and I wondered just how see-through my wet T-shirt might be. He brought a battered hand up to my cheek, his thumb barely brushing my slick skin. "You're so beautiful."

My heart pounded, and I struggled to keep my body from thinking for me. "You've got head trauma."

He almost smiled. "I thought you were beautiful from the moment you banged on my office door and chewed me out."

I pressed my lips together, trying to find a safe place to focus my attention. He filled the entire shower stall, his skin clean and wet, every part of him chiseled. His gym shorts clung to a package I had no business noticing.

His finger caught my chin, lifting it until I met his gaze. "Sorry if I made you uncomfortable. I'm probably a real prize right now."

Every bruise and swollen cut on his ruggedly handsome face only enhanced the spirit inside of him. "You're still way too handsome for your own good."

His legs bent, but not from a lack of consciousness. I rose up on my toes, my lips meeting his halfway. His chest rumbled as he pulled me closer. I couldn't tell if it was a moan of passion or a groan of pain, but it didn't slow the kiss. His mouth savored mine, lingering, tasting, until he parted my lips with his tongue. A sigh escaped my throat as the kiss deepened.

I ran my hands up his chest and around the back of his neck. He took a step forward, pushing me back against the cool wall of the shower. His erection pressed against me, but it didn't wake me from the haze of passion, the urgency of desire. I didn't want to think about reality, about danger, about lies, about the future.

I wanted this complicated man full of secrets and pain and wounds.

Breaking the kiss, he rested his forehead on mine as we both struggled for breath. "If I wasn't so beat up, I'd be stripping you down and taking you right here." He panted a couple of times, and a curl of wet hair dangled over his forehead. "But I'm pretty sure my legs'll give out."

Saved by weak legs. With each breath, reality encroached on the passion he'd stoked inside me. "Yeah, we should get you in bed."

"My thoughts exactly."

"So you can sleep." I turned off the shower and supported him as he got out.

He handed me an oversize bath towel. "I can sleep later."

I kept an eye on him for any signs of dizziness as we dried off, but he seemed steady. Now that I was out of the hot water, my clothes were getting cold. Before I could say anything, he wrapped another towel around my shoulders.

"I'll get you some dry clothes."

His broad shoulders filled the doorway as he stepped out into the carpeted master bedroom. My heart pounded as I reached up to touch my well-kissed lips. I would've slept with him, just like my vision. Shit. What was happening to me?

Dry clothes were the least of my worries.

Chapter Nine

Inside the walk-in closet, I leaned against the wall, sucking in a slow, cleansing breath. I'd been around the block. I'd kissed my share of women, probably more than my share. But nothing prepared me for the firestorm of kissing my mate. She unraveled me. I hadn't been lying. If my body wasn't so beat up, I would've lifted her up and taken her in the shower. The wolf's instinct to claim her as mine intoxicated me.

Only my injuries held me back.

And now that blood made its way back above my shoulders, reality cut through the instinct and lust. If all the old Pack stories were true, that tiny fireball of a woman who stood drenched in my bathroom was the only woman I would ever love.

But she wasn't a werewolf and didn't share the bond that my wolf already recognized. And although that kiss made it clear she might be physically attracted to me, she still didn't trust me. Maybe she never would.

Shit. I didn't even want to think about my future if she walked out of it.

At the back of the closet, I pulled a pair of sweatpants and a plain blue T-shirt off the shelf. There was no way they'd fit her, but they'd keep her warm while her things were in the dryer. I came around the corner to find her bent over, towel-drying her hair. When she straightened and flipped her damp hair down her back, a tentative smile tugged at the corners of her mouth.

"I was starting to worry you passed out again."

I handed her the dry clothes. "Nah, just took me a minute to get my head together."

"You should go lay down. I'll be right out." She closed the door, and I tried not to think about her naked in my bathroom. Too late.

I piled my pillows up and got into bed. Keeping my head elevated would help with the swelling, or I hoped it would. Fighting again tonight hadn't been my best idea. The door opened and my breath caught. Kilani stood in the threshold in my blue T-shirt and nothing else. My gaze ran over her smooth, tanned legs. The baggy shirt masked her curves, but her hardened nipples were impossible to miss. She had the wet clothes in her hands, and the sweatpants were folded on the counter behind her.

"The pants were too big?"

She rolled her eyes and chuckled. "They kept falling down, so I figured I'd be safer without tripping over them." She lifted her wet things. "Can you point me in the direction of the dryer?"

"I'll take them for you."

I sat up and she frowned.

"You're supposed to be resting."

"Putting your clothes in the dryer isn't hard labor."

"Still requires being upright." She came forward and patted my bare foot. "Give your body a break, okay?"

I groaned and settled against the pillows again. "Through the kitchen, it's right inside the garage."

"I'll be right back."

She walked toward the door while I took in the view and wished I'd given her a shorter T-shirt. When she disappeared from the bedroom, I stared at the ceiling, wracking my battered head for my next move. My mate was in my house, in my shirt, and yet she was still miles from being mine.

Earlier she'd known I was going to faint. There was no other explanation for her sudden urge to get in the shower with me. She went to Brightwood. They wouldn't have taken her without some proof of psychic abilities. But she denied it. She wanted the truth, but I couldn't give her that, so why did I expect her to share hers with me?

I was screwed.

"Okay, I should have dry clothes in the morning." She came in and grabbed a pillow before walking to the closet.

"What are you doing?"

She glanced over at me. "Just need an extra blanket."

"You can sleep here." She didn't come any closer. I sighed. "Do I look like I'm in any condition to ravage you?"

That made her smile. A little. "I just don't want to give you mixed signals. In the shower before…" She shook her head. "I'm sorry about that. I'm not looking for…more."

I ran my fingers back through my wet hair, ignoring

the ache in my hand and arm. "What is it with you and that gigantic chip on your shoulder?"

Her features sobered. "I prefer to think of it as protective armor from lying doctors."

A deep growl rumbled in my chest. "You think you want truth, but you don't want mine. Trust me."

She crossed her arms, hugging the pillow. "Try me."

I ground my teeth together. "I don't even know where to start."

She came closer to the bed, her voice warming. "How about starting with your father's condition? Jared told me he hasn't regained consciousness."

"No, he hasn't." My gut twisted. I struggled to cling to my professional distance as a medical doctor instead of a son. "He doesn't respond to any stimulus that I've seen, although my mother claims he squeezes her hand sometimes. You and I both know that could be reflex, not a real sign of cognitive function."

She dropped the pillow and sat on the edge of the bed. "Have you talked to your family about his condition?"

The rage I thought I'd exhausted in the boxing ring came roaring back as I propped myself up. "No, I haven't told them that he's most likely brain dead." I turned, letting my legs settle off the side of the bed, my back to her, protecting me from her compassionate dark eyes. The last thing I wanted was her pity. "I'm way too personally involved to make this decision. He's breathing on his own, so we'd have to withdraw the IVs. He'd get dehydrated and eventually…"

I glared at the ceiling. I couldn't even say the words out loud.

The mattress shifted behind me and her gentle hands

caressed the tops of my weary shoulders. "You've been carrying an awful lot of worry on these shoulders all alone. Your brother said you can't take him to a hospital. He wouldn't tell me why."

There was the million-dollar secret. It went against everything the Pack had ever taught me, but she wouldn't believe me anyway, so what the hell, at least she'd stop asking about it. She already thought I was a liar, so what did it matter?

Nothing mattered anymore.

"My father is a werewolf. We can't risk his DNA, and tissues, being discovered at a hospital."

She stopped rubbing my shoulders. I listened, waiting to hear her footsteps racing toward the front door.

"Your father is a what?"

I turned enough to see her face. "We shift into wolves during the full moon, Kilani."

She sat back on her heels. "If this is supposed to be a joke, it's not funny."

"Yeah, it's far from funny." A humorless chuckle escaped my lips, and I reached over to lift her chin until her gaze met mine. "I *wish* I was joking." Her dark almond eyes searched my face. I waited and finally whispered, "I'm the Pack doctor. I'm their only hope for healing and I can't take them to the hospital for proper care."

Shaking her head, her attention shifted to her bare ankle, her fingers sliding over the turtle tattoo. "I want to see your father."

I blinked. Of the million responses to "I'm a werewolf," asking to see my father hadn't even made the top 100 on my list. "What?"

She scooted up to sit beside me on the bed. "Take me to him tomorrow. I might be able to help."

"I appreciate the offer, but without an EEG and a CAT scan, there's no way to assess the damage. He's breathing on his own, but there's no way to know if he'll ever…" I got up, unable to sit still and finish that sentence. In a desperate attempt to change the subject, I wheeled around toward her. "What does seeing my father have to do with my family being werewolves? Or are you trying to forget I admitted that?"

"Oh, I haven't forgotten." She got up, fierce as she glared up at me. "Are you judging me because I didn't run screaming out of the room? Or maybe I should've laughed in your face. Would that be more acceptable to you?"

"What is your problem?" Usually I was much better at reading women. "You said you wanted honesty. I just gave you a heaping helping of truth and now you're pissed at me?"

"Forgive me for not reacting properly." The fire in her eyes dimmed. Slightly. "Look, I have no idea if you're nuts, teasing me, or if by some crazy chance maybe werewolves are real. I went to a boarding school where the only admission requirement was psychic abilities, so I'm willing to believe there might be other things in the world I don't know about."

She took my hand, her touch soothing the agitation brewing in my gut. "Telling me your secret isn't what set me off, it was your tone. Rage swells inside of you like a cancer. You've been carrying this burden for your brother and your mother, and it's killing you whether you acknowledge it or not. What will happen when taking punches and landing them doesn't relieve the stress anymore?"

I did *not* want to talk about this. I went back to the bed and sat down, staring at my hands. "Fine. Tomorrow morning you call in sick to the hospital, and I'll take you to my dad."

"I'm on the third shift tomorrow. I can see your dad and still make it to the hospital in time."

I snapped my head up so fast, a wave of dizziness blurred my vision. "It's not safe for you there."

"I'm not helpless. I'll be careful. I have pepper spray. And…" She came to sit beside me. "It'll be tough for them to sneak up on me."

"How so?"

She shrugged. "I get hunches."

I smelled the lie between us. Catching her chin, I lifted her gaze to mine. "I admitted to you that I'm a werewolf and you *still* can't tell me you're psychic?"

Her eyes widened before she yanked away from my touch. "I don't know what you're talking about."

"The hell you don't." I clenched my swollen fingers into battered fists. The pain helped to rein in the anger. Before my life spiraled out of control, I used to be a pretty patient guy. Until now, I hadn't noticed just how short my fuse had become.

Having my dominant wolf awake and alert that our mate was close by didn't help. "You went to Brightwood Academy. Tonight you *knew* I was going to pass out. I don't have to be Sherlock Holmes to put the pieces together."

I waited for her to answer, wanted her to take the bait, to feed the fire.

She got up and walked over to pick up the pillow from the floor. "See you in the morning."

In spite of the aches and pains, I beat her to the door. "Wait." Her eyes narrowed and I added, "Please."

She sighed. "I'm not going to talk about this, so we might as well get some sleep."

I pulled my damp hair back from my forehead. "You know, when you're not pushing me away, we make a good team. You helped me save my father and kept me safe from more head trauma in the bathroom earlier. I trusted you with a secret. Why can't you trust me?"

She brought her hand to rest over her heart. "Because something in here is broken."

"And I'm not?" I shook my head. "Look at me." Taking her hand, I pressed it to my chest. "Maybe we can fix each other."

"No."

"No?" I frowned as she pulled away from me.

"Everyone who mattered walked out of my life except my grandmother, and then I walked out of hers. That's how it is with me. You've got your family, your brother. You'll get through this, and you'll find some beautiful werewolf woman and live happily ever after. I'm on a different path."

"First off, there are no werewolf women." I could explain details later. For now, I just wanted to keep her in the room. "Second, I don't know if you've noticed, but I'm a fighter. I don't walk away when the road gets rough."

"Well, I do."

She reached for the door handle and I caught her wrist, yanking her close. "Enough bullshit, Kilani. I tell you I'm a werewolf and you don't freak out. I mention being psychic and you can't get out of here fast enough."

Her gaze lowered to where I held her and back up to my

face. I let her go.

"My psychic abilities got me involved with Brightwood, and one day I got a vision that scared me. I pretended my powers faded. They lost interest. I graduated and put myself through nursing school. I'd rather not have it get out that I still get flashes of the future. Now we've both shared a secret. Happy now?"

My pulse pounded. My mate was not only exotic and beautiful, she was intelligent and wise. Hiding her powers probably saved her from a Nero lab or, worse yet, the jaguar-shifter breeding program Sasha had warned us about.

Too bad she didn't seem to be admiring me likewise. With her hip jutted to the side and her jaw set in a stern frown, it was clear she'd finished with our conversation.

"Is that why you want me to take you to my dad?"

She shrugged. "Sometimes when I touch people, it can jar a vision loose. My gift isn't an exact science, and the things I see are usually only a couple minutes into the future. Pretty useless if you want to keep something from happening or change it, but for a nurse, it comes in handy. If I can sit with him, I might be able to get something to give you answers."

Answers. I'd pay anything for a few of those. Staring into her eyes, there was so much I wanted to say, to tell her, but stringing sentences together seemed impossible.

"Thank you." Without meaning to, I caressed her cheek. She didn't pull away, but she didn't rise up and kiss me, either. I swallowed the emotion choking my throat and whispered, "I haven't had anyone to talk to about this. I… Shit, I don't know what I'm trying to say. I probably should've quit at thank you."

Chapter Ten

KILANI

Seeing the pain in his eyes, hearing it in his voice, almost undid me. The honesty and rawness in his tone had me clinging by a thread, but I reminded myself he just told me he was a werewolf. That werewolves exist.

But if I believed my ancestors could communicate to Grandma Nani through a turtle, how could I dismiss werewolves without at least considering the possibility?

This wasn't helping me keep my resolve.

I stepped back, distancing myself from his distracting touch. "I'll set the timer on my cell phone to wake me up to check on you and your head trauma, but for now, can I go get some sleep?"

He nodded but didn't move away from the door. "You can have the bed. I've got a futon in my office. I can stay in there."

Again he surprised me by putting me first, reminding me that my past relationships had set the bar low. Limbo champion low. "You look like you've been through a meat grinder. I can't let you sleep on a futon."

The corner of his mouth curved into a lopsided smile. My idiotic heart fluttered. "I might need a nurse close by."

I rolled my eyes, fighting to keep from smiling. "We're a little old for playing doctor."

"Who said anything about playing?"

For a guy who probably had a concussion and cracked ribs, he moved like the wind, his lips fusing to mine, his fingers tangling in my hair. My shock ignited into hunger, and unlike our earlier kiss, this time I embraced it.

Why not? Life had no guarantees at the moment. My best friend was dead, and I could be next. Here was this handsome, intelligent doctor who wanted me.

So he had a few demons and claimed he's a werewolf. For tonight, we could comfort each other. I didn't have to let him anywhere near my heart.

Jason backed me toward the bed, our tongues sliding together in a sensual dance. He tasted fresh and wild. I ran my hands up his chest, enjoying the rumble of his pleasure in the kiss. His hand slid under the oversize shirt I wore, his touch heating up my entire body until my nipples were taut, aching for his attention.

And then my phone rang.

"Voicemail," he growled against my lips.

Tempting. It rang again and I broke the kiss, struggling to catch my breath. "Sebastian gave me that phone. He could have news or a warning."

Jason groaned but released me. My legs wobbled as I

hustled to the bathroom where I'd left it charging. Sebastian's name flashed on the screen. "Hello?"

"I only have a minute. My brother is in Reno now, taking lead on this mission to silence you. Did you find Adam?"

"Yes, but he won't help me unless he talks to you first. He thinks I could be bait or a trick or something."

"Wolves." He paused long enough for me to wonder if the call had dropped. "At least tell me you are not alone."

"I'm not. Jason let me stay at his place."

"The doctor?" He groaned. "*That's* who they sent to protect you?"

Jason stalked across the room and took my cell phone; apparently he heard our conversation just fine.

"Listen, asshole, I'm more than capable of keeping Kilani safe." He held the phone away from his ear so I could hear, too.

"Enough with the ego, Wolf. My brother is there with a trained mercenary team searching for her. You may be able to treat her wounds, but she needs more than a doctor to elude them."

I snatched my phone back from Jason. Their little pissing contest wasn't helping me. "Aside from your brother being in town, is there anything else I need to know?"

"I'm being watched so I can't leave yet. I will get to Reno as soon as I can, but I must not appear to be rushing. This is his mission, not mine."

"And in English that means?"

He hissed. I could almost hear his eyes rolling. "I will try to be there by tomorrow night to meet with Adam. I will make contact when I can. Until then, stay alert."

The line went dead. I turned to find Jason across the

room, his back to me with his arm up on the window frame. His head rested against it as he stared into the darkness.

I took a couple steps toward the bed. "Now I understand what a sitting duck feels like."

He didn't move. "I'm sorry about earlier. I should've had my full attention on watching for threats. Usually I have better self-control. But you…you make it tough for me to think straight."

With the mood decimated, I got into the bed. No sense splitting up now; we'd be safer together. "Just for the record, I was the one who offered to sleep out on the futon."

He finally moved, pushing off the window frame and approaching the bed. "This thing between us is more than just a physical attraction for me. Around you something inside…" He tapped his chest and seemed like he might say more. With a sigh, he shook his head and sat on the opposite side of the mattress. "Never mind. I'm sure this seems insane. It sounds crazy to me too, and I'm living it."

"Crazier than telling me you're a werewolf?"

"Let's cross one bridge at a time." He glanced over at me with a chuckle, but his features were anything but happy. "In the morning, I'll take you to see my dad. My mom and my brother will probably be there, too. Then you can decide if we're all nuts."

"And then you'll tell me the even crazier thing?"

He almost smiled. "I'll think about it."

I slid into bed, trying not to allow my earlier vision of our naked bodies to torment me. Now that I was well aware of Jason's kissing ability and the way my body responded to his touch, it was impossible *not* to imagine what would've come next if my phone hadn't rang, bringing reality crashing in with it.

He turned out the light and I closed my eyes.

"Kilani?"

My name sounded beautiful in his deep, rich voice.

"Yeah?"

"Just so you know, doctor or not, I will beat the ever-living shit out of any person who ever tries to hurt you. And if I knew who broke your heart, I'd hunt him down and make him pay."

Too bad he'd have to start with my own mother.

I awoke disoriented. After hightailing it out of New York and across the country to Reno, I still lacked a real home base, but even so, this was *not* my new apartment. A steady heartbeat thumped in my ear. Lifting my head, I stared down at Jason. I was in Jason's house, his bedroom. His bed.

His face was still bruised, but the cut on his eyebrow had scabbed over. He didn't have the swelling I'd expected. We hadn't iced his eye, but other than the discoloration, no one would guess he'd been pummeled the night before. Memories crept back into my consciousness.

Werewolf.

In the morning light, it sounded even crazier than it had last night. But it might explain his superhuman healing.

He opened his eyes, surprising me. For a moment, he just stared up at me. My breath caught in my throat being so close to him. Until now, I hadn't realized his arm was around me while we slept. It had been so natural, like our bodies fit together.

"I didn't mean to wake you. Sorry about that."

He reached up, cupping my face in his hand. "I'm not." His thumb caressed my cheek. "I wish we could stay here."

I chuckled, shaking my head. "I've never been on the run from bad guys before, but I'm guessing being half naked in bed is probably not the best plan."

He raised his uncut brow. "Rain check, then?"

"You don't give up, do you?"

He sobered, his gaze locked on mine. "Not where you're concerned."

I sat up, extricating myself from his arms. Tough to think straight with my hands resting on his toned, bare chest. The heat in his eyes didn't help, either. "Are you still taking me to see your father?"

The bed shifted, but I didn't turn around. Now was his chance to make an excuse. I readied myself. This was *not* the first time a doctor didn't want to bring me home to meet his folks.

"Yeah. I need to check his vitals anyway." He groaned behind me, his joints popping. "And then we should find the mole who tipped off Nero that you were in town."

I got up and went to the door. My clothes were in the dryer. I had some fresh ones in my bag in the trunk of Jason's car, but I wasn't going in the driveway like this. I glanced at him over my shoulder. "I have a shift to work today, too."

"Are you trying to pick a fight with me?"

Was I? "Just reminding you. You can afford a few days off. I can't." I left before he could reply.

Crossing the living room to the kitchen, my gaze wandered to the framed wolves on the wall. If werewolves were real, if what he said was true, then Adam must be the alpha.

That's why Sebastian sent me to him. Sebastian had grumbled on the phone last night about "wolves."

A werewolf pack might be strong enough to hold off a mercenary unit from Nero.

This was certifiably nuts. Being psychic was one thing, but this went beyond any woo-woo I'd ever been exposed to at school. This was believing that there could be another species of humans that shifted into wolves.

I gnawed at my lower lip. Jason's father lay in a bed at home instead of in a hospital. For a doctor, that was going against everything the medical profession demanded for patients who'd experienced anoxic encephalopathy. His father could be in a vegetative state permanently from the lack of oxygen to his brain. There'd be no way Jason would keep him out of a hospital where he could be monitored.

Unless werewolves were real and they didn't want doctors, and scientists in the hospital lab, to discover them. What had his twin brother said? *Our family is complicated…*

I pulled my clothes from the dryer and changed quickly inside the small laundry room, dropping Jason's shirt I borrowed into the empty washing machine. Since our impromptu shower the night before, I didn't need to waste any time on it this morning.

On my way back to the bedroom, I made a pit stop in the kitchen to get some coffee started. I'd hated coffee until I started in nursing. Long shifts taught me to covet the power boost of caffeine, and a bunch of cream and sugar helped to mask the taste.

Jason came out, pulling a moss green tee down over his washboard abs. "Smells like you found the coffee."

"Hope you don't mind." I glanced at the coffee maker. "I

filled it with enough water for both of us."

"Sounds great." He passed by me, the scent of musk and pine teasing my senses. He pulled two travel mugs out of the cupboard. "I went out and got your bag from the car while you were changing. It's sitting on the bed if you want to brush your hair before we go."

He brought my stuff inside without being asked. Again, I was reminded how low my previous relationships had set the bar on my expectations. Part of me wanted to throw a parade in his honor. I wasn't used to simple acts of kindness.

"Thanks. I'll be right back."

After tying my hair back in a ponytail, I brushed my teeth, added a touch of mascara and lip gloss, and tried to tell myself the primping was for my shift at the hospital and not to impress Jason's parents. This wasn't a date; it was a favor. And it might not even work. I could open my mind for visions, but I couldn't force them to appear on command.

In the kitchen, Jason was filling the travel mugs. I watched him for a moment until he finally looked over my way. "Everything okay?"

I shrugged and started adding cream and sugar. "You're a fast healer. I still can't believe you're not swollen up. We didn't even ice your eye, but other than the bruising and the scab over the cut, no one would know you got in a fight."

He put the lid on his mug, and a tendril of steam slithered out the slit in the top like a serpent. "You're still thinking I might be certifiable?"

Stirring, I reached for the lid to the travel mug. "Not certifiable, but maybe not a werewolf, either."

"I can't blame you. If I wasn't living it, I probably wouldn't believe me." He took a relaxed sip of the coffee like we'd been friends forever, but the desire in his gaze said he wanted us to be more. My body responded with a flush of heat, and I hadn't even tasted the coffee yet.

"If this really is true, why trust me with it? We barely know each other. Maybe I'm a crazy gossip."

He laughed and my heart fluttered. "Who would believe you even if you did gossip?"

I took a slow swallow, a groan of pleasure humming on my lips. "If werewolves are real, is Adam your alpha?"

"It *is* real." He turned off the coffee maker and put the cream and sugar away. "And yes, Adam is my Alpha. That's why I need Sebastian to get his ass out here and talk to him so we can get the Pack involved and keep Nero away from you."

The reminder of danger zapped conversation, keeping the drive to his parents' house draped in silence. Quiet gave me plenty of time to second-guess my abilities. I shouldn't have told Jason I might be able to "see" something about his father's condition. After a few weeks of frustration and worry, how disheartened would he be when I couldn't tell him anything, or worse yet, what if the future was bleak?

Would he be frustrated enough to step into that boxing ring again?

And why did I care? It was none of my business. Not really. Were we friends? I did help him bring his father back, and now he was helping me evade Nero. That had to count for something.

He turned in to a wooded community surrounding Lake Stanley. "You're awfully quiet."

"I could say the same about you." Outside the car, birds huddled close together on a power line keeping warm against the brisk fall morning. "Anything I should know about your folks before we get there?"

"Well, you know about my dad's condition." He made a slow right turn, his gaze darting toward me for a second. "And you've already met Jared."

"What about your mom?"

A sad smile curved his lips. "My mom's name is Sarah. She's taking a sabbatical from her commercial real estate firm to take care of Dad. You'll like her. She's smart and probably the strongest person I know."

He pulled the car into a tree-lined brick driveway that led to a stunning stone home with a gabled roof. After he turned off the engine, his attention shifted to me. "She's also certain my dad is going to wake up and be himself." Pain etched lines around his gorgeous eyes. "I've told her that each day he doesn't respond, his chances of a full recovery are less likely, but her hope is unshakable." He broke eye contact, blinking hard before he cleared his throat. "I want her to be right, I do. But I know he's probably already…"

He didn't finish. He didn't need to. I got out of the car and followed him to the front door. He knocked, and Jared answered with an easygoing smile. He obviously carried his mother's optimism.

"Kilani. Good to see you again." He and Jason clasped forearms before they shared a quick embrace complete with back slap. He lowered his voice. "You look better than I thought you would after getting your face beat last night."

Jason rolled his eyes. "It was the other guy who got beat." His soft tone matched his brother's. "You didn't say anything to Mom, right?"

Jared shook his head. "No, but you're going to run out of excuses for those bruises and cuts soon."

He led us inside, and I did my best to keep my jaw from hitting the floor. The vaulted ceiling of the living room went up two stories, with a floor-to-ceiling natural stone fireplace on the far wall. The open staircase leading upstairs had a red gnarled wood bannister. Stunning, yet not opulent. It still gave off the feel that someone lived here. Welcoming.

Jared brought us down a hallway toward a back bedroom. The artwork lining the walls were of wild animals, not wolves, but the life in their eyes tipped me off. I glanced up at Jason. "Yours?"

He nodded. "Yeah."

I took his hand without thinking. "You're really talented when you're not shoving these into boxing gloves."

He gave my hand a squeeze. "And you're sweet when you're not hating me for being a doctor."

I had to smile. "Touché."

We stepped into the back bedroom, and a woman with shoulder-length silver hair and bright auburn eyes, Jason's eyes, set her book aside and stood up. "I was catching Wyatt up on his new James Patterson novel."

She came to stand before me, and I expected to be judged, but she pulled me into a hug. When she stepped back, a bittersweet smile warmed her features. "Sorry. I'm a hugger when it comes to people who save the lives of my family."

"Anyone would have done the same." She wasn't as tall as her sons, but she had at least six inches over me. "I was a nurse in the right place at the right time."

She shook her head, a spark of wisdom in her eyes. "I don't believe in coincidences. You were right where you were supposed to be that day."

If I hadn't been there that day, maybe I wouldn't have

ever met Jason. Could that be part of some greater plan? I swallowed the unanswerable questions and shifted my attention to Jason's dad. I hadn't seen him since the day we got his heart beating again on the floor of the hallway in the medical offices. His coloring looked good, and there was no sign of muscle contractions in his limbs.

Jason checked his vitals, and I got a familiar flash in my mind of what he'd need next. I grabbed a fresh bag of fluids from the shelf and handed it to him as he turned, ready to speak. He chuckled and almost smiled but didn't mention my psychic gift out loud. "Thanks."

"No problem." I took the empty bag from him and disposed of it while he got the new bag started. Sarah sat beside Wyatt, holding his hand, and my chest tightened painfully. How had Jason been shouldering this bad news all alone? She read to Wyatt and chatted with him like he could regain consciousness at any second. How could Jason tell his mother that her husband was never going to wake up?

"Can I get a closer look at your husband?"

"Of course." She stepped aside, but I noticed the questioning glance in Jason's direction.

"She knows, Mom." His voice rumbled behind me as I took the chair at the head of Wyatt's bed. "I told her."

His mother cleared her throat. "That's a big risk. Does Adam know?"

Jared chuckled. "Only the tip of the iceberg, Ma."

I looked back at them. "I'm assuming you're talking about the wolf thing?"

Sarah almost cringed. The hair started to rise on the back of my neck. Before I could say anything, a vision blinded me. Wyatt upright, standing beside Jason. He winked at me. And then it was gone.

I blinked hard, clearing my head. Usually my visions were limited to the very near future within two to five minutes of it happening, like with the IV bag. But even if Wyatt chose now to open his eyes, he wouldn't be standing up on his own for at least a couple of days.

Just like my earlier vision of Jason in bed with me, I had no clue when this one would come to pass or if it was all wishful thinking.

"Are you all right?" Jason kneeled at my side.

"Yeah." I looked past him to his mother. "Sarah, how long has it been since you got out of this house? You should go eat."

"I stay with Wyatt. He'd do the same for me."

"I have no doubt he would, and I'd still kick him out to get some fresh air and have breakfast with his sons, too. " I met Jason's eyes, trying to send him a mental message he'd never hear. "I'm a nurse. He'll be safe here with me, and you can have some fresh air. I'll call if there's any change in his condition."

Truth be told, I needed all of them out so I could relax and trust my gift, but there was no reason not to use the chance for Sarah to get away for a meal.

Jason straightened. "She's right. Get your coat, Mom. We're taking you to breakfast."

"I don't think I can…"

I smiled. "He'd want you to get out, right? He'd make you go eat if he could."

"You're probably right." She sighed, glancing at each of her sons. Finally she went to the other side of the bed and pressed a tender kiss to her husband's forehead. "But just for breakfast and we'll come right back."

"You got it." Jared nodded to Jason and me as he walked his mother out.

Jason sat on the edge of the bed and waited until I looked up at him. "Did you see something?"

I could barely manage a whisper. "Something, but I need more time to figure it out."

He kept his voice low. "I can't leave you here alone with Nero out there someplace. Jared can take my mom out, but I'll stay here in the living room if you need me."

I studied his eyes, the window to his soul. He made no move to shield himself. "You really are a werewolf, aren't you? You all are."

He nodded slowly. "Yeah." He took my hand. "That's the only reason my dad isn't in a facility." He leaned closer and whispered against my ear, "It's also why, unless we whisper like this, my brother and mom can hear every word."

My lips brushed the soft skin below his ear. "Good to know."

"I've got more to tell you." His grip on my hand tightened a little. "Later." He got up, his fingers sliding free from mine. "I'll be out there if you need me."

I watched him go, my pulse still thrumming. I wasn't sure if it was having his body so close to me or the fact that I was starting to believe werewolves might be real. Maybe both. Either way, I needed to clear my head.

Wyatt Ayers had the same rugged features as his sons, with a masculine, strong jawline and a wise brow. Other than the brief flash in my vision, I'd never seen him with his eyes open, but I imagined they'd shine with life. If he still possessed any. I reached for his wrist, counting his pulse. His heartbeat seemed steady.

Down the hall, the front door opened and clunked shut. I stared down at Jason's dad. "I sent your beautiful wife out to get some breakfast. Hope you don't mind. I figured you'd want her to get some sunshine."

A small CD player sat on the bookshelf across from the bed. Music. I got up to investigate. I had no clue what he listened to, but anything would be better than the silence for me to relax. If I couldn't clear my thoughts, I'd never get another vision.

I pressed play and a single guitar plucked a few notes that flooded my eyes with unexpected tears. Neil Diamond's warm baritone sent me right back to the island, sitting on Grandma Nani's knee while she rocked me and sang along to "I Am…I Said."

A secret stash of Neil Diamond songs was on my playlist whenever I needed to feel close to her. And here she was.

Swallowing the lump in my throat, I took my seat at Wyatt's bedside. "My grandma Nani is the biggest Neil Diamond fan in Hawaii." I took his hand, trying not to focus. Forcing a psychic vision meant I'd get nothing. Unfortunately, I didn't have a switch to turn it on and off. "I'm Kilani. I helped Jason the day you were attacked."

I closed my eyes, shifting my attention to the music, to happy memories with my grandmother. Gradually the scene shifted. Wyatt stood beside Jason, both of them smiling in my direction. And then I heard a voice. *I need a little more time. Trying to find my way back. Tell them I'm still here.*

He squeezed my hand, hard, and the connection was broken. "Jason!"

Chapter Eleven

JASON

I sprang from the sofa, racing for the back room. The remote for the television crashed to the floor, exploding batteries behind me. I hardly noticed.

Kilani looked up with tears in her eyes and a tender smile. "He needs more time."

"More time?" I sat on the edge of the bed. "I don't understand."

She patted my thigh with her free hand, the simple touch soothing the adrenaline pumping through my body. "I can't explain it exactly, but he's in there. I think there's some damage from the lack of oxygen, but he's trying to find new pathways. He wanted me to tell you he's still here."

Relief, hope, and joy swelled inside me like a tidal wave. A tsunami of relief. Without thinking, I bent down and scooped her up into my arms, embracing her and laughing.

She squeaked at first, but she didn't wriggle free. A tear slid down my cheek as I buried my face in her hair, breathing her into my lungs. My mate was a freaking miracle. A gift I would never deserve.

"Thank you isn't big enough for what you just gave me."

"Your dad is a tough guy." She held me tight, her breath warming my ear. "I have no idea how long he'll be like this."

"Knowing he's still alive...really alive. That's enough."

I kissed her, hard and needy. I didn't have words for the feelings roiling inside of me like a tempest. Her lips parted, and I growled at the sweet taste of her mouth. Her fingers slid through my hair as she tilted her head and our kiss deepened. I never wanted to let her go. This amazing woman, my mate.

Her soft lips met mine over and over, scorching my soul as she gradually pulled back. "If I had known werewolves were such great kissers, I would've found one much sooner."

Just the thought of her lips touching another man had my inner wolf snarling. "I want to do more than kiss." I placed her feet back on the ground. "But first we've got to get Nero out of Reno."

She straightened her shirt and nodded. "When are you going to tell me the crazier thing?"

"Crazier thing?"

"Yeah. You wanted me to get used to the werewolf idea first."

Mates. Shit, I wanted her to love me before I dropped that bomb. She didn't hate me right now, and she seemed to want me physically, but we'd barely scratched the surface of her heart. I practically had to force her to admit she was psychic. If I told her she was my mate...

All of this was insane. There was no scientific explanation. No way a single touch could determine who I would love. Did I love her? I hardly knew her.

But the instinctive connection through my wolf grew stronger by the second. As impossible as it seemed, I had no doubt I'd die to keep this woman safe. Give up my life in a heartbeat.

Was that love? Maybe. Probably.

She stared at me. "Well?"

My brother's truck pulled up the driveway. "They're back."

"They are?" She frowned. "How do you know that?"

"Some of my senses, like my hearing, are enhanced even while I'm not in wolf form."

"To go with your fast healing."

I shrugged. "We might heal a little faster than you, but not much. Hearing and our sense of smell are definitely the most noticeable. We're stronger than humans, too."

Her smile warmed her features, shining in her eyes. "Okay, it's really weird to hear you call me a mere human."

"I didn't mean it like that." She had me grinning now, too. "Werewolves have a different genetic makeup, that's all."

"Honey, we're home," Jared called as he opened the front door.

I turned toward the hallway. "We're back here with Dad."

Mom brushed past me to sit in the chair by my dad's head. She kissed his forehead and took his hand. "Missed you, Wyatt. I had an extra piece of bacon for you."

She gasped and smiled up at me. "He squeezed my hand. Did you see that?"

"I think he missed you, too." Kilani walked around and turned off the music.

I hadn't even noticed it was on. How was I going to keep her safe when anytime I was near her she became all that mattered?

My mom beamed. "I'll be right here when you're ready to open your eyes."

"Thanks for kicking Mom out for a little while." Jared came behind our mother and rubbed her shoulders. "She needed a little break."

"No problem." Kilani returned to my side. "I'm happy to come by and sit with him whenever I can."

"You're an angel." My mom's gaze shifted between us and finally landed square on me. "She's your... That's why you told her about..."

Oh shit. I shook my head, interrupting her realization. "Kilani is a friend in trouble, Mom. I'm helping her out."

Kilani's posture stiffened beside me. *Damn it.* But there was nothing I could do right now. There was no way to fix whatever I'd just broken if my mom started planning a wedding. I'd just gotten Kilani past thinking werewolves were fictional and that I was nuts. I couldn't have my mom babbling about mates for life.

"She's got a shift at the hospital, so we'd better get going. Keep me posted on Dad's condition, okay?"

My mom nodded and went back to talking to my dad. With that bullet dodged, I gave my brother's shoulder a squeeze. "Talk to you soon, bro."

He smiled at Kilani. "Be careful out there."

"We will. Thanks." She walked out without a second look in my direction.

"You've got your hands full with that one." Jared tipped his head toward the door. "I like her."

"Me, too." I grinned like an idiot in spite of the current situation. Couldn't help it.

Kilani waited at the front door. Silent. At least she remembered there was danger out there looking for her and stayed inside.

I opened the door a little, taking in a slow breath. One more while scanning the trees. Nothing unusual. Satisfied there were no scents I didn't recognize, I reached back for her hand. She walked around me and out to the car.

Damn it. Biting back a growl, I closed the door and followed.

Inside the car, I started the engine but didn't take it out of park. "Want to tell me what's wrong?"

"I'm fine."

"Oh, please." I shifted my attention out the front window, hoping to stop myself from saying something I might regret later. "We may not have known each other long, but I can see you're not happy."

"I know better." She rolled her eyes and glared at the trees. "This shouldn't bother me. I've been through it more than once. When your mom greeted me with a hug earlier, it threw me off. I lost sight of where I stand. I'm just pissed I let it surprise me."

A humorless chuckle escaped me before I could stop myself. "Where you stand?" My grip tightened at the bottom of the steering wheel, that all-too-familiar frustration simmering in my gut. "What are you talking about?"

She groaned and shifted in her seat. "Your mom thought I might be your girlfriend, and the horror that her son, the doctor, might be sleeping with a little island girl nurse was too much for her. This isn't the first time I've seen that face. You saw it, too, and back-pedaled me into the friend zone like a champ."

I opened my mouth to reply, but for a second I was speechless. "Whoa." Turning off the ignition, I ground my teeth, gathering my thoughts. "You think my mom and I give a rat's ass that you're Polynesian? Give me a break. I wouldn't care of your skin was green."

"Easy to say that when we're alone in a car." She pointed toward the house. "But in that room, your mom put two and two together, and the shock on her face said it all. She was already picturing her grandchildren looking nothing like her son, and you covered it so she wouldn't worry." She gulped a breath, the anger dissipating just enough for me to glimpse the pain hiding underneath.

Shit. I never meant to hurt her, but how would I explain about mates without her getting a restraining order?

I stared at her profile as she gazed into the distance. Who had ever made her feel like she was anything less than a beautiful miracle? I'd kill the bastard, or maybe hurt him bad enough he'd *wish* I'd kill him.

Usually I didn't fantasize about getting even, but my protective wolf was closer to the surface right now than I'd ever experienced. Instincts to keep her safe colored every thought and decision.

I ran the back of my fingers down her soft cheek until she met my eyes. "Kilani, I would never be ashamed to tell the world you were mine, if that were true. You're smart, tough, intelligent, and so beautiful."

She blinked back tears as she rolled her eyes. "Again,

easy to say that while we're alone in the car."

"Wouldn't you have been equally pissed if I had told my mom you were my girlfriend when I hadn't even bridged that with you yet?"

Sighing, she shrugged with a nod. "Probably."

"I opted for the easiest out for everyone."

"It doesn't change that even if I was your girlfriend, your mother would never accept me into your family. Her expression made that perfectly clear."

I raked my hand through my hair. I wasn't going to be able to get out of this without telling her about mates. If giving fate the finger were possible, I'd be flipping her two birds right about now.

"Remember that other thing I needed to tell you about?"

"The crazier-than-werewolves thing?"

"Potentially, yeah."

She turned in her seat a little to face me. "It has something to do with your mother?"

"No. Not really." My chest tightened. I cleared my throat but my voice still sounded raw. "Wolves mate for life. Werewolves are no different." I showed her my hand. "At Adam's house when you reached out to examine the bruises on my hand...I knew."

A crease marred her brow. "Knew what?"

"When we touch our mate, skin to skin, the wolf recognizes her." I waited while she put the pieces together.

"You think I'm your..."

"No, I don't *think*. I *know* you are."

She unbuckled her seat belt and bolted out of the car. I hustled around, putting myself between her and the woods. "I didn't want to tell you yet. I'm sorry. I know it sounds crazy. I didn't believe it either until you touched me."

"This is beyond insane. How can I possibly be your mate? I'm not a werewolf. We hardly know each other. Does Nadya know her boyfriend is a werewolf? Is she his mate?"

I kissed her. I didn't have all the answers, and I had no clue how to explain the fear that I might lose her, that she might reject me. Was this how she felt when she misread my mom's reaction?

Her soft lips brushed mine as I wrapped her in my embrace. She fit in my arms perfectly, made for me. I rested my forehead against hers. "Can we go back inside so I can tell my mom the truth? Trust me, she already loves you. I only said what I did because I didn't want her to blurt out that we were mates before I told you myself."

Although her voice was barely a whisper, I had no trouble hearing her. "I don't know how to handle any of this."

"I don't, either."

The corners of her lips turned up, almost a smile. "Not often you hear a doctor admit something like that."

I chuckled and kissed her forehead. "Not many doctors are werewolves."

She rewarded me with a laugh. For a second, I worried my heart might leap out of my chest. "When did my life get so crazy?"

I took her hand, walking her back toward the house. "I've been asking myself that same question lately."

Chapter Twelve

Mates. Insanity. But if I could believe Jason and his family shifted into wolves one night a month, how much further around the bend was a mate? Pretty far. Destiny couldn't possibly be determined with one touch.

Of course, most people would say no one could see into the future, either.

Jason opened the door, and I stepped into the house, my pulse pounding in my ears. What if I didn't want to be Jason's mate? Would he be destined to be alone? I glanced over at his tall, chiseled frame and he flashed me a smile that could give a nun weak knees.

No way he'd be alone. He probably hadn't been alone since high school.

We walked down the hallway, my mind whizzing a million miles per hour. I barely knew this man. Besides being gorgeous and smart and making me laugh, I'd seen his art-work. He had the passion of an artist and more than a few pent-up anger issues to go with it.

But I didn't know his favorite color, or his favorite flavor of ice cream, or music, or movies… Did any of that matter?

We came in the back bedroom and Sarah smiled up at us. "I heard you come in. Did you forget something?"

Jason gave my hand a squeeze. Her gaze shifted to our joined hands. A smile brightened her features as she got to her feet. "I was right. I knew it."

She embraced me, and the warmth of her affection brought the tears flooding to my eyes all over again. She pulled back, smiling. "You're the one. He found you."

And in that moment, I wanted to be the one. I wanted a family who didn't walk out when the road got rocky. I want-ed a man who I could trust with my battered heart.

She released me and hugged Jason. "Why didn't you tell me?"

He chuckled. "You've forgotten how crazy it sounds to non-Pack members. I just barely got her to accept that we shift once a month."

I sat down in the chair next to Wyatt's bed to give Jason and his mom some room. Jared appeared in the doorway and grinned as he leaned against the doorframe.

Their mother chuckled. "Oh, I'm well aware of how crazy it sounds. Your father told me I was his mate *before* he admitted he wasn't exactly human."

Jason raised a brow. "And you believed him?"

She nudged him and turned to look at Wyatt. "No, I thought he was trying to get into my bed, but secretly, it was a romantic notion, like the old arranged marriages, only this one is arranged by fate instead of family."

"Fate…smarter…than any of us."

The raspy whisper silenced us, sucking the oxygen out of the room. All of our attention shifted to Wyatt. I held my breath as Sarah rushed to the other side of the bed, taking his hand. A tear spilled down her cheek. She kissed his forehead.

"Yes it is, Wy."

We waited, but he didn't move. And just when I started to doubt he had actually spoken, his hand gripped mine. "Fate…was good to my boy…the day…she chose…you."

Jason came up beside me, giving his dad's calf a squeeze. "Dad? Can you open your eyes?"

Again we waited. And I got a flash in my head of Wyatt standing and embracing Sarah. I struggled to find something to give me a hint to when or where they were, and I noticed a cake with two names. Then it was gone.

I tipped my head up. "Jason, is there a birthday coming up? There was a cake with more than one name."

He nodded. "Adam's twins are going to celebrate their first birthday."

"When?"

"Next month."

I looked over at Sarah. "Wyatt will be on his feet with you at that party."

She wiped a tear, smiling. "How do you know?"

"It's a hunch." I glanced at Jason, appreciating that he still hadn't outed my gift, not even to his family. Reaching across the bed, I put my hand over Sarah's and Wyatt's joined hands. "I used to go to Brightwood Academy with Nadya. I get visions, little video clips of the future. Just now,

Wyatt was on his feet hugging you at a birthday party."

A sob choked her as she rested her head on her husband's chest. Her mate. I got up, letting go of Wyatt's hand. Jason pulled me into his arms, kissing the top of my head, and I accepted the comfort, still unsure I would ever be able to wrap my head around all of this.

Jared cleared his throat, and we stepped back. He tilted his head slightly and grinned. "I'm glad my brother finally told you. What you do with it now is up to you."

"So I still get a choice in the matter?"

"That's the kicker for us." Jared glanced at Jason for a second before meeting my eyes again. "The wolf inside us recognizes you and we're hooked, for life. You become the other half of our soul, but you're human. You don't have a wolf pushing his instinct on you. We know the minute we find you that you could walk away and reject us. I'd bet money Jason will do everything he can to keep that from happening, but you're the one with the final say."

I hadn't considered that side of it.

Jared stepped up and clapped a hand on his brother's shoulder. "Add to the mess, my brother didn't believe in mates, so he got a double helping of reality and panic."

I looked up at Jason. "And you believe it now?"

"Definitely."

A clock somewhere in the house chimed, snapping me back into reality. Human reality. "I need to get to work."

Jared moved out of our way, but his grin faded. "You think that's safe?"

"No." Jason took my hand. "But she's dead set on going anyway."

"Want some backup?"

Jason nodded. "I'd love some. Until Adam gets proof Kilani isn't some sort of trap, he won't get the Pack involved. Sebastian's supposed to be in town later tonight…"

"'Til then, I'll help keep an eye out for any Nero ops."

"Thanks, man." Jason hugged his brother and took my hand again. "See you soon, Mom."

Sarah straightened with a gentle smile. "See that you do, and bring Kilani with you." Her gaze moved onto me, her expression softening. "I remember what a confusing time this was for me, too. My best advice? Follow your heart. The rest will come."

The awkward silence in the car was killing me. We were only about halfway to the medical center. But I couldn't think of anything sane to talk about. What could I say? *So, if I decide to walk out on you like I did my grandmother and cousins back in Hawaii, will it doom you to be alone forever?* Or maybe something like, *So when do I get fur and sharp teeth?*

Ugh. I took a slow breath. We needed to talk before I made myself insane.

"Your mom likes Neil Diamond?"

He nodded, keeping his attention on the highway. "Yeah."

"My grandma Nani loves him. She claims she's his biggest fan on the islands."

"Has she ever seen him in concert? My mom says he puts on a great show."

I shook my head. "No. Or at least not as far as I know."

"Sounds like you miss her. What's keeping you from

talking to her?"

Suddenly this was deeper conversation than I had intended, but I'd already told him about my visions, and he'd not only believed me, he'd kept my secret. Maybe I was starting to trust him.

More likely I was just sick of being alone. Trust wasn't exactly an area where I had much experience.

"I left for Brightwood even after she said no. Looking back on it, I have no idea how they were able to enroll me without my guardian's consent, but I didn't think about it at the time. I was an angry preteen who thought she knew everything."

"You think she's still upset with you?"

"Maybe." I swallowed a ball of emotions I'd never shared before. "I'm still angry at my mother for walking out on me. Why wouldn't Grandma Nani have those same feelings about me?"

"Your mother walked out on you?"

He turned onto the hospital's street and I prayed for green lights to escape this conversation. At least he couldn't look at me and drive at the same time. "Yeah. I was six. I came home from school and Grandma Nani was waiting for me. She said Mom took a job on the mainland. I asked when I'd get to move over there with her and Nani said I couldn't. I'd be staying with her from now on.

"I wrote letters, prayed, and cried, but my mother never came back for me and never explained. And as I got older, I stopped being sad. I've been angry ever since."

He parked the car around the back, far from the hospital entrance. He took my hand. "You were a little girl who needed her mother. You have every right to be mad. But I bet your grandmother is too worried to stay upset about you leaving against her wishes."

I rubbed the bridge of my nose, willing the tears back. "I can't call her now. Even if I knew her number, I could end up leading Nero right to her."

"Once Adam gives the okay for the Pack to get involved, Nero won't be able to touch you. Your grandmother will be their next target."

"They might've already gone after her once. I tried to warn her." My stomach twisted into a sick knot. "If she didn't know anything the first time around, why would they go back?"

"To Nero, she'd be leverage to get to you." His voice softened a little. "She's your family. I think we should bring her here so we can protect her too."

My heart clenched as a vise of regret tightened around my rib cage. "Sebastian thought they might question her to see if she could tell them where I was. They could already have her for all I know."

He lifted my hand to his lips, distracting me from the cesspool of guilt for a second. "If they had her, they wouldn't bother coming to Reno. Not with the Pack here. They'd make *you* come to *them*. I'm sure of it."

I stared into his eyes. Confidence and courage blazed in his gaze. For the first time since I'd met him, my instinctive distrust for doctors, for men, for anyone who appeared to care about me, faded. That voice I'd grown so accustomed to hearing inside my head, reminding me to be wary, to watch for lies, to cut and run, was silent.

"Kilani?"

His tone carried a raw tenderness, no sign of that

infuriating medical practitioner bedside manner. I wasn't sure I could speak.

"Yes?" I squeaked out.

"Are you all right?"

I laughed. I couldn't help it. "I'm sitting in a car with a werewolf who thinks I'm his mate, waiting to go inside to work where I may or may not meet some guys from Nero who want me dead, and my grandmother, who I haven't spoken to in years, is probably in danger because of me." I wiped a tear with a humorless chuckle. "I'm totally fine."

He smiled and leaned in to kiss my forehead. I closed my eyes, drinking in the comfort of his masculine scent.

"Okay, that was a dumb question." He squeezed my hand and released me to pull the keys from the ignition. "I'll be watching for Nero inside the hospital, and Jared's covering the exits. We'll keep you safe. In the meantime, we need to find out who tipped off Nero and told them you're here. Then we can silence him."

"I have no clue who would've told Nero anything. I haven't been here long enough to really make any friends, and even so, I'd never tell them the real reason I was in Reno anyway."

"It wouldn't have to be specific. Nero may have offered money for anyone with information on new nurses."

"I'm not the only new person on the payroll. Besides, hospitals have new nurses all the time, per diem, part time, full time. I wouldn't be anything special or out of the ordinary."

"Not on paper, but…" He rested back against his seat. "If Nero made a list of potential hiding places for you and added Reno to the list, they would've come around offering a reward for information on new nursing staff from New York, since that was the last place you'd been. They might've given out a visual description, too. You may be using an alias here, but you're still a Polynesian nurse from New York. That's a much smaller pool of people. Definitely worth checking into if someone gave them a tip."

New York. My conversation over pizza with Todd from the stroke floor flashed through my head. There was no way Todd was an informant. But still.

"I split a pizza a couple nights ago with a nurse on the stroke floor. He can't possibly be the one, but I did mention moving from New York."

"It's a starting place." He gripped the bottom of the steering wheel tight enough to bring out the muscles in his forearms. Was he jealous? "What's his name? I can check him out while you're working."

"Todd. I don't remember his last name, but he works on the floor just above mine." I shook my head. "There's no way he's in contact with Nero. He's not that type."

"If money is involved, there is no type."

I stared out at the building, suddenly wishing I'd taken Jason's advice and called in sick, but I was too proud to admit I might've been wrong. Pride won out. I got out of the car. "I need to get changed."

"We didn't bring any clothes…"

"I've got scrubs in my locker."

He came around to my side, but he didn't touch me. All his attention was focused on the parking lot, the hospital. "Be careful. Call my cell if you see anything off."

"I could if I had your number."

He broke his visual scan of the area, cursing under his

breath. "Sorry. I forgot to give it to you."

We swapped numbers. He also gave me Jared's just in case. Hopefully I wouldn't need to use either one.

I headed inside. Adrenaline bound up every muscle in my body, but so far no visions. I chose to take that as a good sign. My whole life, a flash of premonition usually preceded danger. I'd have to trust my track record.

The automatic glass doors parted and Stan tipped his hat from the welcome station. "Good to see you, young lady." His smile faltered. "Everything all right?"

Did it show? I drew in a breath, struggling to mask the anxiety eating me up from the inside out. "Yeah, I'm finc. Some car trouble, but hopefully it's nothing major."

He relaxed and nodded. "Nothing worse than an unreliable vehicle."

"I agree." I walked by, calling over my shoulder, "Good to see you, Stan."

"Likewise, Kelly."

I was getting better at not being tripped up when I heard my alias. Maybe I wouldn't need it much longer. If Jason was right, and Sebastian could convince Adam I wasn't a threat, the Pack would help me and Nero would leave me alone.

And go after Nani.

I punched the elevator button harder than I meant to, glaring at the ceiling to keep the unwanted tears at bay.

Suddenly the elevator faded away and Jason lay on the ground, blood trickling from his nose. Before panic could grip me, I searched for details, clues to time or place. Ropes surrounded him in a square. The damned boxing ring. *No. Come on, Jason, no more beatings.* I spun around, hoping to gain more. An older guy counted. Someone else called out third round.

And then I was back in the elevator.

He wasn't fighting right now. When? If I warned him, would that keep him from climbing into that ring again? Not likely. From what I'd seen, he was every bit as hardheaded as me, and against my better judgment, here I was at the hospital for my shift. How could I stop him from fighting?

The doors opened, and the scent of disinfectant and rhythmic beeps of the machinery welcomed me, calming my jumbled nerves. This was my universe. No guessing, no fear, just hard work healing those who needed extra help.

A room number flashed in my head and I went to the right. I could put on my scrubs in a second. Inside, the sleeping patient's arm crimped the oxygen tube. The monitor wasn't buzzing yet, but it would soon. Carefully I untangled the tubing without disturbing her and watched her levels stabilize.

Satisfied she was taken care of, I headed into the break room, grabbed my extra scrubs from my locker, and quickly changed in the restroom. Two hours flew by in a blur of IV bag changes, blood draws, and checking vitals.

With a few minutes to myself, I ducked inside the break room for a bottled water. Being busy definitely helped to calm my fears. It hadn't been a mistake to come in after all. Maybe Sebastian was wrong about Nero. Maybe they came to Reno on a hunch without knowing where I worked.

Grabbing the black Sharpie from the table, I labeled my water bottle and stowed it in the fridge. When I stepped into the hallway, a vision of Jason flashed through my head. He had Todd pressed against a wall. Todd's eyes widened with terror, and blood dripped from his lower lip. I turned my focus, catching sight of gauze pads and tape before it faded.

A supply closet. *Shit.*

My stomach twisted as I pulled out my cell and hit Jason's name. It went to voicemail. *Damn it.* I pressed Jared's number, my fingers trembling. He answered on the first ring.

"Hello?"

I ducked back inside the break room, keeping my voice low. "Jared, it's Kilani. Jason didn't answer his cell and there's trouble on the fifth floor."

The air rushed past the phone speaker; he was already on the move. "On my way. Where are you?"

"Fourth floor."

"Stay there. I'll find him."

And he was gone. I stared at my phone for a second before I slid it into my pocket. If I hurried, I might be able to stop Jason. My visions were usually at least a few minutes into the future. I jogged to the elevator, calling to the charge nurse at the desk, "I'll be right back."

The doors opened on the fifth floor and I looked down the hallway. Which way? To my left, a muffled cry was followed by a slamming door. With my heart hammering in my chest, I chased the sound to a supply closet. Farther down the hall, a nurse paged security.

I had to hurry.

Chapter Thirteen

JASON

After Kilani entered the automatic glass doors safely, my cell phone buzzed. "Yeah?"

"I'm casing the north side of the building. No scent of any jaguars, but if Nero sent a human team, we're screwed."

Hearing Jared's voice relaxed me a little. We'd patrolled together on many new moon nights to keep the jaguar shifters from hunting in our territory. Besides being my twin, he was my partner, and when he had my back, I could focus on other things.

"I'm on the south side, main entrance. No sign of the jags here, either. Sebastian told Kilani his brother was here with a team from Nero. Even if the team is human, Sebastian's brother is a jaguar, so we should catch his scent. I'm going inside. She told one person she was from New York. It can't be a coincidence that a day or two later, Nero is here in Reno."

"Keep me posted. Be careful."

"You too, Jared."

I slid my phone back into my pocket and made my way through the cars toward the front doors. As I got closer to the main entrance, I caught Kilani's scent, awakening my wolf and derailing me from the task at hand. I ground my teeth together, forcing the animal part of my spirit to back off. We both wanted to be with Kilani, but right now, our mission was to find the mole who tipped off Nero that she was here. If I could find him, I might have a chance at getting information from him to get to the Nero ops before they discovered us.

At the elevator, I pressed the button and waited for the doors to open.

"Dr. Ayers?"

A leggy woman with long blond curls down her back headed straight for me. Barb Turk. I hit the lit arrow three more times.

The doors opened just as she touched my arm. "Jason?"

There was no pretending I didn't see her anymore. "Barb? How have you been?" Now the damned doors opened. "I've gotta run—"

"I'm going up, too."

She followed me into the elevator, the prison doors closing behind her.

"I'm so glad I ran into you. I'm in town for a few days if you want to meet me for dinner."

Barb was a pharmaceuticals rep with a *Sports Illustrated* swimsuit body and ambition almost as bright as her bleached teeth. I'd gone out on one date with her, drank too much, and woke up in her hotel room bed.

She'd been trying to get me back there ever since.

I pushed the button for the fifth floor. "I'm seeing someone right now."

"No strings, then."

Her expensive perfume assaulted my heightened senses as I shook my head. "I'm really not interested, but there are plenty of doctors in this building who would be thrilled to take you up on the offer."

"But you're the doctor I want." She flipped her hair back over her shoulder. "We were good together. Why do you keep putting me off? I'm not asking for marriage, just a fun night."

"I already told you, I'm seeing someone." The bell rang for the fifth floor. Thank God. "Sorry, Barb. I—"

She grabbed my hand. "I don't see a ring on your finger. You don't need to be straight-laced with me."

"Enough." I retrieved my hand, my patience dwindling. Rapidly. "I'm working."

I walked out, grateful not to hear her impractical shoes clicking behind me. I'd made more than my share of dating mistakes over the years, but Barb Turk had to be in my top five. I stopped at the nursing station for the fifth floor.

"How can I help…" Her badge read *Kendra*, and the name clicked as the nurse glanced up from the keyboard and smiled at me. "Jason?"

I hadn't seen Kendra in…two years, three? She got up and came around to give me a hug. I returned the embrace.

"Did I hear you got married?"

She'd been my longest relationship. After a year together, she'd wanted to move in, and although I should've loved her,

I didn't. At that point in time, mates had seemed like a farce.

The joke was on me now.

We broke up, and she moved on. "Who's the lucky guy?"

She pointed to a picture by her computer screen. "That's David. We just had our first anniversary."

"Congratulations." And I meant it. She deserved a lifetime of happiness.

"So what brings you up to the stroke floor, Dr. Ayers?"

"I'm looking for a nurse named Todd. Is he on today?"

She nodded. "Yeah, I think his shift is almost over. Want me to page him for you?"

"No." I shook my head. "I can find him. Thanks, Kendra. Great seeing you."

"Take care, Jason." She started to say something else, but the phone rang and she was right back to business. It was just as well.

I'd had my fill of visits with ghosts-of-relationships-past for one day.

Listening for male voices, I ventured down the hallway and around the corner. A nurse came out of one of the rooms, his attention on the tablet in his hand. His badge said *Todd*. He looked up and recognition hit me like a Mack truck.

"Wolf?"

Holy shit. Todd, the nurse on the stroke floor, the potential mole for Nero, also ran my underground fight club. The same Todd. *Damn it.* I'd been shooting the breeze with him while he'd been selling out Kilani, leading Nero right to her.

Rage erupted, burning through my bloodstream until my hands trembled with adrenaline. *Damn it.* "Shut up and come with me."

He stiffened. "What are you doing at the hospital? Is

someone in your family sick?"

I grabbed his upper arms and pressed him back against the wall, lowering my voice. "I'm not going to ask again. We need to talk."

He nodded, and I took a step back. Keeping hold of one of his arms, I walked him toward a door labeled SUPPLIES. Once we were inside, I threw him to the far wall, pinning him there. "How long have you been working for Nero? Is that why you invited me to the club? Have you been giving them intel on me, too?"

He shook his head, stammering. "I-I don't know what you're talking about."

"I think you do." I clenched my hand into a tight fist. "And if you don't start answering me, I'm going to jog your memory for you."

"I don't work for them." I pulled my hand back. "Okay, okay. Some guy came in about a month ago, told me to watch for new nurses from New York. There was money in it for the information. He said they were taking a survey or something."

My fist landed in his gut on instinct, before I realized I was going to punch him. He wheezed, collapsing to his knees. I yanked him back onto his feet. "You stupid bastard, Todd. It never occurred to you that these guys might want to hurt her? You led them straight to her."

He gasped for air. "You know Kelly?"

I almost corrected him, but I managed to keep her cover. "Yeah, and now she's in danger. And it's your fault."

"I'm sorry, Wolf. I needed the cash."

"You needed to think, asshole. A survey? No way. You knew it was blood money." I hit him again and when his knees buckled this time, I let him fall to the floor. The door flew open behind me. I spun around to find Kilani, eyes wide.

"Oh Jesus, Jason." She rushed past me to inspect Todd's bloody lip.

I frowned. Was she seriously nursing that waste of skin? "He's working for them. He told them where to find you."

"I'm angry, too. Pissed, in fact." She looked up as she grabbed some gauze pads from the shelf. "But this isn't a boxing ring. This is assault. You could get arrested."

"I don't believe this. You're angry at *me*?" I pointed at the piece of shit she was cleaning up. "This is the bastard who told Nero where you work. He took their money and sold you out."

My pulse pounded in my ears, fury roaring in my head like a lion. I'd never needed to hit anything so badly. I wanted to pummel something until I was too exhausted to lift my arms, until the rage ran dry.

"I know who he is." She disinfected his wounds with a jerky hand. He flinched a couple of times but had the good sense to keep his mouth shut. "And I know what he did." She met my eyes. "But right now, I need to clean up this mess so you don't end up in jail. I need you with me, remember?"

"What the hell?"

I turned around to find Jared in the doorway. Kilani glanced up at him. "Your brother just beat up this nurse."

I narrowed my eyes, struggling to keep my voice down. "*This* is the guy who tipped off Nero, and she's defending *him*."

Jared met my eyes, his tone low and even. "Go walk it off, bro. I'll be sure she stays safe."

"Walk it off? Are you two crazy?" I raked both hands

back through my hair. "This bastard sold out my mate for money and I'm supposed to be calm?"

Jared put a heavy hand on my shoulder. "You don't have to be calm, but beating him senseless isn't going to get us information."

I coiled my fingers into an aching fist, welcoming the pain. Rational thought was out the window, but I managed not to hit my brother. Barely.

"You'll keep her safe."

"You know I will."

I nodded and started to walk away.

"Where are you going?" Kilani asked.

"Ask him." I pointed to the weasel with the ice pack. "He runs the fight club."

The sun faded into the horizon as my tires ground into the pitted, cracked pavement of the warehouse that housed the fight club. Above me, the sky was painted in a sea of turbulent orange and red, mirroring my frustration and anger.

Todd, the guy I'd talked to just last night, the guy who first invited me to the club, also spied for goddamned Nero. Did he know they wanted to kill her? On second thought, I didn't give a shit whether he knew or not. What kind of man gave out personal information about a coworker for money?

Filthy spineless weasels. Pond scum.

And I'd been paying him for a chance to get in that ring, for a little taste of control of my destiny, a vent to release some pressure. I couldn't have known he worked in the building right next door to my office, but as I tore off my shirt in the musty locker room, clear thinking was a distant memory.

With my aggressive wolf so close to the surface, the world seemed more black and white, right and wrong. Todd led killers to my mate. That made him a threat to her. I wanted to kill him.

Instead, I'd take it out on the poor bastard waiting to fight me.

My chest heaved with frustration as I stalked toward the ring, seething for primal satisfaction. A familiar scent hit me between the eyes, as solid as any punch. Jaguar.

Adrenaline exploded through my body. If I weren't a werewolf, this might've been enough pressure to cause a heart attack, but in my current state, all I could think was, *Bring it on, asshole.*

Marv blocked my path. "Wolf. I thought you were resting. You said—"

"Change of plans, Marv."

He shook his head. "Your eye's still bruised up, and your ribs—"

"Are fine." I stared at my opponent's back, willing him to turn around and face me. "Tell Bob I'm in."

Marv sighed, but he did as he was told. Bob's shoulders fell as I approached. He met me at the ropes. "This is a bad idea, Wolf. Go home. Rest up."

"I'm not going anywhere except inside this ring. You can either ring the bell or get the hell out of the way."

Bob pulled the ropes up, and I ducked through. The small bloodthirsty crowd roared as I walked toward the center of the ring. The clipboard with bets and bills passed through the bleacher seats like a wildfire. I rolled my shoulders, my gaze still burning a hole in my opponent's back. He had to have caught my scent, too. He had to know a werewolf had gotten into the ring, but he still didn't turn.

"Next up, our reigning champ, Wolf, will face off with the champ from the Virginia Brawlers Club, Jaguar."

He called us to the center, and the jaguar finally turned. His aloof smirk stoked my fury. His cultured, deep voice didn't help, either. "Well, well. Look what we have here... Wolf."

I couldn't wait to beat the ever-loving shit out of this guy. While Bob rambled through the rules, we stared each other down. No one else in the club understood the significance, the bad blood between my Pack and the jaguar shifters.

Bob finished his spiel and we bumped gloves. The top of a lion tattoo peered out on the inside of his arm, uncovered by the glove laces. The letter *N* emblazoned on the lion's forehead.

Fucking Nero. This jaguar was here for Kilani. I'd kill him.

We circled each other. I ground my teeth into my mouthpiece. He was about my height and build. His jaguar nature would mean he'd be light on his feet and tough to go down unless I knocked him out. He landed a jab to my ribs, reminding me they hadn't healed yet. I answered with a solid right to his chest, bumping him back a step.

He raised a brow in mock amusement, and then unleashed a combination of punches to my abdomen, working me back toward the corner. The post hit me between the shoulder blades as he landed one more punch, growling near my ear.

"You should've known this ring belongs to me. Eye of the tiger."

I shoved him. "But I have the heart of the wolf, asshole."

I pummeled him with jabs to his ribs, then countered with a right to his temple and a left to his midsection. Bob chased us to the other corner. The jaguar's breathing wheezed past his lips, his elitist smirk gone.

We were through talking.

The bell rang and I forced myself back to the corner. My towel hung off the corner, pinned between the ropes. I snagged it and wiped my face, wishing for the first time that I had a trainer in my corner. This jaguar was the toughest opponent I'd met in this ring, and having someone apply Vaseline to help the gloves slide off on impact made more sense now. Sadly, I was worlds away from that.. Our ring reeked of mildew, sweat, and blood. Our punches were landed for glory, to silence the inner demons, not for cameras or endorsement deals.

My gaze stayed on my opponent as I bounced my weight on the balls of my feet, keeping my muscles loose. Because I was a werewolf, my extra strength gave me an advantage even over guys who outweighed me or had a few inches over my arm reach. But this guy was a jaguar.

Neither one of us had the advantage of our animal natures. This would be a gladiator battle to the end.

Maybe then I'd be able to walk away from this place for more than a day or two. Maybe this would calm the beast inside of me.

The bell rang and we rushed to the center of the ring. No dancing around this time. I landed a left to his gut and a right uppercut to his chin. He staggered back a couple of steps, wiping away a little blood from the corner of his mouth. My wolf growled, agitated by the scent.

I waved him closer with my gloves, taunting. "Come on, Jaguar. That all you got?"

He charged forward, his right hand impacting my ribs so hard, stars ignited at the edge of my vision. I retaliated with a left to the head, and when his hands went up in defense, I attacked his ribs with a solid combination. The assault continued back and forth until the bell finally clanged.

In my corner, I struggled to catch my breath. Exhaustion soothed my temper and left an opening for rational thought to creep in. I had to defend my ribs. If they weren't already cracked, they would be soon. How could I protect Kilani with a broken body?

Why was I wasting myself on this fight in a ring? I should've been with her, keeping her safe. *Shit.*

The bell rang, signaling the third round. We walked to the center, no longer fresh, and I contemplated the fastest way to get out of here and back to Kilani. If I got lucky, I could land a solid punch to his jaw and knock him out.

Or I could take a fall.

Pride twisted in my gut. I'd never been knocked out. But none of this mattered. This ring, it wasn't my world. Kilani was. Right now, she was my priority, and I needed to get a fucking grip on this anger that I'd allowed to become my master.

I charged the jaguar, punching his ribs, waiting for my opening to hit his face. If I could knock him out, I would. Otherwise, I'd take the fall. This fight was about to end, one way or the other.

"Jason. No!"

My head snapped to the right. Kilani ran toward the ring. Before I could reply, the jaguar's glove hit my temple. My vision wavered. The room tilted.

And I fell into the darkness.

Chapter Fourteen

Kilani

Jason hit the floor, blood trickling from his nose. The same scene from my vision. And my interfering had caused it. He took his eye off his opponent and… Wait a second…I recognized his opponent.

"Sebastian?" I climbed into the ring as the older guy counted. Sebastian narrowed his eyes, but if he meant to caution me, he could stuff it. "Get me a towel. Now." Sebastian snapped out of his victory daze and went to the other corner. I yanked the rag from his hand. "What are you doing here?"

"We don't use our names in these clubs."

"I don't give a flipping crap what you use here. I need you to find me some ice."

A young, mousy-looking guy jogged up the aisle with an ice pack. He handed it to Sebastian without looking at him, all his attention on Jason.

"No one's ever knocked Wolf down. I told him it was too soon to fight again."

I placed the ice at the back of Jason's neck while I cleaned the blood from his face. "Don't feel bad. He wasn't thinking straight." The kid didn't move. I met his eyes. "Wolf will be okay." I hoped I was right. Glaring up at Sebastian, I asked once more, "What are you doing here?"

"Beating up a wolf, blowing off steam. What are *you* doing here? I thought that doctor was supposed to be protecting you."

"He found the informant who told your brother I was here. He went ballistic. We had to get him out of there before he ended up in jail." Jason's eyes shifted under his eyelids. I stroked his cheek. "Jason?"

"*This* is the Pack doctor?" Sebastian wiped the blood at the corner of his mouth and almost looked…impressed.

Jason blinked and frowned. "Kilani. Where's—"

"Jared is parking his truck. I jumped out and ran in here to save you from yourself."

He chuckled, his swollen lower lip curving into a lopsided smile. My heart stuttered. He reached up to touch my cheek. "You got me knocked out."

"Sorry about that." I'd tell him about the vision later. I'd seen him on the ground in the third round, but I had no idea my running in screaming at him was what put him there. Visions were tricky like that. I tipped my head up toward Sebastian. "Help me get him up."

Jason frowned. "You know this guy?"

I nodded. "Yeah. This is Sebastian."

He shifted his gaze. "You're Sebastian?"

Sebastian pulled off one of his gloves and offered his hand. Jason stared at it, making no move to accept his help. I did my best not to punch them both.

To his credit, Sebastian didn't storm off. "I only offer my hand to a worthy opponent."

Jason iced him for a couple more seconds before he grudgingly took his hand and got to his feet. "You had to wait until I was distracted to get that knockout."

Sebastian shrugged. "If I see an opportunity, I don't hesitate. I take it."

I slid my arm around Jason's waist and told myself it was to make sure he didn't fall over, not because I wanted to hug him and make certain he would be all right. Seeing him go down did something to me. I wasn't sure what exactly it was just yet, but for now, I wasn't letting him out of my sight.

We got to the ropes, and Marv helped me steady Jason despite his grumbles that he was fine. He'd passed out in the shower last night and got knocked unconscious tonight. This was no way to heal a concussion.

I looked back over my shoulder at Sebastian. "Go talk to Adam. We'll meet you at the ranch."

He frowned. "Enough with names; there are ears everywhere."

I didn't bother to look back. Nero's ears were still out in the truck with Jared. Todd wasn't going anywhere.

Jason got changed and sat on the bench in the locker room, his forearms on his thighs and his head down.

"Are you dizzy?"

"Nah. I'm trying to keep my back from cramping up." He sighed, his head bowed. "And feeling like a hot-headed idiot."

I didn't know what to say, so I went into nurse mode. At the sink, I soaked a clean towel in hot water. I wrung it out and folded it before bringing it over to press the warm compress to his lower back.

"Mmm, that feels good."

Hearing the gruff pleasure in his voice had my mind imagining other things that would feel good.

As the heat faded, he finally straightened, his eyes locking on mine. "I'm sorry about today, at the hospital. When I recognized Todd, something snapped." He stared at his red hands. "You were right about my anger being out of control. The fights…it takes more each time to relieve the pressure. Tonight, I realized fighting isn't helping me deal with the frustration and rage. *It's* controlling *me*."

Again, I struggled for something to say. I'd never allowed myself to be close enough to anyone for a soul-bearing talk like this. I wanted to comfort him, but I had no clue how to accomplish it.

His gaze pleaded with me. "What I'm trying to say is, I'm never coming back here. It sounds completely nuts, since we haven't known each other long, but the truth is, you are what matters most to me. I need to stop getting beat up so I can be at my best to protect you and keep you safe." He tugged my hand, pulling me down to sit beside him. "I'm giving you my word right now. I'm through." He tossed his boxing gloves in his bag. "Wolf is out. For good."

I kissed him, gently at first, careful of his injuries, but he pulled me tight, his tongue parting my lips until I moaned with desire. My pulse raced as I tightened my fingers in his wet hair.

When he rested his forehead against mine, he whispered,

"I want to be the mate you deserve." I opened my mouth to respond, but Jason put his finger over my lips. "Jared's here."

We both turned as he rounded the corner to the lockers. "Bro, this place reeks."

"Yeah. I'm sticking to the gym from now on. At least they disinfect the weight room."

Jared's expression lightened. "Glad to hear it."

"I let Todd know that if he goes to the police, I'd be happy to place an anonymous call to the authorities about illegal gambling at an unlicensed fight club." He leaned against the wall, crossing his ankles. "He agreed to let this go before he locked himself in his office here."

"Thanks." Jason got to his feet without any hint of a wobble. Good sign. He grabbed his gym bag and offered me his hand. "We should get over to Adam's."

He and his brother clasped forearms. I kept meaning to ask what that was about, but there were more pressing concerns.

"Call me if you need me." Jared nodded in my direction. "Keep my brother in line for me?"

"You know it." I grinned.

"I need to talk to Marv before we go."

Jared pulled his keys from his pocket. "I'm going to check on Mom and Dad. I'll call you later."

"Sounds good."

Jared headed for the exit, and Jason walked across the front of the bleachers toward the young guy who'd given me the ice pack. I trailed behind, just in case he went down.

"Hey, Marv."

The kid with skittish dark eyes looked up. "Wolf. You're okay?"

Jason nodded. "Yeah. I'm fine." He scanned the club. "Where'd Jaguar go?"

"He left a few minutes ago."

Jason took a slow breath. Was he sniffing to be sure Sebastian was gone? My life was getting way too strange, even for me.

He gave Marv's shoulder a pat. "I'm retiring. You won't see me back here again."

Marv glanced at me and back to Jason. "You got a girlfriend."

Jason chuckled and reached back for my hand, pulling me beside him. "She's pretty wonderful. And I think she likes me better in one piece."

Blushing, Marv grinned and stared at his shoes. Jason dropped his bag from his shoulder and tugged his battered boxing gloves free. "I want you to have these."

Marv lifted his head, his eyes widened. "No, Wolf. I can't take your gloves."

"Yes, you can." Jason put the laces in his hands. "You're the champ now."

Tears swelled in my eyes as I witnessed the joy on Marv's face. He clutched the gloves tight. "I'm gonna miss you, Wolf."

Jason mussed his hair. "You are the *only* thing I'm going to miss about this place." He tilted his head toward the ring. "Okay, I might miss Bob a little, too."

Marv stepped back. "I'll take good care of these."

"Thanks, buddy."

Jason picked up his bag and took my hand. My fingers laced with his like we'd known each other for years. Once we were out of the building I glanced up at him. "That was sweet what you did for that kid."

"He's got a heart of gold, and Todd doesn't treat him as well as he should. I wish I could do more."

He clicked the keys, and the locks disengaged on his car. Jason froze, immediately tense at my side.

"Get in the car and lock the doors," he whispered.

I gripped his hand tighter. "What is it?"

"Get in the car."

"I'm not leaving you." I kept my concerns about a concussion to myself. If someone was nearby, I didn't want him to know Jason was injured.

"It's *you* they want." He walked me to the door and opened it without ever taking his eyes off the parking lot. "Get in. You can be pissed at me later."

I sat and he slammed the door, clicking the locks from his keys. I strained my eyes, wishing I had his vision, and hearing, and sense of smell. His gifts were at least useful. I wanted to help, not be a weak link he needed to lock away.

But without my pepper spray, and no weapon, that's exactly what I was.

A man stepped out of the shadows toward Jason. He wore tailored trousers and a form-fitting turtleneck, but I couldn't make out his face. Again I caught myself wishing I could control my gift on command. I could've kept us from walking into this trap.

The glare of the yellow streetlight kept reflecting off of an ugly-looking hunting knife in his hand. I had to do something. I hit Jared's number on my cell phone, prayed to my *honu* for Jason's protection, and loathed myself for putting him in danger.

Chapter Fifteen

With Kilani locked in the car, I welcomed my wolf closer to the surface. I couldn't shift my form without the full moon, but I embraced his aggression. This guy with the knife came here for our mate. Physically, I was in no condition to protect her, but he didn't know that.

Either way, this asshole wasn't going to lay a finger on her. He'd have to kill me first, and I didn't feel like dying today. "Not sure why you're flashing a knife, but if you value your life, you should move along."

"Cut the crap, Wolf. I know what you are, and unless you've lost your sense of smell, you know what I am, too. I don't have a problem with you or your Pack. I just need the woman."

I kept my focus on his knife, while I listened for more men on the periphery of the parking lot. "Then I guess we *do* have a problem, because she's not going anywhere with you."

He chuckled and his smile struck me as...familiar. This had to be the brother Sebastian warned us about. His sharp features and dark eyes definitely resembled Sebastian's, but the smirk triggered something. Had I seen him before?

"I'll get her one way or the other. I didn't come all this way to fail." He tipped his head toward the warehouse. "You've been wasting your time and energy brawling, and you're unarmed. I'm going to get what I came for tonight, but in good faith to your Pack, I'm offering you an out. You can walk away. Take my offer."

I rolled my shoulders, loosening my aching muscles for one more battle. "The fight club was just a warm-up."

He was at least four inches shorter than me, and unlike Sebastian, this guy lacked broad shoulders. His torso was stout, and he probably worked out, but he was counting on brute strength. I wasn't sure how much I had left, but if I could stay away from the blade and keep my head clear so I could think, I'd have a chance.

Shifting the knife from hand to hand, he shrugged. "So be it, but let the record show I tried not to kill your Pack's doctor."

I raised a brow, clenching my fingers into fists. "You've done your homework."

"It's possible I know more about your Pack than you do."

He still didn't move in. I glanced toward the entrance of the parking lot. He had to be stalling for time.

"You talk big for a guy who's waiting on backup. I'd bet you introduced yourself to me prematurely." I didn't hesitate. Before he could reply, I knocked him to the ground. Landing on top of him, I grappled for the blade. My instincts screamed to head-butt him and snatch the knife away, but given my recent knockout, I couldn't risk it. If I lost consciousness, Kilani wouldn't stand a chance.

Engines hummed in the distance. His team was coming. I needed to get her out of here. I might be able to best one attacker, but werewolf bravado wasn't going to be enough to stop bullets from Nero mercenaries.

I slammed his wrist against the broken pavement, once, twice, but just as I pried the weapon free, his other fist got loose. He clocked me in the jaw hard enough to ignite stars at the edge of my vision. Gripping the handle of the knife, I slammed it down through his hand and scrambled to my feet as he screamed.

A truck pulled into the lot, followed by a Jeep. Adam's Jeep. The cavalry had arrived. Jared drove up closer to us and got out of his truck, leaving the engine running. "Get Kilani out of here. We've got this."

"We all need to go. He has a team. They could be here with firepower any minute. He was buying time."

Aren, my Alpha's twin brother, jogged over. I watched his bum ankle. Even in a crisis, I couldn't separate the doctor from myself any more than I could the wolf. And Aren had no business running on this uneven pavement in the dark. "Kilani has the Pack's protection. Take her someplace safe."

My attacker was on his feet, blood dripping from the hole in his hand. He brandished his blade, snarling. "If your Alpha values the lives of his wife and children, he should stay out of my business."

Aren wheeled on him, careful to keep himself more than

an arm's length away from the knife. "Don't you dare threaten my brother's family, you pissant. I could kill you before your backup arrives. You're only alive because we want you to get a message to Nero."

"I don't take messages." He lunged for Aren, and Jared moved in from behind, catching his knife arm. Aren landed a body shot to his abdomen as a black van pulled into the parking lot.

"Shit," I shouted. "It's Nero. Get the hell out."

I rushed to the car, to Kilani, popping the locks and climbing in. Behind me, Aren bellowed at the jaguar, "You tell Nero to leave Reno. Now. We don't give a shit why you're here. This is Pack territory. Next trespasser won't get a warning."

I slammed the door and started the car. The tires squealed as I punched the gas pedal. "Hold on."

Her scent filled the interior of the car, reassuring my wolf of her safety. I gunned the engine, glad to see Jared and Adam in my rearview mirror behind me.

Suddenly the passenger side mirror exploded. "Damn it! Get down."

Kilani bent over, keeping her head out of view, as I cranked the wheel and hit the accelerator. We skidded out onto the old highway. I watched my mirror, holding my breath. Jared's truck headlights came up behind me.

"Come on, Adam," I growled, gripping the steering wheel tighter and struggling to watch the road in front and the rearview mirror. Finally another set of lights made the turn. Was it Adam or Nero?

My phone buzzed. I handed it to Kilani. She pressed speaker. "Adam's out," Jared said. "Cheney took a hit, but we're clear."

Call waiting beeped. Kilani glanced my way. "It says 'Aren cell.'"

"Gotta run, bro. Thanks for the backup."

"Thank Kilani. She sent out the SOS."

I smiled over at her as she clicked on Aren's call. "Jason. You guys okay?"

"My mirror has seen better days, but we're fine."

"Good. Cheney's got a new battle scar on the back panel, but otherwise we're good. We're headed back to the ranch to be sure Lana and the kids are all right. Adam wants you to drive for a while. Be sure you're not being tailed, then go home. He'd rather not bring Kilani to the ranch and lead Nero to the family."

"Understood."

"Adam's sending backup to your place to keep watch. They should be waiting when you get there."

"Sounds good. Any word from Sebastian?"

"He called. Adam was talking to him when we got the call from Jared. Luckily Adam's Alpha senses were tingling, so we were already headed your way. Adam got the info he needed from Sebastian. We'll talk soon. Be careful."

The call ended. I reached over and gave her thigh a squeeze. "Thanks for calling Jared. I should've thought of that."

"You had your hands full." She stared out the window.

The high of getting away from Nero faded. "Are you pissed at me for locking you in the car?"

"No." She paused. I waited. Finally, she sighed. "I'm upset that you needed to. You could've been killed tonight. Because of me."

"But I wasn't, because of *you*. You called for backup. You're the hero here."

She groaned, resting her head back against the headrest. "So the rest of your Pack could be endangered, too. What if those guys from Nero started shooting before everyone drove away?"

"But they didn't."

"You don't understand."

"No, I don't." I kept watch behind us, but so far, no sign of the black van. "So enlighten me."

"I sat in this car, praying I wouldn't get a vision of something I didn't want to see. How pathetic is that? I'm used to getting involved and saving people, helping. I'm *not* used to being the weakest link. I hate it. I should've been protecting you."

"Protecting me?" I frowned.

"Yes. You were unconscious less than an hour ago. Tussling with that guy was a huge risk. What if you blacked out again?" She covered my hand with hers. "You needed me, and all I could do was sit in the car and make a phone call. I *never* want to be in that position again."

Warmth spread through my chest. I'd never met a woman like her. She was pissed because she couldn't protect me. I wasn't sure what to say. Instead I pulled off the freeway into a rest stop.

"Why are we stopping?"

I turned off the car and handed her the keys. "We're not being followed, and I was unconscious twice in the past two nights. I've got no business being behind the wheel right now."

She took the keys, her lips twitching like she might be

holding back a grin. "You're just trying to make me feel better."

I ran a finger down her cheek until her gaze met mine. "Is it working?"

She rolled her eyes, but her smile broke through. "I can't believe I'm smiling. We could've been killed tonight."

"But we weren't. That's worth a smile, right?"

She nodded. "I guess it is."

"Thanks for watching my back. You may not think you helped, but calling my brother probably saved our lives tonight." I lifted her chin, pressing my lips to hers. Her hands glided up my chest. Her touch sparking my desire in spite of my injuries.

She hummed softly into the kiss. "Not safe out here."

I nodded and stole one more taste of her lips before I straightened. "You're right."

We got out and swapped places. She found the seat adjuster and moved it farther forward than it had been since I drove the car off the sales lot. Next she adjusted the mirrors, and I realized this was the first time I'd ever seen her drive. The more time I spent with her, the more it seemed like I'd known her forever. Moments like this reminded me I had so much more to learn.

She merged onto the freeway and finally spared a peek my way. "I have a horrible sense of direction and no clue how to get to your house, so if you'd like to get back there tonight, you better tell me where I'm going."

My tone deepened a little. "I definitely want to get back there. *Soon*."

A sexy, barely there smile pulled at the corner of her mouth, but her attention stayed on the road. "You're in no condition for the activity you're implying."

I chuckled. "Does that mean if I was, you'd be game for said activity?"

She shrugged and wet her lips. "We did just narrowly avoid death. That's a pretty big turn-on."

"Making love can be very life-affirming."

"Calling it that is a lie." Her smile faltered.

We rode in silence until I pointed out the freeway exit. "Can I ask you something?"

She stopped at the light. "Only if I can ask you something in return."

"Fair enough." I covered her hand on the shifter. "Tell me about the asshole doctor who made you so cynical about relationships."

She glanced my way. "Why?"

"Because I want to understand why we can be laughing or kissing or half naked, and then I say something that makes you think of that dipweed."

"Dipweed?" She chuckled.

"I can't take credit for it. It's my office manager's word. She prides herself on not cursing."

"She's creative." Kilani shifted her attention my way for a second. "Which way am I going?"

I gave her directions and then prodded again. "Back to the dipweed."

"Which one?"

"Oh shit, there was more than one? No wonder you swore off doctors."

"Bingo."

I ran my hand through my hair. "Let's go with the first one."

"His name was Chris." She made the first turn. Most people missed the street sign. She had good eyes. "We met in college. I helped him study and we started dating. He was a year older than I was with blond hair and blue eyes. I fell for him. Hard. He told me he loved me. And on his graduation day, I showed up to surprise him. He was surprised all right…"

She sighed and made another turn. "His parents were there, and I rushed up to kiss him. The looks on their faces made it plain they had no idea who I was. Then they said Marlene was in the restroom." She pressed her lips into a tight line. "I asked if that was his sister, and his mother was quick to correct me. Marlene was his girlfriend. His blond cheerleader girlfriend."

I gripped the handle on the passenger door, struggling to keep my anger in check. Just imagining another guy touching her was bad enough, but hurting her was over the top. "I'm sorry. I'm hesitant to ask about dipweed number two."

"It's my turn to ask you something anyway."

I tried to peer into the shattered mirror for any tails as we neared my place. "Okay."

"Where did all the anger come from that led to that boxing ring?"

My gut twisted. I wanted to impress my mate, not expose my failures. She pulled up the drive and turned off the car. I grabbed onto distraction with both hands. "Let's get inside. I could use some ice for my jaw."

Dirty play manipulating her nursing instincts, but I didn't know what else to do.

"Fine, but I'm not letting you off the hook."

Close enough for me. I took her hand and unlocked

the door. Once the alarm was set behind us, I went to the kitchen for an ice pack. Kilani followed and sat at the bar.

"How's your head?"

Part of me loved her for changing the subject. Maybe more than just part of me.

"It's been better, but I'll live." I pressed the ice against my jaw. "I'm assuming the knife-wielding Nero op tonight was Sebastian's brother."

"Safe bet." She rapped her nails on the granite countertop. "Question is, why did he show up without a gun and back-up?"

"He was quick to inform me he had no beef with the Pack, he just wanted you. I'm guessing if he showed up with his team and weapons, it'd be hard to buy his line that Nero was just here for you."

"Big risk."

"Not too bad. He knew I was probably exhausted and unarmed. Still had his knife ready. Jaguars don't seem to get that werewolves pull our strength from the wolf and our Pack. We're family, and there's power in that. The second he threatened my mate, the wolf clawed its way forward. He didn't stand a chance."

Chapter Sixteen

KILANI

I stared at Jason. Mate. That word again. In front of me stood this man, rugged and strong, and tonight he would've laid down his life to ensure my safety, yet on some level that instinct to distance myself, to protect the little abandoned girl, haunted me. Maybe it always would.

Could fate really plan a man's destiny? And why would fate saddle him with a woman who would put him in danger? He deserved an equal, someone who could be his backup, not his Achilles heel.

But I couldn't deny the pang of jealousy at imagining him with another woman. Time to change the subject. "You never answered me about the anger."

"No, I didn't."

"Does that mean you don't know where it comes from or you just don't trust me?"

He set the ice on the counter and rested his hands on the edge. Every knuckle was swollen and red. He bent his head, his voice low. "Honest answer?"

"Always."

"Relationships are usually easy for me. I've never found the right person, so if things didn't work out, I'd find someone else. Nature of the beast. But you came into my life and turned everything upside down. The stories about mates are true…" He took a slow breath and lifted his eyes to meet mine. "Every second we spend together, this invisible web of instinct and emotion gets stronger. You make me laugh, you call me on the carpet when you think I'm wrong, and I've never been more attracted to anyone. I wish I was a better man for you, and I'm hesitant to share anything that might make you walk out that door."

His heart, his pain, his fear, it all shone in his eyes, and the swell washed over me until tears welled up. I stood and came around to his side of the bar. He straightened, turning to face me. I took his battered hands in mine. "I've never met anyone like you… I…" I shook my head. "I don't know what to say."

"Then don't say anything." His arms encircled me, lifting me off the ground as his lips crushed against mine.

I wrapped my legs around his waist, sliding my fingers into the back of his hair as our tongues twined in a slow, hungry, sensuous dance. He walked us across the room while we abandoned the rest of the world, lost in the passion of the kiss. I didn't open my eyes. I didn't want to break this spell. Tonight was about surrender and damn the consequences. Who knew what tomorrow held?

He lowered me onto the bed. I savored his mouth a few

more times as I pulled his shirt up, my hands exploring his hot skin. The hunger in Jason's gaze sent my heart racing. He broke the kiss long enough to pull the shirt off, exposing the angry bruises on his ribs.

"Are you sure you're up for—"

He pressed a finger over my lips. "I need you."

I kissed his fingertip, nodding. He traced a line down my chin, along my neck, and over my collarbone, his touch searing my sensitive skin until I ached to be naked underneath him. He pushed my T-shirt up, his eyes never leaving mine as he came closer to caress my abdomen with his lips. I reached down to run my fingers through his hair, moaning as his hands slid under my shirt, up my ribs, and finally cupped my breasts.

All my clothes needed to come off. Now.

He nibbled at my naval, his tongue brushing my skin. I writhed, hungry for his attention even lower. I'd never experienced desire like he kindled inside of me. If he kept this up, I'd have an orgasm with my pants on.

His deep voice vibrated against my abdomen. "Take your shirt off for me."

My pulse pounded in response, my body already begging for release. His stare pinned me as I lifted my shirt up, baring my skin. When I pulled it over my head, he unclasped the front of my bra, groaning as his mouth slid up my chest.

His lips hovered over my nipple. "You're so damned beautiful, Kilani." His fingers caressed my other breast, pinching the tip until I gasped his name. He growled in answer. "Say my name again."

He lowered his head, licking my nipple once before sucking it into his mouth. My back arched toward him. "Jason."

A strong arm slid under me, holding me tight as he feasted on one breast and then the other. Heat coiled in my belly and between my legs. Until this moment, I hadn't realized yearning could be such a delicious torture. I never wanted it to end, and at the same time, I wanted him to take me over the edge so badly I could scream.

His teeth teased my taut nipple as he moved his free hand to the button on my jeans. I wasn't sure how much more I could take. My muscles clenched, aching for release. He kissed his way lower. Opening my jeans, he shoved them down, stripping my panties off with them. He ran a finger over my core and I trembled, my hips bucking. He nibbled at my inner thigh, tugging my jeans free from my legs with one hand as he slid his fingers inside of me.

He moaned against my skin. "You're mine."

Before I could say anything, his mouth was on me, his tongue teasing as I rocked into him. Balling my fists in the sheets, my entire body shuddered. "Don't stop…"

He hummed against me, the vibration sending me right over the peak. I tingled from head to toe, every muscle tight, shivering with pleasure. Gradually he slowed his attention, his lips kissing up my body. His hips settled between my thighs, pressing at my opening, rock-hard right through his shorts.

His lips caressed my neck, just below my ear. "I need you…"

Rational thought fizzled at the raw desire in his voice. "Take me."

He got up and pulled off the shorts and underwear. I'd never seen a sexier naked man. In spite of his bruises, every inch of him was strong, molded and fashioned from iron. I wet my lips, the passionate fire building inside of me all over again. He took a step but stopped short of laying down. He turned and went to the drawer in the bedside table.

He pulled out a condom and tore the package. I sat up and held out my hand. "Let me."

His mouth curved at the corners as he placed the foil square in my palm.

"Lay down."

He raised a brow but did as I asked. I took the condom from the packaging and straddled his thighs, just out of his reach. With my free hand, I stroked his shaft, enjoying every pleasurable sound that escaped him. I ran my fingernails along his sac and traced my fingertip up the underside of his erection before sliding the condom down over him.

"You're making me crazy."

"Looks good on you." I crawled a little higher and rose up over him, not quite allowing the tip of his shaft to touch me. "Sure you're *up* for this tonight?"

He laughed and grabbed my hips, pulling me down onto him. I moaned and chuckled at the same time and practically had another orgasm. His body was made for mine. Sex had never been like this, and we'd just started.

I bent to kiss him, and he slid his hands up my back, growling against my mouth. "Sorry. Couldn't wait any longer."

"Mmm..." I smiled, savoring every taste of his lips. "Forgiven."

He rolled us over before I realized he was going to move and rocked his hips into me, picking up the pace of his thrusts. I pulled my legs up, clasping them around his waist, moaning as he penetrated me even deeper.

A moan escaped my throat as he ran a hand down my body, gripping my hip as he kissed his way down my neck. "Hold on."

Before his words registered, he was on his feet, his large hands holding my ass. I clasped my hands behind his neck, riding his thrusts, grinding into him. He pressed me against the wall, working up into me deeper. The cool plaster on my back made me gasp, the sensation intensifying the pleasure and heat between our bodies. He moved one hand between us, teasing me even higher.

"Let go. Take me with you."

My breath caught, muscles pulsing around his rock-hard erection.

He growled against my ear. "That's it. Let go."

And I did, crying out his name as my orgasm slammed into me almost as intensely as his thrusts. Jason pistoned his hips, stoking the fire until he erupted inside me. For a second, I swore time ceased to exist. The world vanished. And for now, it was just us. His arms, his body, his voice were my world.

He trembled against me, pulling me back from oblivion. "Need to put me down?"

He let out a breathless laugh and nodded. "Yeah. Hold on."

I kissed his neck as he walked us back over to the bed and sat on the edge, our bodies still connected. I wasn't ready to let him go. Not yet. Resting my forehead against his, I stared into his eyes.

He caressed my cheek and whispered, "You're amazing."

"You're the one who fought two nights in a row, then took on an armed attacker, and somehow still had the strength to rock my world. I'm pretty sure that makes you the amazing one."

"I never believed in mates. None of this is rational or logical, but here you are. You're beautiful and strong and intelligent." He kissed me slowly and tenderly. "And if those bastards from Nero ever threaten you again, I'll kill them."

I turned my head, nuzzling into his palm. "Hopefully it won't come to that."

I got off his lap and into the bed. Jason followed my lead after a run to the bathroom to dispose of the condom. It shouldn't bother me that he had a stash of them in the drawer by his bed. Where else was he going to keep them?

But I couldn't help wondering how many women had been in this bed before me. How recently? None of my business. But past hurts clawed their way forward as he slid into bed, spooning me from behind with his warm body.

"You're quiet." He wrapped a strong arm around my middle. "Everything okay?"

I rested my hand over his. "My last relationship was a disaster on so many levels. I think I might have PTSD." Sighing, I closed my eyes. "If this mate thing is real, fate sure saddled you with damaged goods."

"Nothing about you is damaged. You're much stronger than you think." He kissed my shoulder. "Turn around so I can see you."

"It'll be easier for me to talk if I don't."

"Want to tell me about dipweed number two?"

I smiled in spite of myself. "He was in residency and I was fresh out of nursing school. We didn't live together yet, but we spent a lot of time with each other. He told me he loved me. I thought I loved him." I bit my lower lip, struggling to force out the words. "I got pregnant."

Jason's hold on me tightened, but he didn't say anything.

"I thought he'd be happy or at least be responsible but…" I opened my eyes, staring at the electrical outlet. "But instead he gave me money for an abortion. He called me an island whore looking for a white doctor to take care of her. He said the baby probably wasn't his anyway, and he'd never be stupid enough to get *trapped* into a marriage over a mixed-blood baby."

His chest vibrated behind me. Was he growling? I cleared my throat, forcing myself to go on. I'd never told this story to anyone before. Saying it out loud was harder than I ever dreamed.

"Apparently my ethnicity didn't matter when we had sex, but he never had any intention of having a family with me. I took his money and found a new job. Instead of getting an abortion, I used it to buy a crib." My voice wobbled. "I had a miscarriage at twelve weeks."

He shifted and rolled me over, pulling me into his arms. Tears spilled down my cheeks as I pressed my ear to his chest, taking comfort in the steady, strong beat of his heart. He kissed my hair and held me while I wept.

"He thought I got an abortion, and I sold the crib. End of story." Jason was quiet, his hand stroking my hair. I waited. Finally I couldn't stand the silence. "Rethinking fate's choice for your mate?"

He moved a little so he could see my tear-stained face. "Not at all. Just trying to diffuse the urge to go back to the club and beat the shit out of someone. That guy didn't deserve you. He wasn't a dipweed, he was a full-blown fucking asshole."

I laughed and cried at the same time. "You got that right."

He wiped my tear with his thumb. "I may be a doctor, but I'm not him. And I'm not going anywhere."

"You had condoms handy right by the bed, and my warning lights started flashing. Not your fault, but it doesn't change the fact that I can't help but wonder if this bed was even cold before I got into it."

"Wow." He frowned and shook his head. "I'm not going to lie to you. I didn't believe in mates, and I haven't been celibate just waiting to find her. I've had girlfriends, but in case you're curious, I haven't had sex in more than six months. For a while I thought maybe Nadya and I might have a spark, but you saw how that turned out."

"Gareth."

He nodded. "Yeah. She touched him and it was over. Mates. I thought they were nuts." He met my eyes. "I never slept with her." He kissed my forehead, his lips resting there for a moment. "I'm sorry I didn't find you before those other guys did, but I'm here now, and if you'll let me in, I'll do my best to make you happy."

The thought of a real future seemed like a fantasy, an unlikely dream.

Right now, staying alive would be enough.

Chapter Seventeen

JASON

"They're coming."

I bolted upright at the sound of her voice, tense and ready. I didn't need to ask who was on the way. "How soon?"

"I don't know." Kilani was already yanking her pants on. I followed suit.

"Did you see how many in your vision?"

"Not really. At least one, but probably more." She shook her head. "I got a flash of your driveway and the view of the wall beside the garage. They had guns."

"Dammit." I pulled on my running shoes. "Luke and Logan from my Pack were on watch here last night."

"I didn't see them."

"Shit." *God, don't let them be dead.*

"I couldn't get a sense of the time. Usually the flashes are just a few minutes ahead, but lately that's been changing."

"Like what you saw with my dad."

She nodded, following me to the door. "And with us sleeping together."

I cocked a brow in her direction. "You had a vision of us in bed?"

"Guys with guns, remember?"

Yeah, I remembered. "Wait here. I'll check things out."

She grabbed my hand. "No more locking me up to keep me safe. They could come in through the window just as easily as through a door. I'm going with you."

"Please, Kilani." No scents other than our own permeated my place, but that didn't mean they weren't right outside. "Stay here. They won't be able to sneak up on me. My hearing and sense of smell—"

"I know. You're the big, strong werewolf. I'm the defenseless human. I'm still not letting you walk into a bullet."

I tried to stare her down, but she didn't budge. If Nero weren't on their way to silence her, I'd probably admire her moxie, but given the real danger, I was tempted to pick her ass up and lock her in my bathroom until I could be sure she'd be safe.

"Ground rules. You stay behind me, no matter what, and if I tell you to hide, you do it, no questions. Got it?"

A muscle in her cheek flexed, but she nodded. Close enough.

I opened the bedroom door, listening for footsteps or any sign someone might be inside. Satisfied we were alone, for now, I took her hand and led her out. Before we got to the door, my cell buzzed in my pocket. I almost hit the ceiling. My nerves were shot. Not to mention the throbbing in my skull. Any sudden turns made the room tilt. Concussion. I was such an idiot. She needed me at my best.

But this was all I had. It would be enough. Had to be.

The text was from Logan. He and his twin brother were younger than me, but they were deadly fighters. *No sign of Nero all night. We're ready to head home.*

I was tempted to let them go, but if Nero showed up before I could get to the car, Kilani would be in danger. As much as it hurt my pride, right now I was in no condition to take them on all on my own.

I texted back. *Wait until we leave, okay?*

Sure.

Kilani handed me some ice. "Put this on the back of your neck for me."

I placed the pack on my hot skin. "What happened to staying behind me?" I rolled my eyes, refusing to acknowledge the ice was already clearing my head.

"'Thank you' would be the appropriate response here. They obviously haven't arrived yet, and you're nursing a concussion. I might not be a werewolf, but I'm not helpless."

No, she wasn't. Not by a long shot. "Thanks." I slid my phone back in my pocket and grabbed my car keys from the counter. "Let's get out of here before Nero pays us a visit."

"Good plan."

The second I opened the front door, the almost imperceptible whistle pierced my ears. "Get down." I pulled Kilani closer to the ground as a bullet sank into the thick oak doorframe. "Sniper. Stay with me."

Shit. I should've figured they'd keep their distance so I wouldn't catch their scent. If I hadn't taken blows to the head two nights in a row, it probably would've crossed my mind they might use long-distance rifles, but in my current condition...

I put a lid on the rage and focused on Kilani's safety. I could be pissed at myself later. Keeping her tight beside me, I sprinted for the car, staggering our path. Asphalt and dirt peppered us as the bullets landed too close for comfort. If they hit my tires, we'd be toast. Suddenly, deafening gunfire exploded around us as Logan scrambled behind the bumper of my car, returning fire.

"Get in; I'll cover you." Logan squeezed off another shot toward the trees in the direction of the sniper.

"You and your brother better be right behind us." I opened the door and Kilani hustled inside, crawling over the gear shifter into the passenger seat.

"We will," Luke answered, cocking a shotgun on the other side of the drive. He aimed the barrel for the thicket of pine trees. "Touch base at the ranch."

"See you there. Thanks." I got in and turned the key. Before the engine warmed, I pressed the accelerator to the floor. I'd never been more thankful for my circular driveway. If I'd had to back out first, we would've been an easy target.

Two more shots echoed as we put more distance between Nero and us. "Are you all right?"

Her soft hand covered mine on the gearshift. "I should be asking you that. How's your head?"

"Hurts like a bastard, but we're alive, so I'll count it under the win column."

"Need me to drive?"

"I'm fine for now. Too wired to faint."

"You better not." She stared at the passenger mirror. "What now? We can't go to my place or the hospital or the fight club. Should we lay low at the grocery store?"

How was it possible for her to make me smile when just a few minutes ago someone had been shooting at us? But I already knew. Nurses were tough under pressure. When someone came into triage screaming with rebar jutting out of their chest, it was the nurses on the front line, calming the patient and making order out of the chaos. No outward panic.

My mate wasn't a werewolf, that was true, but her spirit was every bit as strong.

"We're going to Adam's."

"Nero knows about the ranch, too, right?"

I nodded, merging onto the highway. "Yeah, but he'd need a bigger team to storm the ranch, and he knows it."

"What about Adam's kids?"

The gunfire had cleared fogginess that slowed my thinking earlier. "We're not going to stay long."

She turned toward me. "Where are we going?"

"Hawaii."

"Hawaii?" Adam groaned and got up from the stool. "This is no time for a vacation, Jason. Besides, full moon is coming up in a few days. What if you don't make it back in time?"

"Then I shift there."

His eyes widened. Adam crossed his arms over his chest, his lips pressed into a thin line. Kilani ran her hand up my back, soothing me. Could she sense my agitation? She'd thought my plan was nuts, too, until I explained myself.

"You can't just shift into a wolf in Hawaii. They're not native to the islands. What if someone saw you?"

"I'll have to be sure they don't."

"No." Adam shook his head. "It's too dangerous."

I got to my feet. "Kilani's grandmother will be their next target. They'll leverage her life to get Kilani to come to them, and you know it."

Adam's wife, Lana, and Nadya came in with sleepy-eyed twins. Adam's daughter tottered over and raised her hands to me. I scooped her up, without taking my eyes off Adam. She rested her head over my heart, her soft hair teasing my chin. It was really tough to stay pissed at her dad with her snuggling in like that.

Nadya passed behind me to hug Kilani, while Lana went to Adam's side. "What's with all the grumbling in here?"

Adam slid his arm around his wife's waist. "Nero had snipers shooting at Jason and Kilani this morning, and now he thinks they need to go to Hawaii…"

His voice drifted off and we both turned toward the front door. Sebastian was outside. His scent was familiar to me now. You don't forget the first guy to knock you out.

Adam started for the door, but I stopped him and handed over his little girl. Animal instinct won out over human pride. The Pack protected their Alpha, whether Adam liked it or not. I turned the knob before Sebastian could knock, relishing the tiny glint of surprise in his dark eyes.

"My scent."

I nodded. "Tough to sneak up on us. Why are you here?" I didn't open the door wide enough for him to see beyond me, and meanwhile I scanned the area for anyone else.

"I need to speak with Adam."

"Did you know snipers paid me a visit this morning?"

Sebastian frowned, glancing over his shoulder. "Inside. They could be watching us now."

"Why should I let *you* in?"

He met my gaze. "Because I'm your best chance to help Kilani."

He was playing my weak spot. I gripped the doorknob tighter. "Your brother paid me a visit last night. Friendly guy with a knife and armed backup. I don't remember you *helping* us then."

"Let him in."

The command was plain in Adam's voice. Against my better judgment, I pulled the door back, leaving room for Sebastian to come inside. Lana took Madeleine from Adam, while their son, little Malcolm, hugged her leg. Nadya pried his pudgy hands free, picking him up, and Lana grinned at her sleepy little boy.

I frowned for a second, wishing my head were clearer. Her smile triggered something, but the memory slipped into the fog in my head before I could grab it.

Lana and Nadya disappeared around the corner, wisely keeping the twins far from Sebastian. No doubt he'd get a hero's welcome from his father if he brought Lana or her twins back to Nero. Females didn't carry the shifter gene until Lana, and somehow she'd passed it on to her daughter. Madeleine was a jaguar like her mother without ever being bitten.

A priceless commodity to Nero in their quest to breed the perfect assassin. If they could produce female shifters without ever being bitten and breed them, they could insulate themselves from outside investigations. No more kidnapping women off the streets or grooming young girls with psychic abilities in their boarding schools.

I still didn't have a clue how they actually achieved their goal with Lana, but the money Nero poured into their breeding program had paid off, or it would have if Lana's mother had turned her over to them. Shortly after giving birth, she abandoned newborn Lana on the steps of a church in San Antonio. She spent her childhood lost in the foster care system. Not a great start to life, but in hindsight, it probably saved her from becoming a lab rat under Nero's microscope.

Sebastian walked past me, but not before I noticed the bruise under his eye. I may have gone down last night, but he didn't get out of the ring unscathed, either.

"Why are you here?" Adam asked as I moved to his right side, ready to back him up physically if it came to that.

"Because the snipers were a distraction. My brother has already caught a flight for Hawaii with a two-man team. The others are staying behind in Reno. If they get the shot to eliminate Kilani, they are to take it."

"He's going to Hawaii to grab Grandma Nani." Kilani stood, approaching Sebastian. "You said they already went to Hawaii while they were trying to find me."

Sebastian nodded. "They did. She had no information."

"But they didn't hurt her, right?"

"Contrary to what the doctor may have told you, we are not blind killers. The last thing we want is attention from the police or the FBI. If we couldn't find you, then holding or harming your grandmother would become a liability. We don't take unnecessary risks."

I glanced at Adam, then Sebastian. Did anyone else in this damned room find it strange that the eldest son of

Nero's president was helping us?

"Give me a reason we should believe you. You weren't backing me up last night." He didn't answer fast enough. I pushed it a little further. "It'd probably make Nero's job much easier if you led me into a trap and delivered Kilani right to your brother in Honolulu, right?"

A wrinkle formed in the center of Sebastian's brow, and everyone looked my way. I didn't give a shit at the moment. From what I'd seen so far, loyalty wasn't a concept Sebastian understood.

"I am not here to protect you, or your Pack, or even Kilani."

"That's the first sentence I've believed since you walked through that door." I crossed over to Kilani and took her hand. "So why *are* you here?"

Sebastian's attention shifted to Adam. "I'm here because it's in my best interest to see that my brother is unsuccessful in this mission. I will do whatever it takes to see that he fails, even if it means working *with* you...this time."

The back door closed and Gareth came around the corner and stopped, his shoulders bunched, his voice more of a snarl. "What in the hell is he doing here?"

Tension boiled over in Adam's living room. I took a step, moving so Kilani was slightly behind me, embracing the instinct to shield my mate. Gareth recently discovered Sebastian had killed his twin brother, but we couldn't afford to allow him to exact Pack justice. Killing Sebastian, heir to the Nero empire, would mean we'd never be rid of them, not to mention that Sebastian was offering us inside information we'd have no hope of acquiring without his help.

None of that mattered a hell of a lot to Gareth.

"How is Nadya?" Sebastian's gaze locked on Gareth's, no sign of fear or regret.

The tension eased from Gareth's shoulders. My jaw slackened. The jaguar negotiated my Pack brother's hostility like an artist, turning attention to the one thing that meant the world to his adversary. The one thing Sebastian's insider intel had helped to save. Nadya.

"She's healed."

Sebastian nodded. "I'm glad to hear that."

And for once the bastard sounded sincere. For reasons unknown to us, Sebastian had been the one to alert Gareth that Dr. Granger was doping Nadya, increasing the DNA modification instead of neutralizing it.

I'd been so desperate for a cure that it blinded me. Another check mark under the column of my recent failures and shortcomings. Another drop in the bucket of uncontrollable anger.

Gareth came closer, standing at Adam's right side.

I focused on Sebastian again. "You came here to warn us that your brother is already on his way to Hawaii to grab Kilani's grandmother."

"She's the only leverage we are aware of to lure the target out of the Pack's protection."

Kilani squeezed my hand. "She has nothing to do with any of this. I haven't spoken to her in years."

Sebastian gazed at my mate from the corner of his eye. "She's your only family. It's a safe gamble that you won't let her die for you. Your grandmother is my brother's backup plan."

"We're going to Hawaii." I narrowed my eyes, daring Adam to deny me. "It'll draw Nero away from Reno. Kilani is their target. They'll follow us."

"And then what will you do, Jason?" Adam's voice was clipped, angry. "You'll be in unfamiliar territory, during a full moon, without anyone to back you up."

"We'll find her grandmother before Nero and bring her back here where we can protect them both."

"They have a head start, Wolf." Sebastian rolled his shoulders back. "By the time you get there, she could already be in my brother's custody."

I dropped Kilani's hand and charged Sebastian before I even realized I had planned on moving. "Are you shitting me? You're seriously taking Adam's side in this? Un-fuck-ing-believable." I balled my fist, but soft fingers caught my wrist in an iron grip.

I turned to find Kilani staring up at me, her brow furrowed. "Punching someone isn't going to fix this."

Her lips were moving, but it took a moment for her words to sink in through the haze of rage. Taking a breath, I nodded and faced Sebastian again. "You said they have a head start, but you want to be certain your brother fails in this mission. Are you planning to go to Hawaii to stop him?"

"It's too risky for me to be directly involved. Too much is at stake." His dark gaze flicked toward Adam, then back to me. "I can offer information, nothing more."

"So you're hoping I'll send another Pack member with Jason to be sure they stop him." Adam stepped back, tipping his head toward the large dining room table. "Have a seat. We'll talk."

I went to follow, but Kilani hung back. Turning toward her, my body blocked her face from the others' view. Adam and Gareth would hear us even if we whispered, and

Sebastian probably could, too, but the illusion of privacy was worth something.

"Are you all right?"

"No." Her skin paled, her hands trembling as she met my gaze. Tears shone in her eyes but she blinked them back. "I'm far from all right."

"I won't let anything happen to you."

She took my hand, lacing her fingers with mine. "It's not me I'm worried about."

Chapter Eighteen

KILANI

I took a chair beside Jason, wishing I could unknot my stomach. His rugged profile hypnotized me. While Sebastian spilled details about Nero protocols, I tried to memorize every line and angle of Jason's face.

My vision a couple of minutes ago had left me shaken.

The moment Adam invited everyone to sit, my mind became a movie set, and at centerstage was Jason, shot and bleeding on the ground. The visceral image made it difficult for me to calm myself and search the scene for clues to time or place. It happened on black asphalt. Outdoors, but where?

And more importantly, when?

I had no goddamned idea. What use was this idiotic "gift" when all it did was scare me? And how could I protect Jason from this dark future? Adam's words "without anyone to back you up" kept echoing through my head.

Why in the hell would fate throw us together? If I was really his "mate," it looked like I was going to get him killed.

Across the table, Sebastian answered Adam's questions. Was he one of the shooters this morning? Did he come to this meeting armed?

After the vision of Jason with a bullet wound, my nerves were shot. It would've been upsetting no matter who had been on the ground, but seeing his skin beginning to pale, the crimson stain growing...

This had to stop. I cared about him. Caring *for* people was my job, but caring *about* them was something I usually shielded myself from. When had he broken through my emotional defenses?

Did it matter?

I had to keep that vision from becoming reality. But what could I do, search every person I came in contact with for weapons?

If I didn't get a grip and focus soon, I'd make myself insane.

Lana came into the room, snapping me out of my panic. "Hi, Sebastian. It's been a while."

She stood behind Adam, kneading his shoulders, but the tension in his jawline grew.

"Still happy living among wolves, Little One?" Sebastian raised one brow. Grace used to find the facial gesture cute, but to me, it always came across as condescending. "How many lambs might the stern wolf betray?"

Before I could ask what the hell he was talking about, Lana rolled her eyes. "Shakespeare, right?"

Sebastian almost smiled. "I see living with wolves hasn't dulled your cultured mind."

"From my side of the fence, wolves aren't betrayers." Lana grinned and kissed the top of Adam's head. "You'll get more bees with honey, Sebastian. Just a suggestion."

Jason watched Lana, his muscles tensing up. I rested my hand on his thigh, instinctively rubbing it, offering comfort without any idea why he needed it.

He leaned forward toward Sebastian. "How old did you say your brother is?"

"Why would that matter?" he countered.

"I'm not sure yet." A muscle contracted in Jason's cheek. "But it might matter tremendously."

Sebastian frowned. "Damian is twenty-seven."

Jason tilted his head to gaze up at Lana for a moment. "Huh, strange coincidence. Lana just turned twenty-seven, too."

"Many people are currently twenty-seven, Wolf."

Jason nodded. "You told Lana her mother was dead, but her father is still alive." His hand covered mine under the table. "Did Lana have a twin, too?"

Sebastian got up. "I think you misunderstand my intentions here, Wolf. I came to stop my brother, not to betray my father or Nero."

Jason shot out of his chair. "How is telling us if Lana had a twin betraying your father, exactly?"

Adam and Gareth stood, and I followed suit, wondering what the hell I was missing.

"It has nothing to do with making certain my brother's mission is unsuccessful."

"Maybe not, but it sounds like you'll be counting on me to do most of the legwork for you. A little information on your brother, who tried to kill me last night, seems like a small price to pay for my assistance."

Lana glanced at Jason and back to Sebastian. "You said my father still works for Nero. Do you know who he is?"

Sebastian shook his head. "Your knowledge of Shakespeare is endearing, Little One, but this isn't a play, and some mysteries are better left unsolved." He went to the door. "I will be in touch when I have more information about my brother's location in Hawaii." Opening the door, he took a step outside and stopped, turning to meet my eyes. "I never meant to pull you into this world, Kilani, but here you are. It would be wise to use every *gift* you possess to stay alive."

D own at Adam's barn, the horses nickered as we walked to my car. Adam had parked it inside in the hopes Nero might not discover it. His plan seemed to be working so far, but they already found me at Jason's place, so my Ford Fiesta was probably much less important now.

I pulled the rest of my clothes and my laptop from the back. This would be enough. Lana bought our tickets to Hawaii online, and by dinnertime, we'd be in the air. Surreal.

"You're not alone in this. You can talk to me."

Jason's deep voice and the slow touch of his large hand down the back of my hair had me suddenly on the verge of tears. I laughed and wiped the corner of my eye. "What do you want me to say? We're fleeing to my childhood home to save my grandmother who hasn't spoken to me since I was eleven, not to mention our lives are in danger. I'm just this side of losing my shit."

He pulled me into his arms, kissing the top of my head.

"You are one of the strongest people I've ever met. We'll get through this. I promise you."

I clung to him but kept my eyes open, afraid of what I might see when I closed them. "I had a vision up in the house."

He tried to pull back, but I didn't loosen my hold on him. I wouldn't get the words out if I had to see him. "I couldn't tell when, or where, but you were shot and bleeding out."

"That's not set in stone. We'll be careful."

"I wish we could run away."

"You'll never be able to live with yourself if they get your grandmother."

I sighed and tipped my head back. "Tell me about werewolf women."

He chuckled. "No such thing."

"What about your mother? She's a werewolf, right?"

He nodded. "She is now, but only men are born wolves. Shifting is carried in the Y chromosome."

"How did she turn into a shifter?"

"Why all the questions?"

I wasn't sure I wanted to acknowledge the answer just yet. "I'm curious, and discussing werewolves isn't something we can do in public."

He ran the back of his fingers down my cheek. "When a werewolf finds his mate, if they ever want to have children, he has to bite her. There's a compound in our saliva when we're in wolf form that mutates human DNA to match ours. A month later, she shifts during the full moon just like we do. She becomes a werewolf."

"Does it take that long for them to get the heightened senses, like superhuman hearing and smell?"

"We're also stronger than the average human." He kissed my forehead. "We need to get on the road so I can grab some clothes and get us to the airport."

"Okay, but you didn't answer my question. How long before you get the werewolf perks?"

One corner of his mouth curved up into a crooked smile. "I've never heard them called perks before, but everyone is different. For some it's gradual, and for others their senses are instantly enhanced. But it takes a full month for the final transformation and her first shift into a wolf."

My pulse raced as I pieced all the information together and the realization dawned on me. I couldn't seriously be considering letting him bite me. Could I? We were on our way to Hawaii, chasing after men with guns. If I had his heightened senses and strength, I could be an equal partner, an asset instead of a liability. It made sense. It could also change the outcome of the vision I had. Maybe.

Never in a million years did I dream I'd be weighing pros and cons of becoming a werewolf.

"Are you going to tell me what that was all about?'

"I already told you—curiosity." I wasn't ready to say the words out loud yet. In truth, was I actually *ready* for any of this? I slung my bag over my shoulder. "Guess we'd better go."

Jason surprised me with a slow, lingering, hungry kiss. My heart pounded in answer. When he straightened, my eyes fluttered open and I wished we were going to Hawaii for a honeymoon, not a rescue mission.

I stared up at him, trying to decipher the emotions brewing inside of me. No one had ever looked at me the way he did, like I was all that mattered, and no man had *ever* put his life on the line for me. The only experiences I'd ever had with "love" left me abandoned and broken.

What would I be if he walked away?

Jason took my hand. "Wait a sec, I need to tell you something."

Butterflies filled my stomach. "Okay."

"Before I discovered you were my mate, I couldn't stop thinking about you. I watched you from my office window that day because I couldn't make myself look away. I wanted to learn all your secrets, to hear you laugh and make you smile."

He cleared his throat and ran one hand through his hair. "My interest in you had nothing to do with instincts. I didn't believe the Pack stories about mates were even real. But when you touched my hand and I recognized you for who you were—"

I rose up on my toes and pulled him down, my lips brushing his. Yes, I was interrupting, but in my defense, he was good with words. I wasn't. I wanted to tell him how much I enjoyed seeing him grin and knowing it was because of me. I wanted to open my heart. He was risking his life to protect me. He deserved to know what that meant to me.

But fear tied my tongue in knots. Admitting I needed him, that I cared about him, it opened me up for wounds I couldn't bear to feel again. For now, this was enough.

My feet left the ground as he cradled me in his arms without breaking the kiss. I savored his lips, happy to lose myself in the fire he stoked inside of me. He walked forward. I didn't open my eyes to see where he was taking me. I didn't care. My heart raced, my blood heated, and I yearned to forget Nero. Sex until we were too exhausted to move seemed like a great idea.

"Kilani," he whispered against my lips.

"What?" I sucked gently at his lower lip until he growled.

"I can't get enough of you… But…right now…we need to…" He groaned, surrendering to one more heated kiss. His tongue demanded mine, hungry, as his fingers tightened into a fist in my hair. Seeing the effect I had over him gave me a delicious taste of power, passion, and I wanted more. His other hand slid up my thigh, cupping my ass, squeezing it until heat pooled low in my belly.

He broke the kiss, fighting to catch his breath. "We can't miss that plane."

The plane. My grandmother. Nero. I nodded, keeping my gaze locked on his. "You are one hell of a kisser."

A sexy, crooked smile curved on his lips. "You inspire me."

He lowered me to the ground, holding me tight against him. His erection pressed against me, making his jeans taut. If lives weren't on the line, I might've dragged him into the tack room for more inspiration.

Instead, I took his hand. "I'm still scared."

"I'd be worried if you weren't, but we'll get through this."

Being a part of a "we" was something I'd yearned for and dreamed about since my mom abandoned me while I was at school. Now this handsome, intelligent, brave man stood beside me, claiming me as his own with every touch, every kiss. I should've been happy, but as we walked to his car, fear ran her icy finger down my spine.

Jason might not walk out on me, but what if he died standing at my side?

Chapter Nineteen

Jared opened the door to our parents' house. "Hey, Jason." We clasped forearms and he turned to Kilani. "You haven't run away screaming?"

She smiled, and my pulse pounded with relief. Since we'd left Adam's place, she'd been somber and quiet. "Not yet, although you'd probably all be safer if I did."

Jared stepped back so we could come inside. "Nah, we'd just find trouble elsewhere. You can't protect us from ourselves, believe me."

"We brought over more supplies for Dad. Where's Mom?"

"Back here," she answered, hearing me perfectly.

We headed for the bedroom and found my dad sitting up with pillows propped behind him. For a second, words escaped me. I'd been praying for this for weeks, dreaming he'd look me in the eye one more time, and here he was.

"You just going to stand there? Come in and give your old man a hug."

He didn't have to ask me twice. I crossed the distance in two strides and bent over to embrace my father. He wrapped one arm around me and mumbled about his other arm not working right yet.

I straightened and cleared my throat, struggling to find my voice. "It'll come, Dad. Your body just needs a little more time to heal."

"You try laying in this bed for weeks and then talk to me about time and patience."

My mom chuckled. "He must be feeling better, because his mulish tendencies are back in full force."

Hope and happiness radiated from my mom's smile. I wasn't sure I'd ever been more grateful. I took the bag of supplies from Kilani and handed them to my brother, then I caught her hand, lacing my fingers with hers. If she hadn't come into my life and used her gift to see my father's future…what if we hadn't given him enough time? What if we pulled the plug on his care too soon?

There was nothing I could offer to repay her. All I had was myself.

"How long will you be gone?"

Jared's voice jarred me from my thoughts. "Not sure yet. I brought enough to keep Dad taken care of for ten days just in case."

He frowned. "Ten days? There's a full moon in there."

"Yeah, there's a good chance I'll be on my own for this one."

"Bad idea, bro." He crossed his arms. "Adam signed off on this?"

"Not happily. But we've got to get Kilani's grandmother to Reno so the Pack can protect her from Nero. She's their only leverage to get Kilani to turn herself over."

He ground his teeth, contracting a muscle in his cheek. "I'll go with you."

"Mom needs you here. With Nero in town, we can't risk leaving her and Dad vulnerable." I clasped his shoulder. "Keep our folks safe for me."

Mom stood and embraced me, her voice buzzing against my ear. "Promise me you'll be careful."

I held her tight and kissed her hair. "I love you, Mom. I'll be home as soon as I can."

Kilani stiffened when my mom released me and focused on her. My mom had no clue about my mate's previous bad experiences with prejudice. While my parents didn't hold any of those judgments in their hearts, I still sent up a silent prayer that my mom wouldn't say anything that could be misinterpreted.

"I heard through the grapevine that your grandmother is a big Neil Diamond fan."

Kilani nodded slowly, her dark eyes flitting toward me and then back on my mom. "She claims she's his biggest fan on the islands."

My mom smiled, although it didn't reach her worried eyes. "If it helps get her to come back here with you, please let her know he's coming through Las Vegas soon and I have a spare ticket with her name on it if she'd like to go with me."

Kilani's eyes widened, shock plain on her face, before she grinned. "If that doesn't get her to come back with us, then nothing will."

My mom winked. "Good. I can't wait to meet her."

"And she'll save me from having to sing another chorus of 'Sweet Caroline.'" My dad met my gaze and smiled. "You take care of that little lady. I'll keep working so I can open the door when you get home."

"There's no rush, Dad. Sitting up and talking are huge improvements. It'll come with time." I brushed my hand against the small of Kilani's back, guiding her to the door. Good-byes weren't my strong suit. "See you soon."

Jared followed us to the door and pulled me into a tight hug. "Don't take any chances over there. Find her grand-mother and get back here."

"Will do." I stared into his eyes for a moment. If I didn't make it back in time for the full moon, this would be the first time we'd ever shifted apart. And if I didn't play my cards right, we might be apart permanently. "I'll be back. Watch out for Dad for me."

After grabbing some clothes from my place, I drove toward the airport. Kilani had been pretty quiet since we left the house. Seeing the bullet holes in my driveway and front door was a harsh reminder of the reality of the danger ahead.

Signs for the airport started showing up on the interstate. We'd be in the air soon, on our way to Hawaii, to her past. The urge to shield her swelled, but there was no way I'd ever find her grandmother without her help, let alone convince the elderly woman to follow me back to Reno.

After the car was parked, I grabbed our duffel bags be-fore she could complain.

"You're the one with a concussion; you shouldn't carry the bags." Her voice soothed tension I didn't notice growing in my shoulders.

"First off, they don't weigh that much, and secondly, my head feels much better. I'm fine."

She rolled her eyes and brushed her hair back over her shoulder. "You're not fine." She walked ahead. Even under her breath, her words were plain to me. "But who am I to talk. I'm not fine, either."

I followed close behind, giving her some space. When you were a werewolf, you learned pretty quickly that our super hearing could be annoying to others when they muttered under their breath. Whether or not it was intentional, it was still eavesdropping.

Waiting in the security line, I conjured up Sebastian's brother in my mind. Damian Severino. After Kilani's last vision, it was even more important that I stay on my guard until we were back with the Pack.

I chose to see her premonition as a warning, not a real outcome.

Something else was bothering me. Why wouldn't Sebastian tell us about Lana's father? He was hiding something. Why? I kept replaying last night after the fight, his brother standing under the yellow streetlight in the parking lot with a knife. Something about him seemed familiar. I'd never seen him before. But still…

"Do you want window or aisle?"

Kilani had her carry-on and her ticket ready. I didn't even notice our flight had been called for boarding. If I couldn't get my head together, this trip could end badly. "Why don't you take the window so you can see the island when we get closer?"

"I'd rather not."

"All right." I slung my backpack over my shoulder and walked ahead of her down the Jetway. The only good thing I'd done so far was upgrading our tickets to first class. We'd have more room, better food, and no stranger sharing our row. I hoped that meant we might talk a few things out, but that would depend on my mate.

We got seated, our carry-ons stowed, and a flight attendant took our drink orders. I could only watch the luggage being loaded on the plane for so long. I shifted around and took her hand. "You've been awfully quiet."

She shrugged. "Could say the same for you."

"I'll share if you will." She didn't say no. "Okay, I'll go first. My head is still a little foggy, but something about Sebastian's brother was familiar. I just can't put my finger on it."

"I couldn't see him very well; the light kept reflecting off his knife. Did he look like Sebastian?"

"Not really. He's shorter and more solid." I dodged a backpack as a late-comer rushed onboard. "This wouldn't be a big deal, but Sebastian got defensive...and it's got to be about Damian."

"You asked him about Lana's father."

I nodded. "And he wouldn't give me a straight answer."

"Maybe Lana's father is Sebastian's superior or something."

I blinked. Clarity smacked into me like a two-by-four plank. "The only person higher up than Sebastian is Mr. Severino himself." Good thing I'd already buckled my seat belt or I would've shot out of my seat. "That's it. That's how I recognized Damian. He reminded me of Lana."

"Lana?" Kilani raised a brow.

"Yes. Damian smiled at me, and then later at the ranch when Lana started to smile...it was the same. And they're the same age, too."

"You think Damian and Lana are related?"

The thrust of the plane's takeoff barely kept me down as the pieces fell into place. "It makes sense. Lana had a twin, but only her twin was delivered to Nero. Her mother left her behind, hoping she'd save her from spending her life as a lab rat."

"You think Sebastian knows?"

"Yes." I gripped the armrest on my seat as we gained altitude. "He didn't admit anything, but he was the one who brought us a flash drive with the breeding experiment Lana's mother participated in. When he delivered the information, he conveniently left out the identity of her father, but he told us he was alive and still working for Nero."

"Her mother?"

"Eliminated." Just like they'd been ordered to handle Kilani. Silenced forever.

Over my fucking dead body.

"Why would Sebastian want to keep that a secret?"

I shrugged. "No clue, but the more I think about it, it makes sense. After Sebastian stole that file, he stopped pursuing the mission to bring Lana back to Nero. They ended up bringing in Sasha to finish the job."

"Sasha? As in Nadya's sister the police detective?"

"She wasn't a detective at the time. Long story." I took another swallow of my Coke. "But if I'm right and Damian is Lana's fraternal twin, then Sebastian is her older brother... he's related to her twins, too." I raked a hand through my hair. "Jesus. Malcolm and Madeleine are Severino's grandchildren. Shit."

"Maybe you're wrong."

I sucked in a slow breath and met her eyes. "I'm not. I can feel it. I need to warn Adam."

I struggled to calm my mind. If I was right, and I'd bet everything I was, then my Alpha's mate and their twin toddlers were in more danger than we realized. Nero wanted Lana because she'd been the first female-born shifter, and now she'd passed that along to her daughter, and somehow, even though Lana was a jaguar, her son was born a werewolf like his father. The secrets in their DNA could change Nero's breeding program forever, making their supply of shape-shifting assassins never-ending.

Did Sebastian give his father that information? That was the million-dollar question.

I passed my empty cup to the flight attendant and did my best to box up my concern. There was nothing I could do while we were 35,000 feet above the ocean.

Leaning over, I brushed my lips to Kilani's temple. The fresh scent of her hair, her skin, calmed the tempest twisting inside me. "So, your turn. What's been keeping you so quiet?"

Chapter Twenty

Kilani

He made it sound so simple. But my thoughts had been running in circles for hours, and I couldn't keep up anymore. I was going back to Hawaii to find my grandmother who hadn't spoken to me in more than ten years, I'd seen Jason's death in a vision, and then there were the mercenaries from Nero after us.

At this point, I was clinging to calm by a thin thread greased with butter.

"I'm not sure where to start." That about covered it.

"The beginning?"

I nudged him with my elbow. Somehow, in spite of my near panic, Jason could still make me smile. "The beginning. Okay…I've never been back home for a reason. When I left for Brightwood, I made the trip without my grandmother's consent, and she never contacted me, so I didn't reach out to her, either. Now it's been years, and I have no idea what to expect. I assume she's still angry with me, but…" I cleared my throat and gazed past Jason, out the window. "Deep down…I'm scared she just doesn't care."

Jason took my hand, drawing my attention back to him. The setting sun coming through the jet's window made his hazel eyes brighter, fiery, and the set of his jaw, the cut healing on his eyebrow, they all came together into a masculine package that stole my breath. Why couldn't we be going to Hawaii for a romantic getaway?

Because life was anything but fair. I'd learned that lesson firsthand more than once.

"Whatever kept your grandmother from contacting you doesn't really make a difference anymore. It's time to let it go and start over. You've both lost time you'll never get back." He kissed my knuckles. Watching his lips caress my skin was a welcome distraction from the dread and worry. "No matter what the future holds, I'm not going anywhere. I'll be here for you."

God, had anyone ever "been there" for me? It was like he offered cool water after I'd been lost in the desert. A little voice whispered, *Too good to be true*, but I did my best to ignore it.

I'd already given him my trust and my body, but my heart remained locked away, and I forgot where I hid the key.

"Easy to say that now. You haven't met my family yet. It's not neat and tidy like yours."

"Really?" He chuckled, shaking his head. "Is that what you think? Our Pack is a lot of things, but neat and tidy? No way. Love isn't always pretty, and it's usually during the ugliest moments when you discover just how strong it can be."

I wanted to believe him. "We should get some rest."

He didn't prod or push, surprising me. Instead, he wrapped his arm around my shoulders. Settled in against his chest, I tried to forget about assassins, past hurts, and even the new ones waiting for me when we got to the islands.

In the steady beat of Jason's heart, I found peace.

We landed in Honolulu. The scent of fresh flowers on the cool evening breeze swamped me, drowning me in a wave of unwelcome memories. My mother teaching me to weave leis and find sand dollars on the beach. And the afternoon my grandmother wiped my tears and promised me she'd take care of me after my mom walked out of our lives.

Jason squeezed my hand. "I've never been to Hawaii before. Does it always smell so..."

"Yes." I nodded, shoving my childhood into a dark corner. "I never realized how amazing the air smelled here until I went to New York. I took it for granted."

We collected our bags and caught a cab to the hotel. We planned to spend the night in Honolulu and catch the first plane to Maui in the morning. Jason checked us in under Lana's reservation. Nero would be looking for Jason or me, so hopefully Lana's name would fly under the radar. For all we knew, Damian and his men were already over on Maui anyway.

"It's late, but I need some food." He handed me a room key. "Probably a substantial amount of food."

I chuckled in spite of my mood. Jason had a knack for

sensing when I needed to get out of my own head or something. Supposedly I was the psychic, but maybe there was more to the mate thing than I realized.

"Is this big appetite a werewolf thing?"

He nodded, leaving our things at the bell desk. "Yeah, our metabolism runs fast, so we need food and plenty of it. The perk is, we never gain a spare tire around our middles."

"I bet Weight Watchers hates you guys."

"Now you understand why secrecy is so important for us."

I laughed and slid my arm around his waist. "What are you in the mood for?"

He glanced down at me with hunger in his eyes, a decidedly sexy hunger that had nothing to do with food. My body warmed. I wet my lips and he tightened his hold around my waist, his voice low, almost a growl.

"Maybe we should go to the room first."

There was a delicious power in witnessing the effect I had on him, in seeing his desire. He didn't hide it from me. That honesty turned me on even more than his chiseled body.

"While that's tempting…" I took his hand. "I'd like to see the water."

He nodded and kissed my forehead. "Sounds good to me."

We made our way through the lobby area and outside. The Sheraton was right on the water, and with the bright, nearly full moon, the froth on the waves glowed in the silvery light. My breath caught in my throat as the waves crashed onto the sand.

Home.

I tugged Jason out to the beach. We pulled off our shoes

and rolled up our pant legs while the local band playing poolside belted out "Louie Louie."

"I have shorts in my bag." Jason laced his fingers with mine. "I should've changed."

I chuckled. "If we'd gone to the room, we would've stayed there."

"Definitely." He grinned and my blood warmed.

We walked down to the water. The cool water rushed around our ankles and a giggle bubbled up from my throat. "Oh, it's colder than I remember."

"You probably splashed around during the day."

I nodded. "I used to collect sand dollars with my mom. She'd tell me stories about how mermaids used them for money."

"This must have been a great place to grow up."

"Yeah. For a while it was…" The moonlight sparkled on the water, and for the first time, I realized thinking about my mom hadn't made me angry.

Another wave came in hard, splashing up our pant legs. Jason jumped back, laughing. "Shit. That one surprised me."

Behind us, the band broke into a cover of "Hungry Like the Wolf." I smiled up at mine. He was sexy even in soaking-wet blue jeans. "Dance with me."

He chuckled, glancing down the beach. "I'm not much of a dancer."

"You can't listen to this song and not move to the beat." I let my hips sway to the pulsing drumbeat as I took his hand. "There's no one out here to see. Just feel it."

He rolled his eyes but gradually started to move with me. The waves crashed and raced toward us, but I barely noticed. I couldn't take my eyes off of Jason. Once he got over being self-conscious, he could move. I danced around him slowly, enjoying the hunger in his gaze.

As the band finished and started a new song, Jason pulled me close, my breasts pressed tight to his chest. "This wolf is very hungry."

I ran my hands up his chest. "Dancing can tell you a lot about a person."

He raised a brow. "I'm afraid of what I just told you."

I laughed as another wave drenched us. "You like to be in control, but the second you allowed your body to respond to the beat, your instincts took over and you danced. You surrendered." Kissing his chest, I whispered, "You have an artist's passion trapped inside your analytical mind."

Jason lifted me up, and I wrapped my legs around his waist. His forehead rested against mine. "I've never liked dancing." He started to sway with the music and the tide, turning us slowly. "But maybe I just never had the right partner."

His lips claimed mine as the waves broke around us. My pulse raced, my body warmed, and gradually he broke the kiss. "You make me feel invincible."

But he wasn't invincible. None of us were, and my vision of him bleeding from a gunshot wound was never far from my consciousness.

"Tell me what it's like out here through your eyes and ears, with your wolf senses."

He slowly lowered me to the ground and took my hand. Together we walked down the shoreline. "We're walking into the wind, so not only can I smell all the food, but if I concentrate, I can tell you one of the band members forgot deodorant. The waves make it tough to hear conversations."

"And how do you know they're not out here watching us right now?"

"After my fight with Damian, I'd recognize his scent in a heartbeat. He's not on this beach. I didn't pick up his scent in the airport, either, but with all the people coming and going, his scent was probably gone by the time we got there."

"So he couldn't sneak up on you?"

Jason shrugged. "It'd be tough. Maybe if he was downwind he could take a shot?" He looked down at me. "Can I ask you a question now?"

"Sure."

"Is this about your vision? Because I don't see it as set in stone. We're being cautious, and we can change the outcome."

I sighed and swallowed the lump in my throat. "I made a pact with myself to never get involved with another doctor, but that night at Adam's ranch, when I found out your first-aid kit was Bactine and Band-Aids and your first love was art, not science…" I shook my head and stared out at the waves. "You're a good guy, Jason, and all I bring to the table is danger."

He came around in front of me and lifted my chin to meet his eyes. "Here's what you bring to the table. You're smart and strong. I've never seen anyone so calm under pressure. The day my dad was attacked, he would've died without your help, and when Damian met us in the parking lot, you were cool enough to call my brother for backup. You probably saved us both." He started to smile. "And you saved me from cracking my head open in my shower even though I'm a terrible patient."

I laughed, remembering the way he groaned about the

Bactine stinging. "You really are a bad patient."

"And tonight you got me to dance." He pointed to his chest. "Me. The non-dancer. And you know what?" I shook my head. "I sort of liked it."

I grinned. "So when this is over, you might take me dancing?"

He kissed my lips. "Definitely." He pulled back, smile fading. "I need to tell you something."

My pulse jumped a little. "Okay."

"If things go bad here, I need you to know that…" His voice was raw with emotion. "Somewhere in this crazy mess, I fell for you. And if that vision you had comes true, I want—"

"I want you to bite me and make me like you."

His eyes widened at my interruption. "What?"

"It's the only way I can help you and not be a hindrance. I see that now."

He frowned. "You don't have to do that. Not yet." He took my hand. "Being changed by your mate is a commitment. Lifelong commitment. I'd be lying through my teeth if I told you I didn't want that with all my being, but before you interrupted I was trying to say…I love you. And I'm willing to wait twenty years if that's what it takes for you to see that those aren't empty words like you've heard in the past. When you need me, I'll be there. You don't need to change a thing."

A tear spilled down my cheek as I rose up on my toes to kiss him. His strong arms held me tight as our lips parted. My tongue tangled slowly with his while my mind reeled, replaying his words over and over. This wasn't an "I love you" gasped after sex, or a manipulation. He hadn't asked for anything in return.

What could I give? All I brought to the table was trouble and danger. Unless he changed me. If I had the senses he did, combined with my visions, I could save him. Was I ready for a lifelong commitment? Was he? Some small part of myself, the little lost girl, reminded me that my own mother walked out on me and never came back. What if Jason discovered the flaw inside me that sent her away?

My chest tightened as I pulled back, aching to escape the doubt and fear roiling inside me. "You're probably starving."

He growled against my lips. "Not for food."

I caught his lower lip with my teeth, whispering into the kiss, "We could order room service."

"Probably safer to stay inside." He hummed against my lips.

Oh, he was preaching to the choir.

We both grinned. Jason grabbed my hand and hustled back to the hotel.

I woke in a cold sweat. Jason still slept peacefully beside me. I sat up, rubbing my ankle over my *honu* tattoo. The sea turtle came to me in my dream. Through his eyes, I saw my grandmother. Her face was in shadows, a bonfire blazing behind her as she danced. Her hands told me a story. A warning.

The men in gray were back. They were on Maui asking about her. She left her home, the one I shared with her so long ago. The turtle turned, offering me a view of the rainforest and the waterfall. The cabin. Grandma Nani was staying in her spiritual getaway. When I was little, I'd go with her, watching her work. The skills of a true Kahuna were passed down to family. No outsiders.

But I left home before she could teach me. Had she taken in another apprentice in my place?

My *honu* let me see my grandmother one last time. Her dance had changed, slowed. Fire flickered in her dark eyes, her skin gleaming with sweat. I struggled to concentrate, to hold onto the dream. Using her body, she wove an urgent message.

Stay away.

I pulled my knees into my chest. Could she have any idea that we were already on the islands? My grandmother didn't have visions like I did. She gained information from the winds, the waves, the animals and rocks. Our ancestors lived in these islands, and a Kahuna could sense their presence, receive their messages.

Jason stirred beside me. "Something wrong?"

"My grandmother contacted me in my dream. She wants us to stay away."

He sat up, running his hand slowly up and down my spine. "She's trying to protect you."

"Or I'm not welcome here."

"No way." He kissed my shoulder. "I don't believe that for a second."

"I wish I shared your conviction." I grabbed a rubber band from the nightstand and put my hair up. "The Nero team is on Maui. She isn't at her house."

"She told you where she was?" He glanced at the turtle on my ankle. "How does this *honu* thing work exactly?"

"Nothing exact about it." I shrugged. "He guards my family line, and when we summon him, sometimes he can connect with our bloodline across the miles through dreams and meditations. That's how I warned her that they were looking for me a few weeks ago."

"And she got the message?"

"As far as I know. It's not like sending an email. The meaning isn't always clear in dreams, and other times it never comes through at all."

"Gareth has something like that."

"Really?"

Jason nodded, peering over at the clock. "His mom was part of the Paiute tribe, and while Nadya was fighting for her life, he found out he was a dream walker."

"Wow. So he doesn't need a go-between?"

He shrugged. "I'm not clear on how it works, but according to Nadya, he entered her dreams and helped her. He could connect with her wolf, hold her spirit on this side."

"Our *honu* delivers warnings and messages. I'm not sure he could physically help us."

"Getting the message that they're already on Maui and the location of your grandmother is help enough." He got out of bed, naked, still bruised but strong. "We should get out of here. The sooner we find her, the sooner we can get back to the Pack."

"Harvest moon is tomorrow night."

He nodded and pulled on a pair of underwear. "Yeah."

"Her cabin is tough to get to. There's no way we'll get her and get back to Reno in time."

"I figured." He picked up his shirt. "Sounds remote enough that I should be able to shift up there without being seen, right?"

I used to play in the forest while my grandmother held her spiritual retreats. There were places where the vegetation was impenetrable and you couldn't see farther than a few feet ahead, let alone blaze a trail. What if he wandered off as a wolf and couldn't find his way back?

"There aren't many people up there, but it's not like the woods in Lake Tahoe. The forest on Maui is thick. Hikers get lost all the time."

He came and sat next to me on the bed. His gaze drifted over my face. "You're my mate. My other half. Whether you're ready to believe it or not, it doesn't change that it's true. My wolf can track you anywhere. If you stay at your grandmother's cabin, I'll find my way back, no matter what." He ran his fingers along the edge of my jaw. "You're my north star, Kilani. Being near you makes my heart, my soul, and my wolf whole for the first time in my life."

My mouth went dry. I cleared my throat, struggling to dislodge the lump of emotion choking me. I leaned in and brushed my lips to his, wishing for the millionth time that we could just hide away. I opened my eyes, losing myself in the intensity of his stare.

"I can't figure out how to open my heart. I want to, but I'm so terrified that if I did and then I lost you, I'd never recover. It'd probably be easier if you weren't everything I ever dreamed about. You're smart, sexy, and a little rough around the edges…"

The corner of his mouth pulled up into a crooked, boyish grin that melted the heart I was so desperate to protect. "You don't have a monopoly on fear. Until we kick Nero's asses out of Reno—and trust me, I have every intention of doing that—you're a target. If anything happened to you…" He shook his head, breaking eye contact. "Can't even think about it."

I covered his tight fist and kissed his cheek. "If you make me a wolf like you, I'd be stronger and more help in the ass-kicking department."

Jason got up from the bed and stalked over to pick up the duffel bag. "You still don't seem to get it. There's no turning back. I won't trap you into loving me. Right now, you still have a choice. You can still walk away. I hate the shit out of the thought, but I care about you, and I'd never want you with me, wondering if it was all a mistake."

We packed up the room in silence. I chewed on his words. He made it clear, he wanted to change me, to make me his, but this wasn't a traditional relationship. This was mate for life. Two halves of one soul. The romantic dream I'd carried around most of my life.

But my mother and two different men snubbed out that flame, crushing it into ashes, and I didn't know how to believe again.

We caught a cab to the airport to grab the flight over to Maui. Jason held my hand, but he kept to himself. Normally silences made me nervous, worried someone was disappointed or angry with me, but with Jason, I could think. He was giving me space.

Giving me a chance to decide what I really wanted. It shouldn't be that difficult, but this wasn't deciding between a banana and a pineapple. The only thing that was certain was my desire to keep my vision from coming true. Jason would not end up shot, lying in a pool of his own blood. Not while I was still alive.

Was that love? Maybe.

I had today to figure it out. Tomorrow night was the full moon.

Chapter Twenty-One

JASON

While Kilani sat at the gate, I gave Adam a call. He answered on the first ring. "Everything all right?"

"For now. We're waiting for our flight over to Maui." I lowered my voice. "I figured something out last night and it involves your family."

His tone sobered. "I'm listening."

I took a deep breath. "Sebastian's motives for stopping his brother have been bothering me."

"Yeah, me, too."

I nodded even though he'd never see me. "I think Damian is hoping to win favor with their father, maybe bump Sebastian out of line to inherit the company."

"You could be on to something."

I clenched my fist. Adam wasn't going to be as calm about the next part. I cleared my throat. "This affects us because ever since Damian came at me with a knife, something about him seemed familiar, and yesterday when Sebastian got pissy about Damian's age, it confirmed the last piece of this puzzle."

"You lost me."

"When Lana smiled last night, I realized why Damian looked so familiar." I paused, but he didn't reply. "Adam, I think Damian is Lana's fraternal twin."

"Holy shit." Adam groaned under his breath.

"Yeah." I glanced over at Kilani. "I think that's why Sebastian never took Lana to his father. He brought me a flash drive with the breeding experiment data but no mention of the father's identity. Because he realized he's Lana's older brother and that makes Severino—"

"Fuck," Adam interrupted, his breath puffing into the phone. "You're telling me that my kids have Nero blood."

"Yeah."

"Their grandfather is the lunatic who ordered the hit on your mate."

"And I'm guessing Sebastian hasn't told him or they'd have a much bigger force beating on our back door."

"Damian must not know..."

"I have no idea, but you and your family need to have backup at all times until we can nail Sebastian down on this."

"And you need to grab Kilani's grandmother and get your ass home. We need to circle the wagons. Splitting up the Pack leaves us vulnerable."

"I know. We'll be back soon."

"Thanks for the information. Not what I wanted to hear, but I'll protect them."

Our flight number blasted across the PA system. Kilani

got up.

"Gotta go. Talk to you soon."

I dropped my phone in my pocket and jogged over. Kilani glanced up at me as we got in line to board. "How'd he take it?"

"About how I expected him to. If I'm right and the twins are Severino's biological grandchildren, we're never going to get that bastard to leave us alone."

"But he doesn't know, right?"

"We won't know for sure until we find Sebastian again."

To call Maui beautiful did it a disservice. The stunning views of the ocean on one side and the lush jungle on the other made driving perilous. Kilani contacted one of her cousins who loaned us his Jeep, saving us from paying for a rental and potentially alerting Damian and his team that we were on the island. Having the wind in my hair, the clean scent of the air, and Kilani's tan legs bared in a pair of cut-off shorts beside me, shit, it was tough to remember we were in danger.

Last night, I'd said the words. *I love you.* Out loud. Never before had I said that to anyone who wasn't a relative. I glanced over at Kilani as she pulled her long hair around her shoulder, containing it with one hand. Shifting my gaze back on the road, a smile tugged at my lips. Last night she'd coaxed me into dancing, and later I fed her grapes while we basked in the afterglow of making love with the balcony door open and the roar of the ocean blotting out the rest of the world.

I wanted more nights like that. More time to hold her in my arms, to hear her laugh and make her smile. I loved her.

She didn't return the sentiment. It probably would've stung, but her kiss was answer enough. I'd meant what I said about waiting for her. Unlike me, she'd spoken those words to two men before me, and they'd both broken her heart and her trust.

I'd have to be patient, but she was worth every minute.

She glanced my way. "Hopefully Nero is still sniffing around Grandma Nani's house down by the beach. My cousin said they came by his surf shop yesterday, but he told them he thought she took the ferry to Molokai to treat a sick girl who couldn't travel."

"I hope they bought it."

She nodded. "At least it'll slow them down a little. Either way, the cabin is off the grid, so even if someone mentions it to them, there's no address to enter into their GPS."

She directed me up winding roads with switchbacks and sudden drop-offs that had me tightening my grip on the wheel. The road to Hana was only about fifty-two miles on the map, but between the hairpin turns, sheer cliffs, and narrow bridges, we'd been driving for more than an hour and, according to the mile markers, we were only halfway there.

After another twenty minutes, Kilani pointed to a turnout filled with tourists, Hawaiian artisans, and a cart full of fresh fruit. I parked the Jeep and turned toward her. For a second, I couldn't speak. She stared at the jungle, the wind sliding through her silky hair. I memorized her profile, wishing I had my charcoal and a drawing pad handy. Every part of her, from the gentle slope of her nose, to her full lips, to the curve of her chin, called to me.

I shifted in my seat. Memories of making love to her the night before crept into my mind. How in the hell did I ever get so damned lucky? Kilani was beautiful, strong, wild, and…mine.

"Everything okay?"

She glanced my way and forced a smile. "We hike from here."

"All right." I climbed out of the Jeep, wishing I could lift the burden from her shoulders. What if her grandmother was still angry with her? There was no way that could be true. But why hadn't she visited or called Kilani? It didn't make sense.

That uncertainty hurt my mate, which in turn agitated the wolf inside of me. It didn't help that the full moon was so close. I took a deep breath, searching for any sign of Damian's scent. Fruit, sunblock, Doritos, and humans. No hint of a jaguar shifter. Yet.

I'd stay alert. They could be anywhere.

I handed Kilani her backpack and she took off down a barely marked trail. I followed, ducking underneath branches and brushing past ferns. A light drizzle blanketed us. Not enough to wash the sweat from my skin but just enough to make my shirt even wetter. After we'd hiked about a mile, she slowed.

"We're almost there."

"Good." Did she sense my discomfort? "How did your grandmother make it out here alone? This isn't a beginner's trail."

"Grandma Nani knows this island better than anyone. She could make this hike in the middle of the night without moonlight overhead."

We crossed through a thicket of trees and Kilani pointed. "There it is."

I narrowed my eyes in that direction. Trees, vines, ferns, a waterfall, but no cabin. "I don't see it."

"You will."

Her grin stunned me for a second. She hadn't smiled since we'd been in bed last night. I jogged a couple of steps to catch up to her.

"See it now?"

And there it was. A little cabin, painted the same color as the forest, with yellow trim that blended with the tree bark. No wonder I hadn't seen it. Camouflaged so perfectly into its environment, a trained Green Beret wouldn't have found it.

A woman came out onto the tiny porch, and Kilani stopped so fast I almost plowed right into her.

The woman squinted. "Kilani?"

She nodded, rushing for the steps as the older woman came down to meet her. They embraced, and I tried to figure out who this woman could be. There was no way she was old enough to be a grandmother to a grown woman. Maybe it was Kilani's aunt? I kept my distance, allowing them some private time, while I took a closer look at the cabin.

"You shouldn't have come."

I turned as Kilani stepped back, crossing her arms, defiant. "That's the first thing you have to say to me? Seriously? I'm here to take you someplace safe. I had to come."

The woman clucked her tongue. "I am safe *here*." She glanced my way. "Who is this?"

Kilani held a hand out to me. "Grandma Nani, this is Jason Ayers."

"This is your *grandmother*?"

Grandma Nani chuckled. "I'm going to like this one." She sobered and came closer. "You are not... You are..." Her dark eyes sparkled in the sunlight as she stared up at me. "You are a moon child. She calls to you."

I glanced at Kilani and back to her grandmother. "I guess I like the moon all right."

"Psh..." She shook her head and walked back toward the cabin. "Come inside. We need to talk."

I tugged Kilani to my side, whispering, "How could she know... You haven't said anything about me to her..."

"No, I haven't, but I told you the island speaks to her. Maybe our ancestors told her about you? I didn't stick around long enough to be her apprentice, so I'm not sure how it works."

"I can't tell her about the Pack."

Kilani laced her fingers with mine. "Your secret is safe with me, but it sounds like the wolf is already out of the bag, so to speak."

The scent of eucalyptus, sage, and gardenia assaulted me as we sat down inside. I'd never be able to smell Damian and his team until they walked into Nani's living room. Less than ideal.

"Mind if I open a couple windows?"

She rolled her eyes. "This is my only hope of covering your scent from the hunter who searches for me."

I got up, frowning. "How do you know all this?" Uncertainty didn't sit well with me and quickly edged toward anger. "What the hell is going on here?"

"Sit." She went to the tiny stove and tipped the kettle into three Asian teacups. "Has my granddaughter told you nothing about me?"

"She told me you're a Kahuna."

"That I am." She placed the handle-less teacups on a small bamboo tray. "Do you understand what that means?"

"Not really."

She handed Kilani a cup of steaming tea and turned toward me, narrowing her eyes. "Do you understand what *sit* means?"

Every culture had different rules and signs of respect, but this wasn't my grandmother or my spiritual advisor, and I wasn't going to be ordered around until I had some answers. "First tell me how you can possibly be Kilani's grandmother. You're probably younger than my mom."

She almost smiled and glanced back at Kilani. "He is as headstrong and demanding as you." Sipping her tea, she met my gaze. "Kilani is the first of the women in our family to finish school and go to college. I had her mother when I was fourteen, and she followed in my footsteps when she had Kilani."

"How do you know I went to college?" Now Kilani was on her feet, too. "We haven't spoken since I was eleven years old. You never even called."

Nani's fire dimmed slightly, her shoulders dropping as she placed her teacup on the counter. "We have much to talk about."

"Damn straight we do, but we don't have time now." Kilani put her cup beside her grandmother's. "Those men don't want to question you this time. They want to hurt you to get to me. We need to take you back to Reno. Jason's… family can protect us until the threat passes."

Nani shook her head. "You shouldn't have come."

"Stop saying that." Kilani pulled her hair back from her forehead. "You can be angry at me for leaving against your wishes later. It's not safe for you here. We need to go."

Lightning arced through the dark clouds, followed by the deafening crack of thunder. I walked over to the screen door just as the angry sky opened up. Large drops of tropical rain pelted the roof of the cabin.

I called over my shoulder, "We're not going anywhere right now."

"Please, you two. Sit."

Kilani took a seat on the wicker loveseat, leaving a space for me beside her. Once we were settled, Nani took the rocking chair in the corner. Kilani popped her shoes off and shifted to tuck her feet up. I noticed Nani was also barefoot. My tennis shoes weren't going anywhere. If we had to run, I'd be ready, even if I had to carry them both.

"The reason I sent the *honu* with my message to stay away was to protect you, not because I didn't want to see you. I have missed you, my little mynah bird."

Kilani's grip on my thigh tightened. I covered her hand with mine in support, reminding my wolf this was not our fight.

"I knew you didn't want me to leave the island, but I was just a kid. I thought I knew what I was doing. You never called, never sent a letter, never visited." Kilani broke eye contact, staring into her lap. "Did you even notice I was gone?"

Nani opened her clasped hands, her fine fingers tapping out a silent melody on her legs. "Can your friend wait on the porch so we can talk freely?"

Kilani shook her head. "I have no secrets from Jason."

My pulse jumped at her declaration. She couldn't tell me she loved me yet, but she trusted me. I stared at our joined hands, the bruises fading from my knuckles. I loved her, but I still hadn't answered her question about the fight club, the rage.

"Fine." The clouds blocked the setting sun, leaving us in shadows. Nani lit a candle beside her chair. "Do you still have visions of the future?"

Kilani nodded.

"Did your mother ever tell you that she had the gift, too?"

Kilani stiffened. "No."

Nani sighed. "I failed her."

"What are you talking about? *She* was the one who left *us*."

The sour scent of fear stung my nostrils. What was Nani hiding?

"She did, but not the way you think."

Kilani pulled her feet out from under her, leaning forward on the loveseat. "Please tell me what's going on."

Nani's gaze met mine for a moment, pleading, but for what, I had no idea. I ran my hand up Kilani's back.

"Your mother didn't go to the mainland. She drove her car off a cliff on the road to Hana. She left me a note." Candlelight sparkled in the tears welling in Nani's eyes. "She was never strong enough for the visions. They terrified her and stole her free will. I tried to help her, but I couldn't silence the gift. Nothing I did worked. She was my child." She cleared her throat. "I didn't know how to tell you."

"A note? She…" Kilani shook her head and shot up from the loveseat, her voice choked. "You told me she had a job, that she abandoned me. She's…dead?" She swiped at a tear on her cheek. "How could you lie to me about this? You made me hate her. I thought there must be something wrong with me." She gulped in a breath. "I need some air." I got up to go with her, but she caught my wrist. "Alone."

"Damian is out there with orders to eliminate you. I can't let you go out by yourself."

She pointed at the downpour. "I grew up in this jungle, not them. They'll never find me, especially not in the storm."

"It's too dangerous."

Her gaze met mine. The raw pain in her eyes broke me. "You said you can find me no matter where I go. Just give me a few minutes' head start. Please, Jason. I don't have a death wish, but if I don't get out of this cabin right now…" Her eyes fell onto her grandmother, her lips tightening. "I will hurt someone."

"Five minutes and I'm out that door to find you."

"Thank you." She rose up on her toes to kiss my cheek and whispered, "They're not coming up here yet. We're safe for now."

I wished I could be as certain as she and her grandmother seemed to be. It wasn't a risk I was willing to take. Kilani slipped out, the screen door slamming behind her.

"I never meant to hurt her."

"You have got to be kidding me." I wheeled around to face Nani. "How exactly did you figure telling her that her own mother didn't want her anymore wouldn't hurt her?"

Nani got out of her chair and straightened her back. "I was young and scared. My daughter killed herself because of the visions, and my granddaughter had the same gift. I couldn't lose them both."

"But you did."

"At least she's still alive." She broke eye contact. "I did chase after her." She collected the teacups. "When I got to Brightwood, they explained their mission to teach these girls to accept their gifts, to use them not fear them. I'd failed her mother. Who was I to think I could protect Kilani from the same fate?"

I ran a hand through my hair, struggling to rein in my thoughts. "Why not send her a letter? All this time she thought you didn't care, that you were angry with her."

Nani stared at her feet. "I never wanted her to come back here. After losing her mother, I was too frightened that I wouldn't be able to save my little mynah bird, either." She lifted her head, meeting my eyes. "The morning I found that note, I couldn't save my daughter, but the ancestors deafened Kilani's gift, sparing her from seeing a vision of her mother's fate. I didn't know what else to do. If she discovered her mother's gift caused her to take her own life, what if Kilani did, too?" She shook her head. "Anger is stronger than fear. I'd rather have her hate her mother and me than worry her gift might drive her insane."

Was she right? Had Kilani's anger and bitterness kept her alive, driven her to succeed on her own? I had no clue and no time to ponder it. "I've got to go find her."

"There is a waterfall not far to the north. It was her favorite spot as a little girl."

"Do you have a weapon here in case they show up?"

She waved off my warning. "The ancestors will keep them away."

I rolled my eyes. "Kilani told me they're not up here yet. I'm guessing she had a vision, but stay alert and get the hell out if they come knocking. I'll be back soon."

The tropical rain pelted me, soaking my shirt in an instant. Finding Kilani's scent through the wind and rain would be tough, but with the full moon so close and my mate nearby, my wolf would have no trouble. My sense of direction was unfazed by the storm. I headed north, listening for the sound of a waterfall.

I found her clothes first. Adrenaline shot through my body like lightning. I started to pick them up when Kilani called my name.

"I'm down here."

About four feet below was a pool, fed by the waterfall. And Kilani treaded water, naked, staring up at me.

I frowned. "Did you forget trained killers are looking for you?"

"I told you they're not up here yet. I had a vision. They must've seen Lana's hotel reservation in Honolulu. They're on Oahu now."

Relief threatened to bring me to my knees. "Why didn't you tell me?"

"You said you'd be five minutes behind me. I needed to get out of there." She dipped her head in the water, smoothing her hair back. "Are you coming in?"

She didn't need to ask me twice. I stripped off my wet clothes and shoes, dropping them beside hers, and dove in. The water in the pool was slightly cooler than the rain, refreshing. I came up and pulled her into my arms. She clung to me, her lips against my neck.

"I wish there was something I could do." And I meant it.

She leaned back, meeting my eyes. "Follow me."

Chapter Twenty-Two

I swam to the falls and waited for Jason. Shouting over the crash of the water, I pointed down. "There's a cave behind the waterfall. Take a big breath and hold my hand."

He didn't question. He took my hand, his gaze locked on mine, making it hard to catch my breath. I tightened my grip and turned toward the falls. The mouth of the cavern was only a couple of feet below the surface, but the rainy, twilight sky made it tough to see in the dark. I could find it in my sleep, but I didn't want to leave Jason behind. Hand in hand, we found the opening and swam through, then pushed up, popping our heads up inside the rock cave.

He scanned the chamber, his arm sliding around my waist. "This is cool. How did you find it?"

"I spent a lot of time up here as a kid, and one day I was diving in the pond and saw the opening." I kissed his chin, pulling his attention back to me. "I've never brought anyone here before."

He sobered and swam to the ledge. The muscles in his back tensed as he lifted himself out. He sat on the edge, his feet ankle-deep in the water.

"What's wrong?" I asked.

"I need to tell you something, but there's no way I'll get it out with you naked in my arms."

I wanted to lose myself with him and forget Grandma Nani's lies, but apparently it would have to wait. "Okay."

"You told her you had no secrets from me, and I've been keeping one from you."

I kicked harder, treading water. "I'm listening."

His head was down. I couldn't see his eyes. "You asked me where the rage comes from. I never gave you a straight answer. Fear kept me from it, and after talking to Nani, I see that's bullshit now." He lifted his chin, his gaze locking on mine. "I love you. That's stronger than my fear that you'll think less of me or walk away."

He cleared his throat. "I never wanted to be a doctor. My dad was a veterinarian and usually handled any Pack injuries, and on some level, I thought he always would. Then Jared and I were in high school and thinking about the future, and we lost someone in the Pack."

I got out of the pool and sat beside him. I took his hand in mine, lacing our pruned fingers together. "What happened?"

"Malcolm, Adam's dad, was our Alpha, and his mate, Martha, was sick. My dad was pretty sure it was cancer, but animal chemo wasn't going to cut it…"

"And she couldn't go to the hospital."

"Exactly." He turned toward me, water dripping from

his hair. "We all watched her waste away because she was a werewolf and we had no doctor who could help her. Jared and I were honor students; we both got scholarships and went to college as premed students. He was going to be a doctor and I was going to be a surgeon."

"Your brother, the carpenter?"

He nodded. "Don't let Jared fool you. He's really intelligent. There was an accident in college, and he ended up dropping out."

"You gave up being an artist, and then being a surgeon, because your Pack needed a doctor."

"Yeah. I understood, but things started to change the night Malcolm was shot."

"Someone shot Adam's dad?"

He stared into the water. "There was a fire fight with Nero and he took a bullet to save Lana. She was pregnant with the twins. The kicker was, I could have saved him. The bullet pierced his spleen. I could have removed it, and he'd be alive to play with his grandchildren." He picked up a tiny stone and tossed it. "He ordered me not to risk it, not to take him to the hospital. Doing surgery in the dirt without any assistance wasn't going to happen. In the end, I watched him die in Adam's arms."

He groaned and met my eyes. "That's when this fire started inside me. I gave up everything to be the healer for our Pack, and even then, my hands were tied. Boxing at the gym helped relieve the pent-up frustration. But six months later, Nadya came to the Pack for protection. One of Nero's mutant wolves kidnapped her and bit her. I didn't have a clue how they mutated the DNA. She'd die if I couldn't figure it out. So I took a risk and reached out to Adam's uncle.

He's a general in the military. He arranged for a scientist from Nero to come to Reno and assist me in treating her."

His hands tightened into fists. "Instead of saving her, he was juicing her up. When we found out and called him on it, he attacked my father with potassium chloride. I couldn't get my dad the care he needed, either. The anger was eating me up from the inside out. When Todd approached me about the fight club, I accepted the invitation. At least there, I had control over my destiny."

I lifted our joined hands to my lips. "In med school they teach you to beat death, to save lives, and you leave on a pedestal feeling like a god. You *think* you can decide who lives or dies. But the truth is, none of us can."

He slipped his hand free of mine. "What good is being a healer when my hands are tied? I love these people. They depend on me." As he met my eyes again, the pain and fear were plain for me to see. "My father and Nadya both almost died because of my mistake."

"But they didn't."

"Malcolm did." He took a slow breath and lowered his voice. "I can't lose another person."

And there it was. The rage that he'd allowed to take over his life. His perceived weakness and failure. He'd laid it out before me. No more secrets. I caught his chin, turning his head to meet my eyes.

Again, I found words hard to come by, but finally my lips moved and I whispered, "I love you."

No normal person would've been able to make out my words over the background noise of the falls, but my mate caught every word. My mate. Mine.

I leaned in and kissed him, again and again. He returned

the hunger, his tongue parting my lips. My pulse raced with desire as I ran my fingers up his wet chest, exploring every chiseled muscle. I needed this. I needed him.

Turning, I slid my leg around his waist, straddling his lap. He moved his hands down my back and lower, gripping my ass and pulling me tight against him. His erection pulsed between us, teasing me until I ached for him to be inside me.

"Condom," he growled.

"I don't care."

His teeth grazed my lip as he lifted my hips. The tip of his shaft brushed my core. I shuddered. His gaze held mine. "You're sure?"

I nodded. "I want you. Now."

He didn't hesitate, penetrating me so deeply I cried out. My nails dug into his shoulders, and I rocked my hips, grinding against him. We kept our eyes open, our noses touching as we gasped, sharing each other's air. Every rock-hard inch of him was made for me, stoking the fire inside my soul.

His lips brushed mine. His growl, vibrating through me. "I claim you. My mate. Always. I love you."

He brought one hand between us, his finger teasing me until I trembled in his arms. I pressed my forehead to his, eyes open, passion laid bare for him to witness. "I love you, too."

My muscles clenched around him. He thrust his hips up into me harder and faster, and finally he erupted inside of me, holding me so tight I could barely breathe.

I never wanted him to let go.

When we swam out of the tunnel and came up in front of the falls, the storm had passed and the moonlight sparkled on the rock pool. Jason broke through the surface beside me and we cut through the water, swimming closer to shore. Once my feet could touch bottom, I stood and stared at the moon above us.

"This time tomorrow, you'll be a wolf."

He took my hand, lifting it to his lips. "Yeah."

"So even if we grab Grandma Nani and get to Honolulu on the first flight over, we'll never get back to Reno before dark."

"Nope."

I turned toward him, marveling at his profile in the moonlight, the water shining on his skin. "You're not concerned?"

He stopped staring at the moon and looked down into my eyes. "When we left, I'd made my peace with shifting here. I'll be careful."

I rubbed my lips together, struggling for the right words. "I want to be your mate."

He cupped my cheek. "You already are."

"You know what I mean. Tomorrow night."

"You're sure?"

His eyes searched mine, and in that moment, I realized I'd never been surer of anything in my life. "You told me that you would always be here for me, and I want to do the same for you. I want to be your partner, not your weak spot."

He held me in his arms and kissed me long and slow and deep until my entire body molded against his. I laced my fingers behind his head, my heart pressed close to his, and a wave of emotion crested, hitting me so suddenly, I didn't realize tears rolled down my cheeks. A hot tear dripped onto Jason's chest. He broke the kiss and rested his forehead against mine. Concern lined his eyes.

"What's wrong?"

"Nothing." I laughed and wept at the same time. "I thought I was in love before, but it never... Instead of weak, I feel... God, I wish I had words. Usually the thought of caring about someone turns my stomach, like I'm standing on shifting sand. But it's not like that with you. I..." I rolled my eyes. "I suck at trying to say something romantic."

Jason chuckled, stealing another kiss. "Loving me is enough. That's all the romance I need."

"I do love you." I nodded, another tear sliding down my cheek. "So make me a big strong wolf already."

Jason laughed, dunking us both under the water. I wrestled free and swam for the shore. Crawling out, I made it to our clothes first. Jason followed and grabbed his shirt.

"So, what about your grandmother? What do we tell her?"

"About you turning into a wolf tomorrow night?" I shrugged. I wasn't ready to think about Grandma Nani and open that ugly box of emotions. "I think she already knows. I have no idea how, but she does."

"And how are you holding up?"

I pulled on my pants and immediately couldn't wait to get them off. Cold and wet and stuck to me in all the wrong places. I shook out my legs. "I'm still pissed at her. I can't wrap my head around how she could possibly think it would hurt me less to think my mother didn't want me."

"For what it's worth, she was in shock and mourning her daughter at the time. You had visions of the future, too. She thought if you were angry with your mother it would make you stronger than being afraid and worried you might suffer the same fate."

I hadn't allowed myself to remember my mother in years. If she wasn't thinking about me, I sure as hell wasn't going to waste my time on her. But that barrier was gone now. The visions of the future had tormented her.

"I can remember my mom putting on makeup every morning to cover the dark circles around her eyes. She had nightmares. Maybe they were visions. When I started seeing them too, she took me on a picnic at the beach and told me about free will. She wasn't even twenty years old yet, but to me, she was everything. She said nothing was carved in stone. I believed her, but maybe she'd been trying to convince herself."

Jason came to my side, fully dressed, and took my hand. "Right or wrong, your grandmother never stopped loving you or your mom. She made a mistake, a big one, but the ball is in your court now."

He was right. Every word. If anyone understood how short life could be, it was a nurse. But I'd just learned my mother had never left me for a job. She didn't decide there was something wrong with me and walk out of my life. She had died.

And my grandmother let me spend years hating her. Whatever her reasons, I never got the chance to mourn for my own mother, and deep down, I thought something was wrong with me, I was incapable and unworthy of being loved. My heart clenched in my chest.

"I don't know how to forgive her for this." I squeezed his hand and started back, my stomach tight with uncertainty. "My whole life, every hurt, it all stemmed from her lie. I believed her. I thought no one wanted me."

"It also made you the amazing, strong woman you are now. Maybe the visions would have frightened you more if you knew they drove your mother to suicide? We'll never know. But I'm grateful that you ended up in Reno, in the hospital. Without you, I would have lost my dad, and I might not have ever found my mate."

I'd never considered what my life might've been like if I had stayed on the islands. Would I have been a teenage mother like my mom and Grandma Nani? Jason stood tall, powerful beside me as we made our way back to the cabin in the moonlight. Right or wrong, good or bad, I wouldn't trade my life for anything.

And I wouldn't let Nero take it from me.

The screen door squealed and I cringed, half of me hoping Grandma Nani was sleeping. She set her book aside, stood up, and opened her arms. I froze for a moment.

"I am sorry, Kilani. Please forgive me."

Tears welled in my eyes for the abandoned little girl inside of me, and I ran into my grandmother's embrace. She held me tight, running her hand down my wet hair.

"We've lost so much time, mynah bird."

I clung to her, breathing her in. She still smelled like fresh rain even when she was dry. "I'm sorry I never came home."

"No." She gripped my shoulders, pulling me back to meet her eyes. "No. *You* did nothing wrong. *You* found a future. Here there were only ghosts. You made a life, chose a good partner. I am so proud of you."

Over my grandmother's shoulder, Jason sat on the love-seat. He caught me staring and winked. I closed my eyes and drank in the love.

In the corner, my phone beeped inside my backpack. I frowned and went to retrieve it. Flashing on the screen was a text from Sebastian.

He knows you are on the islands and Honolulu is your only way off. He will take his stand at the airport.

I dropped my phone back in my bag. "Getting home is going to be tricky."

Closing my eyes, I struggled to recall details from my vision—could we have been in an airport? But all I saw was Jason's blood.

Chapter Twenty-Three

JASON

A bird babbled outside the window. I squinted at the sunshine filtering through the bamboo shade. "What the hell is that?"

Kilani rolled over, spooning my back. She kissed my shoulder. "That's a mynah bird."

"My alarm clock is less annoying."

"Yeah, they're pretty chatty. That's how I got my nickname." She nuzzled close to my ear, her teeth teasing me. Much better way to wake up than the damned bird. "I had long black hair and I chattered constantly. My mom and grandma called me their little mynah bird."

I rested back on the pillow and she snuggled against my chest. Waking with her in my arms was quickly becoming my favorite time of day. I traced a circle on her back. "I should get up and be sure we're still alone."

"Sebastian's text said the Nero team is watching for us at the airport in Honolulu."

"Yeah."

"You don't believe him?"

"I'm not ready to bet your life on Sebastian's information." Kilani blinked hard and gasped. "Cover your ears."

"What? Why?" But I was beginning to recognize her tell when a vision was coming on. She almost always closed her eyes. Hard. And when they opened again she was in action.

Nani burst into the room singing at the top of her lungs. I didn't understand the Hawaiian lyrics, but the message was clear as she raised all the shades. Time to get up.

"Much to do, mynah bird." She tied the final cord around the cleat on the wall and met my eyes. "Big night for you."

I sat up on the futon, careful to keep the sheet around my waist. "Why do you say that?"

"Must we continue this game?" She placed her hands on her hips. "Tonight is the full moon. Tonight you embrace the wolf."

"Do you hear how crazy that sounds?"

Her eyes sparked with mischief. "Doesn't make it any less true, right?"

I glanced at Kilani, who was doing her best not to crack up. Happy was a great look for her. I wanted to spend the rest of my life making her laugh.

"How do you know all this?"

Nani went to the door and stopped. When she turned, the teasing was gone, replaced by a spiritual calmness. "Our ancestors watch over her. They came to me in a dream and showed me my granddaughter's mate, both sides of him."

She closed the door behind her, and I fell back onto the

pillow. "Your grandmother is something else."

"Yes she is." Kilani nodded. "When I was little, she told me that the wind, the waves, the rocks, the trees, the animals, they're all connected, and our ancestors can communicate through them. I left home before she could really teach me. The best I've done is meditating and connecting with our family *Aumakua*, our protector, the *honu*. The sea turtle used to be my friend when I got lonely on the island." She kissed over my heart. "We need to get up and get dressed for breakfast. As you've probably noticed, there's no lock on that door."

That got me moving. I pulled a clean T-shirt and cargo shorts from my pack. Luckily we'd reached the cabin before the real rain started. I'd had my fill of wearing wet clothes.

Nani fed us a delicious breakfast of banana pancakes with coconut syrup. I'd never been a huge fan of pancakes, but she changed all that with one meal. Kilani and I washed the dishes and made a game plan for our exit the next day. Nani swore she could make an oil that would mask my scent from Damian, but I wouldn't be able to pick up his scent, either. If the oil was strong enough to cover me, that's probably all I'd smell, too. Big sticking point for me.

There had to be another way.

I left Kilani and Nani in the cabin to pack her things for the trip to Reno while I surveyed the area for any sign of Damian and his team. Part of me almost hoped I'd find something, since at least then it would be obvious which side of the fence Sebastian was playing right now. The only person I could be sure he looked out for was himself.

After a couple of hours mapping the land around the cabin, I was satisfied we were alone. I also had a much better idea of the terrain. Tonight, when I shifted, I would need to keep from being seen. Challenging task. During the full moon, my wolf relied on instincts. I still had some influence, but the animal was definitely in charge.

The night Malcolm, my previous Alpha, was shot at Lake Tahoe, he lay on the ground bleeding, and I'd forced myself to shift back into my human form. My shock drove the wolf back. I'd never overpowered the animal inside of myself before. It hurt physically and psychologically, but I had done it. And if it came to that tonight, I'd do it again.

Hunger pains reminded me it was past lunchtime, but I wasn't ready to go back to the cabin yet. Instead, I jogged back to the waterfall. Standing at the edge of the pool, I stared at the fine mist of water hovering around the falls that spilled into the pond. Kilani wanted me to change her. One bite and she'd be a wolf, welcomed into my Pack family as my mate. She'd be mine completely. I should've been eager.

But being a werewolf came at a price.

She'd have to live in Reno. The heart of a werewolf's strength was his or her Pack. Without it, a lone wolf struggled during full moons to keep from being discovered and from surrendering to blood lust. Dead humans risked our secret being revealed to a world that shot first and asked questions later. If the police caught them, humans would find out we existed, so rogue wolves were usually dealt with by nearby Packs.

But that wasn't what held me back. I closed my eyes, replaying that fateful night in my mind. Me telling Malcolm we needed to get him to the hospital so I could repair the internal bleeding, and him refusing.

Commanding me as my Alpha not to move him. To let

him die.

I rubbed my eyes and looked up at the clouds. If Kilani were a werewolf, I'd never be capable of letting her go. I'd risk my Pack, my entire race, and take her to a hospital. Save her. I'd put her life above everyone else's.

If she remained human, we could still get married, love each other, and live a normal life for the most part. But we wouldn't be able to have children.

She'd bought a cradle for the baby she never carried to term. My gut clenched. She'd wanted that child.

I stared at my reflection in the pond, the ripples distorting my face. Until this moment, I'd never considered children. I loved Adam's children, little Malcolm and Madeleine; being their Pack uncle brought me joy and laughter. But a father...

This wasn't a decision I could make on my own. I needed to talk to Kilani. But if she still chose to be a werewolf...

I'd cross that bridge when I got there.

The screen door wailed, announcing my arrival. Kilani came out from the bedroom with a box of pictures. I frowned. "Glad it was me and not Nero coming in?"

"Wow." She put the box on the counter. "You're in a great mood."

"Just worried that you're forgetting the danger."

She came closer, chin up, not the least bit intimidated. "Between my visions and my grandmother's messages from our ancestors, we knew it was you. So what's the real problem here?"

The urge to punch something simmered in my gut. I

took her hand. "We need to talk. Alone."

Kilani pulled free of my grasp and went into the tiny kitchen area. "I'll be right back, Grandma Nani."

She returned to my side and handed me a banana, a short stubby banana.

"What's wrong with it?"

"Nothing's wrong with it." She smiled up at me, derailing my frustration. "It's a Hawaiian banana. We call them apple bananas and they're delicious."

"You think a banana is going to mellow me out?" I raised a brow.

"I think you're hungry, and this will help."

My stomach growled, outing me. She chuckled and I peeled as Kilani and I walked out of the cabin. I found a big rock for two and we sat overlooking a lush green hillside. I finished the banana and rested my hand over hers.

"I need to talk to you about tonight."

"Okay." She glanced up at me. "The full moon."

I nodded. "You asked me to change you, but I'm not sure it's the right call. At least, not right now."

She straightened, pulling her hand away to cross her arms. "You told me it's forever. Are you second-guessing if you want to be with me?"

"No. Not at all." I ran my hand up her back, hoping it might coax her to relax, but she remained stiff and stoic. "But we can be together without changing you. We can date, live together, get married… If you become a werewolf, you'll be tied to Reno, to the Pack, and if anything happens to you medically, you'd have werewolf DNA too, so I wouldn't be able to take you to the hospital. It would be like my dad and Malcolm all over again. I'm not strong enough for that. I couldn't sit by and watch you slip through my fingers just to keep our secret from the humans."

My voice choked, wobbling. I cleared my throat, staring off into the distance. "I'm trying to tell you I'm scared."

"And you think I'm not?" She slid off the rock and stood in my line of vision, forcing me to meet her eyes. "I told you I loved you, and I meant it. But I will *not* be your handicap. I won't be locked inside another car again while you fight my battles. And I've got news for you—if there's a medical emergency in the Pack, I'll be assisting you from now on. You don't get to carry all the responsibility on your shoulders all alone. Not anymore."

She paused and stepped closer, taking my hand. "That vision I had hasn't changed, Jason. Maybe if I'm a werewolf, if my senses are enhanced like yours, we can make the outcome different." She squeezed my hand. "Please. I can't lose you, either."

I stared into her eyes, my heart pounding. If I changed her tonight, there would be no going back. What if the past repeated itself?

It wouldn't matter if we didn't try for a future.

"I'm not going anywhere." I stood and pulled her into my arms, kissing her hair, breathing her in. Gradually I loosened my hold on her and stared down into her eyes. "Wait for me by the waterfall tonight."

She nodded. "Will I turn into a wolf, too?"

"Not until the next full moon. The bite will hurt, but it'll heal up pretty fast." I lifted her hand, my lips caressing her knuckles. "Hold out your hand. The wolf will do the rest."

Nani filled us up with Spam and rice as the sun dipped lower into the horizon. The large orange harvest moon would be overhead soon. With the time difference in Hawaii, I figured my brother and the Pack were already howling around Lake Tahoe. Strange to imagine running alone tonight.

"Will the moon child sense the danger of the road? Will he stay back?"

I glanced at Nani. Tomorrow we'd be home in Reno. She would be surrounded by the Pack. Time for a little trust. "I scouted the area today. The wolf should recognize the safe areas. He won't wander close to the road and humans."

She collected my plate with a smile. "I never dreamed there would be a wolf on my island."

"Just for one night." I stood up and stretched. "Thanks for dinner. I better get outside. Keep the door locked, just in case."

Nani glanced up from the kitchen sink. "We are protected."

God, I hope that's true.

Kilani came to my side. On her tiptoes, she kissed my cheek and whispered, "I'll see you soon."

The wolf growled inside of me. With the moon and our mate so close, it was dangerous for me to stay. The last thing I wanted was to shift in Nani's cabin. I pressed my lips to Kilani's forehead and smiled down at her. "Stay safe."

I opened the door and stepped outside. The night was clear and warm, perfect for a run. I jogged to the north, deciding I'd leave my clothes by the waterfall. After the wolf claimed Kilani and bit her, I planned to force him back and shift back so that I could check her wound. After Nadya's violent reaction when Nero's mutated wolf bit her, I was a little gun shy. Kilani should be safe, but I wished I could be certain.

At the pool I stripped off my clothes, sweat dripping into my eyes. It was time.

Shifting hurt like being drawn and quartered, maybe worse. Even the movies that portrayed a grisly transformation didn't scratch the surface of the real thing.

I growled, struggling to keep from screaming as my legs gave out and I fell onto my hands and knees. My back bowed up, cracking and snapping as every vertebra reformed and my tailbone regenerated. The bones in my fingers, all my knuckles, and my feet shattered, rebuilding into paws. I panted, no longer able to speak or cry out; my lips and vocal chords didn't resemble a human man's anymore.

Hair pushed through my skin, like thousands of needle pricks all over my body. My jaw elongated, teeth growing and changing form. Inside I fought to slow my breathing, surrendering to the change. Through the haze of agony, I tried to focus on my anatomy, marking what had changed and how much farther I had to go. My ears were the final transformation, stretching and elongating.

And finally I was whole.

The wolf stood, shaking off the dirt from his thick fur. We stretched and bolted into the darkness, free. He chased after a mongoose, riled up some bats, and tracked a deer. Deep within, I encouraged the wolf north. Kilani would be waiting at the waterfall and once the wolf caught our mate's scent, he wouldn't give up the trail until we were reunited.

After getting sidetracked by the unfamiliar smell of a wild boar, my wolf finally ran north. We skidded to a stop, sniffing the air. The wolf pricked its ears. The crashing of the waterfall was close. The wind shifted, and we found Kilani's scent.

The wolf took off in search of our mate, and deep inside I prayed this wasn't a mistake.

Chapter Twenty-Four

A huge red-brown wolf broke through the ferns, surprising me. Survival instincts kicked in, and I stumbled backward, almost tumbling into the water. This was Jason. Had to be. There weren't wolves on Maui.

I forced my feet to stop, but there was no slowing my pulse. My heart galloped in my chest like a thoroughbred. "Jason?"

The wolf tilted its head, panting. His tongue lolled out, exposing long, sharp teeth. Shit. This was going to hurt. I rolled my eyes. Of course it would. This wolf had fangs long enough to pierce all the way through my hand. Was Jason still conscious inside?

Question I should have asked *before* I begged him to bite me.

"Can I have a minute first?" I knelt down. He was taller

than me now, but he didn't attack. "Would it be okay to touch you?"

I held my breath, grateful he didn't leap forward and maul me. He came closer until we were nose to nose. My hand trembled as I stroked his neck. His coat was thick and smooth. Up this close, I recognized the bright hazel eyes. Jason's eyes.

"You're amazing."

He licked my cheek, and I laughed, my fear and trepidation fading.

"Gross." I wiped my face and straightened up a little so I could scoot beside him. "So you're all right with me petting you?" He rubbed against my legs in answer. I scratched behind his ears and kissed the top of his head. "I'm a little nervous."

The large wolf laid on his belly next to me. I followed his lead and sat in the dirt too, sliding my hand down his back. His cold nose bumped the fingers of my free hand, and before I could snatch it away, his jaws snapped closed.

I gasped, the jolt of pain stealing my scream. He immediately released me and tenderly licked at the wound, doctoring it. Tears rolled down my face, but I had to laugh.

"Wolf spit isn't sanitary."

He chuffed and continued his nursing until the blood was gone. In the bright moonlight, six puncture wounds oozed, but he hadn't torn my skin. No stitches. The wolf got up and started walking away.

"Stay with me."

He looked back, whined, and walked behind the trees. I started to get to my feet to follow when wet popping sounds stopped me in my tracks. Bones cracked, joints dislocated, and I plopped back down, wishing the waterfall were loud enough to cover the horror happening a few feet from me.

After what seemed like the longest ten minutes of my life, Jason came and sat beside me. I expected a naked man like the werewolf movies and TV shows, but he had his shorts and T-shirt on. They weren't even ripped up.

"You're dressed."

"I left my clothes here when I shifted earlier." He took my hand, careful not to touch the bite. "I wanted to be able to help you if things didn't go according to plan."

He turned my hand over, examining the other side. The moonlight glinted off the sweat rolling down his face. How difficult had it been for him to shift back so quickly?

I nudged him with my shoulder. "If wolf spit was disinfectant, I'd be in great shape."

"It's our saliva that changes your DNA and makes you like us. He was probably just being sure you were ours." Jason kissed my forehead. "I'm sorry there's not a better way to do it."

"I think he was trying to be gentle. He distracted me first."

Jason lifted my hand into the light again and finally started to smile. "You're healing."

"What?" I jerked my hand back, inspecting it. Two of the puncture wounds had already closed and the others were fading. "It's impossible."

"It's the mate bond. We become one and the wound turns into a scar. You should be fully healed within an hour."

"But I won't change into a wolf?"

He shook his head. "Not until next month."

"When will I have the heightened senses?"

He shrugged. "It's different for everyone. Some people notice their hearing is better right away, and some have an enhanced sense of smell. Most of the time your strength and speed is increased within the first twenty-four hours."

I stared into the darkness, waiting for X-ray vision to kick in. Would I be able to tell that I could see farther than before? I opened and closed my hand, marveling at how quickly the wound was healing.

"I hope it kicks in fast for me. Tomorrow is going to be tricky with those guys watching for us at the airport."

Jason took my hand. "I didn't claim you and change you so you could protect me from one of your visions." His gaze searched mine. "I'm serious. Just because you're a werewolf now doesn't make you indestructible. A bullet or a stab wound will kill one of us just like any human. I need you to be safe."

"And I need that for you, too." I broke eye contact, staring at the moonlight sparkling on the water. "Maybe we should just stay here? We could try to wait them out."

Jason tossed a pebble into the pond, sending out ripples of light. "We need the Pack if we're going to keep you and your grandmother away from Nero. If we stay and hide out here, they'll just send a larger team and we'd be outnumbered."

I hadn't thought of that angle. I rolled my head, hoping to get the buzzing in my ears to stop. "Have you warmed up to Grandma Nani's scented-oil plan?"

"No. If I can't track him, he could sneak up on us without warning."

I sighed, staring up at the stars like they might have the answer. "Do you have a different plan to get through the airport without them spotting us?"

"I do, but you're not going to like it."

Every muscle in my body tensed. I crossed my arms over my chest. "What did you have in mind?"

"Damian is a jaguar shifter. He's familiar with our scent, but he doesn't know you're a wolf now. He and his team will be after me. If I'm out of the picture, getting to you should be simple. They don't know you're more than human. That's our ace in the hole. I can distract him and get him chasing my scent, while you and your grandmother get on the plane. Tell the gate agents she needs early boarding, and I'll meet you guys on the flight."

"Split up?" My brain short-circuited for a second. I shook my head, stuttering. "N-No. No, there's no way… No. He'll kill you. I've seen it."

"He won't. I'll be ready for that. I won't let him get close enough. As long as he chases me, you and Nani can get on that plane."

"There's got to be a better way."

He raised a brow. "I'm listening."

I got up and dusted off my backside.

"Where are you going?"

"My hand is healed. I'm going back to the cabin. Grandma Nani might be able to help."

He stood, but he looked less than convinced.

"I'm serious. She knew what you were without us telling her anything, right? She's a strong Kahuna. Don't doubt the power of our ancestors on these islands. They protect her."

Candles flickered in the tiny living room. Grandma Nani sat on a woven bamboo mat with her legs crossed. Her eyes opened the moment I stepped inside. "What have you done, mynah bird?"

I frowned. "I don't know what you're talking about."

She was on her feet much faster than I expected, biting into her lower lip. Without a word, she grabbed my hands, quickly running her finger along my new scar.

"Maybe I should be asking Jason."

She let go of me and muscled past to get into Jason's personal space. He was so much taller than her, she had to tip her head all the way back. She looked like she was trying to see into space. I gnawed at the inside of my cheek. This seemed like a really bad time for inappropriate giggles.

"What did you do to my granddaughter?"

He raised a brow. "Your granddaughter is my mate, but I think you already knew that when we arrived."

"Kilani was still human, Kahuna magic in her bloodstream. You've tainted her." She swatted his arm, clearly not intimidated by his size or the fact he was a huge wolf less than an hour ago. "I never got to train her. She doesn't understand the powers she possessed. Now she will *never* know."

He ground his teeth together, his nostrils flaring, but he kept his voice even and controlled. "Becoming a werewolf, and being my mate, has *not* tainted her. Kilani is stronger now, her senses heightened. Our bite doesn't change who she was, it just adds to her abilities."

She narrowed her eyes and spun around to face me. Clutching my wrist, she pulled me into the modest kitchen area. A pot bubbled on her two-burner stovetop.

"Smell this, mynah bird."

I leaned closer, took a deep breath, and coughed, stumbling backward. The room tilted as I slid down the wall.

"Are you insane?" Jason yelled somewhere in the distance. "What did you do to her?"

He was beside me. I couldn't see him, but...I recognized his scent. My sense of smell was heightened. Whatever Grandma Nani had in her pot, the effect must have intensified with my new werewolf blood changing me.

I floated, weightless somehow, struggling to identify the scents that assaulted me. Seaweed...rainbow eucalyptus bark...and...popolo, Black nightshade.

"Popolo." I opened my eyes, squinting at the candlelight. Apparently my vision was now enhanced, too, and thanks to my grandmother's concoction, my pupils had to be the size of quarters. "Seaweed, rainbow eucalyptus, and nightshade. You knew it would knock me out."

"Only if you still had my blood in your veins." Grandma Nani knelt down, examining my eyes. "I didn't realize your new abilities would increase the potency. It should have made you dizzy, not leave you knocked out on my floor."

Jason scooped me up and carried me around my grandmother over to the loveseat. He held me in his arms even after he sat down, but his gaze was locked on Grandma Nani.

"You could have hurt her with your little test."

She took her favorite chair. "Only if I had used the green nightshade berries. They were ripe. There was no real danger." She sighed, staring at her hands. "I owe you an apology. It surprised me when the wind whispered that Kilani was changed. I thought she was lost to me."

I rolled my eyes. "I've been lost for more than ten years."

Part of me wanted to reel the words back in, but Grandma Nani didn't seem fazed. Apparently it was going to take some time for the abandoned girl inside of me to heal.

She lifted her head. "I always believed you'd come back when you were ready and I would teach you our ways. You are my only grandchild with gifts. The last of my line. Every generation there are fewer of us left. If we don't pass down our legacy, the Kahuna magic will be lost."

"But you just proved she's still got it, right?" Jason loosened his hold on me so I could sit beside him.

"Yes." The candlelight flickered in Grandma Nani's dark eyes. "And I will need her magic to help us get to the mainland."

Jason and I glanced at each other and back to her. "You have a way to get us into the airport without being spotted?"

She smiled and nodded. "We will make it rain."

Chapter Twenty-Five

JASON

"Rain?" I raked my hands through my hair. "How exactly is that going to help?"

Nani scooted forward, perched on the edge of her chair. "They can't get weapons past the security checkpoint, so they must wait for us outside the airport. If we make a downpour, the water will keep your scent from traveling and alerting them, and everyone will be covered with umbrellas."

I sat back, pondering her idea. "That could work."

I wished we could just fly from Maui into the Honolulu airport and switch planes, but no doubt Nero had connections to check the manifest. They'd be waiting for us to land. We'd be sitting ducks. But our plan to fly into a smaller airport and drive over to the Honolulu International Airport was far from perfect. The lesser of two evils.

Kilani popped her bare foot out from under her and

leaned in. "We could stay together under umbrellas. They'd never spot us."

"Maybe not outside, but we'd be vulnerable inside waiting in the security line. We can't wander around a busy airport with our umbrellas open."

"If they come in, they risk being caught on security cameras or by the TSA officers." Kilani kneaded the tension building in my shoulder. "It could work."

Fear blew through my gut like a bitter tempest. I was fucking sick of not having any control over my life. Putting my trust for our safety on a Hawaiian rain spell did nothing to ease the frustration.

"You can bring Kilani up to speed on Kahuna magic by tomorrow morning?"

"Yes." Nani winked at my mate. "She has the power. I will show her how to tap into it."

I gave Kilani's thigh a squeeze. "I need to check in with Adam."

"Will he be…able to answer his cell phone yet?"

"They're three hours ahead of us. He should be home by now." I stood and headed out the door before anyone else said anything to me. Pressure pounded in my head. I should be reveling in my new mate, teaching her about her new abilities, not stomping around outside, aching to pick a fight.

Didn't change a goddamn thing.

My cell buzzed in my pocket. Adam's name flashed on my screen. "You beat me to it."

"What the hell happened last night? When were you going to tell me?"

I frowned. "Tell you what? I was about to call you to make arrangements for our arrival at home tomorrow."

"We can talk about that later." Even through the phone, the Alpha command colored the sound of his voice. "You shifted alone, and you bit someone."

My grip on the phone tightened. "How could you possibly know that?"

"I've told you before, since I ascended to Alpha, I sense things about the Pack." His tone darkened. "Including our Pack numbers growing."

"Shit. Did Gareth get this kind of reception when he changed Nadya?"

"I wasn't happy that he didn't warn me first, but we had already accepted her into our Pack before he bit her."

I cracked my neck, my weight shifting between my feet. Punching something would've been amazing right about now. "Are you saying Kilani's not welcome?"

A pregnant pause and Adam sighed. "Thank God."

I ran my free hand down my face. "Please tell me what the hell is going on?"

"You shifted alone on an island with no native wolves. When I sensed you'd bitten someone, I didn't know who it was. I didn't know if your wolf attacked someone and now we had a rogue wolf in our Pack or what."

"Give me some credit. I'm not stupid."

"You've also never shifted away from the Pack."

True. I took a breath.

"Sorry, man." Adam's voice lost the Alpha undercurrent. He was back to being my lifelong friend and Pack brother. "How's she doing?"

"She handled it really well. Nothing like what happened to Nadya."

"Good. We should plan a welcoming party for her when

you get back. You're still coming home tomorrow, right? Any sign of Nero?"

I nodded. "Yeah, we're flying out as early as possible. Sebastian sent Kilani a text that Damian moved his team to the Honolulu airport. They know that's our only way to the mainland."

"Shit."

"Exactly. Kilani's grandmother has a plan. She's a Kahuna."

"She surfs?"

I chuckled, shaking my head. "No a true Hawaiian priestess, a Kahuna. She's pretty amazing. But assuming her idea works, we still need to keep her out of Nero's hands. Since they're well aware of the location of the ranch, and my place, and Gareth's garage…we're running out of places to hide her."

"We can put her up at a hotel and have her lay low."

I stared up at the stars. "I was actually thinking of having her stay on the Paiute reservation with Chloe, Gareth's god-mother. Nero has no clue about Gareth's ties to her. There would be no reason for them to be sniffing around by Pyramid Lake."

"You want me to talk to Gareth."

"Yeah. If he could get Chloe onboard, we could meet someplace public and pass Nani over to her. Nero would never find her, and they'd lose their bargaining chip with Kilani."

I waited.

"I'll see what I can do. Call me from Honolulu before you get on the plane and I'll lay the final plan out for you."

"Sounds good. Thanks, Adam."

"Jason?"

"Yeah?"

"Congratulations, man." The smile was plain in his voice. "You found your mate even though you didn't believe they existed."

I chuckled in spite of my worry. "Now I just need to get us home without being captured, shot, or both. Piece of cake, right?"

"Be careful."

"Will do."

When I opened the door to the cabin, Kilani and Nani stared up at me from bamboo mats on the floor.

"Everything okay?" Kilani moved to stand, but Nani grabbed her arm.

"Not yet. We still have work to do."

"Didn't mean to interrupt. How's the rain-making coming?"

Kilani glanced at her grandmother and back up to me. "Still dry, but we're getting closer."

Her scent had intrigued me before, but now that her inner wolf had awakened, the attraction was even more intense. I clenched my fists to keep myself from grabbing her off the mat, tossing her over my shoulder, and carrying her to the futon in the bedroom.

"I'm going to try and get a little rest so I'm sharp tomorrow."

"Okay." She nodded, her cheeks flushed with color, her eyes sparkling with desire. Blood pumped through my veins, hitting me square in the groin. Never in my life had I wanted anyone so urgently.

"You should…sleep, too." I shoved a hand in the pocket of my shorts, hopefully masking my raging erection.

Nani turned her head, gazing at each of us and shaking her head. "I do not think she can concentrate much longer with you so close by."

I chuckled and forced myself to walk away. In the bedroom, I stripped down and dropped onto the bed, wishing there was a cold shower handy. I'd have to go back to the waterfall. Instead, I laid on the futon, a sheet draped over me, hard enough to pound nails, and prayed the Kahuna lesson would be over soon.

I dreamed of home. The full moon shined on Lake Tahoe. The Pack howled in the distance. I stepped into the cool, still water, staring at the silver moon in the sky, wishing for my mate. Something splashed to my right.

Kilani. Naked.

She approached me with a warm smile. Kneeling in the shallow water, she slid her soft hands up my calves. *So real.* Her fingertips glided farther up my legs. I growled as her feather-light touch teased even higher, barely tracing along the length of my erection until I ached for more contact. Her lips caressed my abs, her warm breath on my skin. I buried my fingers in her thick, silky hair.

Her teeth brushed my neck, her scent filling my lungs, and I tightened my grip, growling against her ear. "Dream come true."

She lifted her head, moonlight shining on her face. "Shh. Grandma Nani just fell asleep in the front room."

Although her body covered mine, I wanted to be even closer. Sliding my hands down her back, I gripped her ass, pressing her hips even tighter. But when I tried to roll her underneath me, she held her own, pinning me to the mattress.

She nipped at my bottom lip with her teeth, a sparkle

in her dark eyes. "I'm already changing. My sight, hearing, and strength. So, *mate…*" That word had never sounded so damned sexy. She placed her finger over my lips. "I've wanted you all night, but I'm in charge, and you have to be quiet."

I kissed her chin, her soft mouth, and smiled. "I can be quiet if you can."

I slid one hand between her legs. She was wet and ready. I growled without meaning to. She hummed against my chest, nibbling at my nipple.

"You're playing dirty," she whispered.

"Did you want me any other way?"

She lifted her head, wearing a sultry smile that almost made me lose it before we began. "I love you dirty."

Aw fuck. My mate was the sexiest woman I'd ever met. I needed to distract myself or things were going to be over way too soon. She started kissing lower, about to scoot out of reach, but I didn't let her go. I shifted her hips up closer, toward me, my fingers working to make her scream.

At the moment, I didn't give a shit who was sleeping in the other room.

Suddenly her lips slid over me, hot and wet down the length of my erection. I ground my teeth, struggling to keep the growl in my chest as her tongue teased the tip.

She sucked slowly as she glided up my shaft and whispered, "Shhhh…"

I grinned. Two could play this game. I gripped her thighs and lifted one leg, placing it on the other side of my head, opening her to me.

"Shhhh…" I kissed her mound, exploring her folds with my tongue. She moaned and laughed at the same time as she took me back into her mouth.

The more I pushed her toward her climax, the more she tempted me. We were both going to win…very soon.

She worked her mouth down my shaft a few more times and then sat up. Before I realized she was moving, she'd already shifted herself around, straddling my hips. I ran my hands up her legs, memorizing the perfection of her body in the moonlight. My mate.

I never had a clue I could love someone so much.

She lowered herself slowly, closing her eyes, her jaw dropping slightly in a silent moan as I slid deep inside of her warm body. I'd never be able to get close enough to her. She leaned down, kissing my lips as she ground her hips into mine. Against my mouth she groaned. "I hate being quiet."

A breathless chuckle escaped me. "Me too. Once we're home…"

"Lots of noise."

I caught her lip in my teeth. "Definitely."

Neither of us mentioned the danger or the chance we might not make it home. Tonight we were invincible. Her body contracted in my arms, her inner muscles clenching, taking me right over the peak with her. I held her tight, kissing her again and again as the aftershocks rocked us and the warm tropical breeze washed over our sweaty bodies.

"I love you, Kilani."

"I love you, too."

And for tonight, that was enough.

Chapter Twenty-Six

Kilani

We hiked out just after sunrise. I should've been exhausted, but between the afterglow of the amazing night in bed with Jason and the adrenaline of knowing trained guys with guns were waiting for me in Honolulu, I was plenty alert.

Jason led the way, I followed behind him, and Grandma Nani brought up the rear. He didn't let either of us carry our bags. Apparently his concussion was healed, and he wasn't going to let me help. I might've protested the alpha streak, but for now, I let him be.

My vision of him lying on the ground bleeding from a gunshot wound tormented me every time I closed my eyes. Having my hands free might make the difference. If I could hear the click of the trigger or see the sight on the rifle, I could shove him clear of the line of fire.

Or at least that was my plan.

Hopefully it wouldn't come to that.

We reached my cousin's Jeep and Grandma Nani raised a brow. "Your cousin loves that Jeep. He must've missed you."

"I promised him we'd be careful with it."

We climbed inside. My grandmother insisted on sitting in back, so I took the passenger seat beside Jason. He made the harrowing drive back down the road to Hana in pretty good time. My cousin had already arranged our flight back to Honolulu.

In an effort to stay below Nero's radar, he bought the tickets to fly us into the smaller Kalaeloa airport on Oahu. It only recently started accepting commercial flights, and Nero would probably only be scanning the airline manifests from Maui to Honolulu International. We'd land a few miles away, undetected. A twenty-minute shuttle ride would get us to the main airport, and with the help of Grandma Nani's downpour, hopefully we'd reach our plane to the mainland without incident.

Or at least that was the plan.

We pulled into the Kahului airport on Maui and texted my cousin. He met us in front of the terminal and I handed him the keys to his Jeep.

"You're going to come back soon and buy me dinner, right, cousin?" He hugged me tight. I forgot how great family could be.

I nodded. "I definitely owe you."

He turned and shook Jason's hand. They were almost the same height—Jason had him by a couple of inches, but my cousin had some Samoan blood on his mother's side, so even though he might've been a little shorter, he was solid and seemed larger than life.

"You take good care of my cousin and Grandma Nani."

Jason smiled. "I'll do my best."

Grandma Nani embraced him, closing her eyes and murmuring to him in Hawaiian. She pulled away and held him out at arms' length. "Aloha au iaoe."

"I love you, too, Grandma." He kissed her forehead.

She took our hands, stacking them before placing hers on top, holding them together. "Ohana. Nothing stronger than family." Her gaze lingered on each of our faces. "Time to go."

She dropped her hands and walked toward the small terminal. We all straightened, freeing our hands.

Once we were settled on the small plane, Grandma Nani on the aisle, Jason at the window, and me in the middle as a buffer, she took my hand, her expression all business. "We must prepare."

"You told me all I had to do was be open so you could tap into my energy, my spirit."

"Yes, but I need you to start now. Clear your head of guns and dark visions and think of a tropical storm. Close your eyes and breathe it in. Smell it, feel the rain on your skin. Find your spirit within. You are Kanaka Maoli; let it bloom inside of you."

I followed her instructions. Jason twined his fingers with mine, sensing my need for him, for our wolves to be joined. How all of this wove together with my Hawaiian spirit was a mystery to me, but his touch strengthened my concentration.

My *honu* came forward, his shell sparkling in many colors. He swam closer, and when I stared into the water, watching for him, my reflection startled me.

I was a black wolf.

The sea turtle poked his head up, tilting it each way, examining me from all directions. I leaned in, sniffing at the *honu*, recognizing the familiar scent of my childhood on Maui. The wolf and the turtle tested boundaries, the turtle snapping at the wolf's paws and the wolf swatting at the turtle's shell. Playing.

I fought the urge to open my eyes and break the spell. Grandma Nani had worked with me most of the night on my concentration. Today, I would be a conduit for her power, a source for her Kahuna magic to tap into to help her focus the clouds.

While I centered myself, she sat beside me calling on the ancestors, calling the Great Mother, asking for the sky to be dark, the storm clouds heavy with rain. Protection. By the time we landed in Honolulu, an otherworldly peace settled over me. I embraced it, praying this would keep me open for Grandma Nani's plan to work.

I tried to be conscious of the scents around us, but I had no clue how I'd recognize Damian or any other jaguar shifter, since I'd never technically smelled them before, but I hoped if I got used to human scents, maybe our Nero friends would be "different."

Jason was a man of few words today, his attention focused on the crowds and our surroundings. The way he stalked through the jungle and the airport, I never would have guessed he was a doctor. He moved like a warrior, ready for a fight. Every muscle tight, jaw set, eyes scanning. I did my best to keep up and stay out of his way, while struggling to maintain the peace and power of an open channel for my grandmother. A wobbly tightrope walk for sure.

Once we were on the shuttle, Grandma Nani patted my thigh. "This will work, mynah bird. Faith is power. No doubts, no worries. Stay focused."

I nodded and wished I'd get a vision with a brighter outcome. But for now, my gift was silent, just like my mate.

I looked over at Jason. "How are you holding up?"

He shrugged without taking his eyes off the traffic ahead. "I'll be better when we land in Reno."

"Is Adam meeting us at the airport?"

He nodded. "Yeah, he'll be there, and Gareth is coming, too."

"As in Nadya's boyfriend, Gareth? Why?"

He finally turned his attention on me, keeping his voice low. "His mother was part of the Paiute tribe. His godmother still lives on the reservation, sort of off the grid, like Nani's cabin. I'm hoping she'll be there too so we can introduce her to Nani. I think it'll be safest for your grandmother if she can stay with Chloe and not anyone in the Pack, since Nero seems to know so much about us."

"Shouldn't we ask Grandma Nani first? She probably thinks she's staying with us."

"Since they know where I live, that's not a good idea."

I glanced at Grandma Nani. She stared out the side window. "Have you been listening to all this?"

She didn't move, but her lips curved into a peaceful smile. "The Paiute are old ones like our people. I would like to meet her."

That was good enough for me.

As we neared the airport, the sky darkened, and angry clouds moved in to cover the sun.

"Looks like a storm coming in," the driver called back to us. "Hope your flight isn't delayed."

"Hope not." Jason pulled out my grandmother's bag and unzipped the duffel. He handed each of us an umbrella. "Maybe it'll blow over quickly."

"Never can tell." The driver shook his head.

Grandma Nani winked at me, completely confident in the coming rain and the subsequent dissipation of the foul weather. I wished her unshakable faith would rub off on me. I had no clue if anything was happening. She muttered at the sky in Hawaiian under her breath, but if she was using my energy, it didn't seem to affect me. Although I'd never asked if I would feel her magic, I assumed I'd at least notice something.

Stay calm. At peace. Welcome the honu.

I kept my mantra going in my head. It couldn't hurt. By the time the shuttle pulled in to the terminal, his wipers were working overtime and visibility was still hindered.

Jason gathered our bags and took my hand. "Ready?"

"As I'll ever be."

We popped our umbrellas open and stepped out into the mad rush of travelers.

Chapter Twenty-Seven

I gripped Kilani's hand tighter than I should have, but I couldn't help it. I'd never been this tense in my entire life. Every breath through my nostrils brought in information to process. Perfume, hairspray, halitosis, babies who needed changing, cologne barely covering the need for a shower, they all assaulted me as we pushed through the rain and the people toward the glass doors.

Every time I was bumped, a growl rumbled in my chest. My wolf was clawing to the surface of my consciousness, understanding the concern for our mate and unsure of where the threat might be lurking. This was dangerous, and it had nothing to do with Nero.

"Can I help you with your bags?"

"No." I pushed past the skycap to the doors and ushered Kilani and her grandmother inside. We were about to lose the cover of our umbrellas. I nudged Kilani. "Be sure Nani puts her hood up before she closes that umbrella."

We all wore hooded sweatshirts from Kilani's cousin, hopefully masking our identities from behind. I collected the umbrellas, shaking out the water before stuffing them back into the larger duffel.

"I'm not picking up any strange scents."

It was going to take a little while for me to get used to dating a werewolf. I hadn't realized that the entire time I'd been scanning the airport, Kilani had been doing the same.

"Me neither. Let's hope that means they were outside and we're in the clear." We headed for the security line.

"Excuse me, ma'am. I'm going to need to see some ID."

A male TSA officer had Nani's elbow. By his scent, he was human, but his heart was pounding.

My eyes narrowed. "Is there a problem?"

He lifted his head. Dark sunglasses covered his eyes. I couldn't read him. "We have an alert out on an abducted female. Just checking IDs."

He wore a black wristband. Nero. Had to be. "Bullshit."

The officer reached for his sidearm, but my punch was faster. The uppercut to his jaw landed solid. He collapsed on the ground, unconscious, and someone screamed, "Terrorist!"

Damn it. I growled to Kilani and her grandmother, "Run. Find a bathroom, stay away from security cameras, and lay low."

They took off, and I tugged the wristband back, exposing the black lion's head tattoo with an *N* emblazoned on the cat's forehead. Nero.

I scanned for Damian. *Come out here, you chickenshit.*

More TSA officers ran toward us. They'd discover this

wasn't one of their own soon enough. I couldn't risk getting arrested. I took off, toppling suitcases and pissing off travelers. Anything to slow the TSA agents. Once I lost them, I ducked in a bathroom and pulled off the hoodie, stuffing it in the trashcan on my way out. Outside, the dull roar of activity remained centered around the downed would-be TSA agent.

I sat on a bench and took out my cell.

"Oh, thank God," she whispered. "You're okay."

I closed my eyes, focusing on her voice. Kilani was safe. "Where are you?"

"We're coming out of a bathroom in the food court."

"Wait. Ditch the hoodies first, then meet me by the Burger King."

"See you soon."

"Be careful." I put my phone back in my pocket.

Opening and closing my right hand, I drank in the ache from my sore joints. It was almost unsettling how much I enjoyed punching that guy, allowing the anger to explode. I found an empty table in front of the Burger King and waited.

The second Kilani came into view, the wolf inside of me howled. I got up, weaving through the tables, my gaze locked on hers until I had her safe in my arms again.

I kissed her hair. "Let's get on a plane."

She nodded, pulling back as Nani approached.

Her grandmother stared up at me and gradually started to smile. "You protected me and my granddaughter."

I held her gaze. "I always will."

She patted our joined hands. "Enough danger for one day."

I wished I could believe her, but my gut told me this was

just the beginning. When I clocked the Nero agent, I figured it would draw out the rest of the team to finish the job, but no Nero mercenaries or Damian showed up. It was too easy. Something was off.

In the security line, I kept watch as I placed a call to Adam.

"Jason? You guys are okay?"

"Minor bump in the road, but I wanted to see if you could get Sasha to meet us at the airport back home."

Adam paused. "Talk to me."

"I don't want to bet our lives on Sebastian's intel. We had a run-in with one of Damian's goons here in Honolulu, but no sign of the jaguar himself."

Adam's voice deepened. "You think Damian is back in Reno."

"I think there's a strong possibility, and Sasha is our best with a gun."

"I'll call her right now."

"Thanks, Adam."

I put my cell away, and Kilani ran her hand up my back. With her heightened hearing, I had no doubt she got both sides of the conversation, but it didn't matter. I had nothing to hide.

"You think he's already there."

I shrugged, still deciphering every scent and scanning every face. "I think it's a distinct possibly. I attacked one of his team, and there was no backup."

"Decoy?"

"Maybe? Either way, I'd rather be safe than sorry." I glanced down at her warm eyes. "Just once, I'd like to have some control over my life."

I stared out into the throngs of people, grinding my teeth as I struggled to swallow the hot rage bubbling beneath the surface.

One way or another, I was going to get Nero to leave my mate the fuck alone.

Chapter Twenty-Eight

KILANI

Even though the heat of his skin warmed me through my shirt, Jason was miles from me. Hard to believe last night we'd been so connected. Since we'd left the cabin on Maui, he'd been distant. Maybe he needed to be.

He dozed off on the flight over the ocean, his forehead resting against the window. The sunlight bathed his face in light and I drank in the peace on his features. I wished I could freeze the moment and hold it in my hands forever. We'd never get off the plane, and I'd never have to face the reality of my vision.

Sighing, I rested my head and closed my eyes, praying for a new glimpse of a new future. I was a werewolf now—that should count for something, change the trajectory of the future. Maybe we already had. If I were still human, maybe he would've been shot in Honolulu.

I waited, trying to clear my head. Nothing happened. What good was a gift if I couldn't use it when I needed it?

I opened my eyes again and Grandma Nani gripped my hand. "Rest, mynah bird. Rest now while we can."

There was no way I could sleep. Not now. But I tried to placate my grandmother.

The captain's voice startled me from my unexpected nap. Apparently I'd been more exhausted than I realized. We were on the descent into Reno. The weather was clear and cool, and Jason was already alert. All business.

"When we land, Adam will be waiting for us at baggage claim. Sasha will be there, too, and she's always armed. We'll have Gareth take Nani and we'll go in the other direction. If they're waiting for us, they'll need to split up. They'll be weaker."

I took his hand. His palm was cold and clammy. "Are you trying to convince me or yourself?"

He pulled away from my touch. "I'm not even sure anymore."

"You're not in this alone."

"It's not me I'm worried about."

I frowned. "You should be. You were the one in my vision, not me."

"I'm being cautious, but I can't let anything happen to you. If that puts me in danger, so be it."

"My feelings exactly."

He caught my chin, lifting my face gently to meet his eyes. "Do *not* take any risks for me. I've been a wolf my whole life. I can handle this. As long as you're okay, that's what matters."

I nodded and settled in for landing. If he thought I would stand by and watch him get shot, he had another think coming, but I kept it to myself.

If I was Nero's target, why would Jason be the one bleeding in my vision?

If I could piece the puzzle together, I could change the outcome. And I had every intention of changing it. Jason would not bleed today. Not if I could help it.

J ason finished his call with Adam while we waited for the cabin doors to open. He leaned in close, keeping his voice so low, I probably wouldn't have been able to hear him if he hadn't bitten me.

"Adam, his brother Aren, and Sasha got to the airport early. They've been canvassing the entrances and exits and haven't found any evidence of Damian or Nero. Hopefully it's a good sign. Maybe I was wrong and we lost them in Honolulu."

I wanted that to be true so badly I could scream. "Where are we meeting them?"

"Aren and Sasha are staying in the shadows around the parking lot to cover us if there's any trouble. Gareth and Adam are waiting at baggage claim. Nadya and Chloe have a car ready in the short-term parking lot to take Nani once we're sure they're not being followed."

"And we're going home with…"

"Adam is taking us in his Jeep. He's parked a little farther back in the lot."

"We're not splitting up anymore?" There was no certainty any of our plans would work, but changing it up now worried me.

"Since they haven't found any trace of Nero, we're staying together. Safety in numbers."

I took a deep breath, trying to fortify myself and draw on my core grace-under-pressure nursing skills. "Okay, so we get out and head for the short-term lot."

He nodded and kissed my temple. "Let's get home."

The cabin door on the plane opened, and we filed out and up the Jetway. My stomach tightened into nauseous knots. I cleared my throat and blinked hard.

The vision flashed again, and this time I recognized our shadows. Outside. The shooting would happen outside.

I grabbed Jason's hand. "We can't go out there."

He frowned. "We can't stay in the airport, either. What's wrong?"

"The vision. I just saw it again. There were shadows. We were in the sunshine."

A muscle in his cheek flexed. "Sasha and Aren are covering us when we go out, and they've already searched for any trace of Damian and his team. Are you sure it was at the airport?"

I struggled for more detail, but it faded before I could find anything new. "No. I can't be sure."

"Then let's get out while we have protection. We'll get Nani someplace safe and then see if we can find Damian. I'm sick of running. Time to turn the tables and find *him*."

Thousands of butterflies swarmed in my stomach. What if I pressured him to wait and staying in the airport ended up giving Damian time to arrive? Guessing games like this were the path to madness. There was no way to know what would cause my visions to come true.

The night I'd seen Jason unconscious in the ring, it

turned out to be *my* fault. If I hadn't interfered and run in to save him, he would've seen Sebastian's punch coming. He could've protected himself if I hadn't gotten involved.

Fear paralyzed me. The stakes were too high.

Jason took my hand, his touch yanking me back from the void. "Kilani, we can do this. We'll be careful."

I nodded, taking strength in the commitment in his eyes.

Nani pointed to the right and broke the silence. "This is getting us nowhere. The sign says the exit is this way."

Jason squeezed my hand before we separated, keeping my grandmother between us. Since Nero wouldn't risk shooting me in a crowded airport, Grandma Nani would probably still be their target like she was in Honolulu. Abduct her and coax me into their custody.

Not if I could help it.

My new heightened senses were on overload. Between the throngs of people bumping into us and the adrenaline pumping through my veins, I worried my head might explode.

"Try to tune it out." No human, including Grandma Nani, would've heard Jason's whisper, but I understood every word.

"How?" I glanced his way, but his focus was straight ahead.

"Instead of trying to examine every sound and smell that hits us, dismiss them, let them go until you find one that shouldn't be here."

I dodged a roller bag. "I have a lot to learn."

"I'll help you." His eyes met mine for a second. "You're doing great. We're almost there."

My heart clenched. I never dreamed I'd find such a perfect lover, friend…mate. Why couldn't it have been under better circumstances?

We walked through baggage claim and Adam and Gareth waited by the doors, larger than life. Hope bubbled inside of me. Maybe we were going to make it after all. Even if Damian had split his team between Honolulu and Reno like Jason suspected, we had three male werewolves, a jaguar shifter detective with legendary aim, and her werewolf mate, and Nero didn't know I was a wolf now, too.

Jason and Adam clasped forearms, then he turned and did the same with Gareth.

Adam approached me, clamping his large hands firmly around my forearms. "Welcome home." His green eyes commanded respect, boring into me until I lowered my gaze. What the hell? He caught my chin, gently raising it. "Your wolf is surrendering dominance to the Alpha. Once we formally bring you into the Pack, your wolf will settle in."

Awkward. I cleared my throat and pulled my grandmother closer. "Adam, this is my grandma Nani."

Adam shook her hand like a normal person. The arm clasping must've been a Pack thing. "Great to meet you. Welcome to Reno. I'm sorry it's not under better circumstances."

She smiled up at him. "Thank you." She chuckled. "My granddaughter didn't mention how handsome this Pack is."

"Nani." I nudged her.

Adam grinned and gripped Jason's shoulder. "Sasha and Aren are out in the short-term parking keeping watch. Nadya will take Nani out to Pyramid Lake."

Jason nodded. "We're still riding with you?"

"My Jeep is a couple of rows back." Adam tipped his head toward Gareth. "Sasha's taking Gareth in her car."

"So we're just walking to the parking lot? No running or

hiding?" My pulse picked up the pace.

Adam made eye contact with each of us before he finally nodded. "I wouldn't let you walk out there if I thought you were a target. We've done all we can to ensure it's safe."

Jason took my hand. "Stay alert. Assume they could be anywhere."

Grandma Nani took my other hand. "The sooner we get out, the sooner I can see this Pyramid Lake I keep hearing about."

I smiled and squeezed her hand. "We'll keep you safe."

Adam and Gareth walked ahead with Grandma Nani, Jason, and me bringing up the rear. The sun blinded me for a second and the dry breeze shocked my skin. We were *not* in Hawaii anymore.

I didn't need to be an empath to hear the sizzle of tension in the three males in our group. No wonder Nadya waited in the car. She must've gotten better at shielding herself over the years. Living with a Pack of werewolves had to be a challenge.

My panic level sank a little lower with each row we passed in the parking lot. We were going to be okay.

The vision that had been tormenting me for days flashed again, and this time I was able to see part of a green fender. With my heart pounding in my ears, I scanned the cars. Three rows up, a green sedan was parked in the end space. I didn't have time to explain myself to the men. Jason might be dead by then.

I searched ahead, but I didn't see or smell anyone.

Then I looked up at the four-story long-term parking structure next door to the lot. Someone stood up on the top floor. I tried to get a better look and something glinted in the sun.

"Kilani? What's wrong?"

No time. We were five paces from the green car. I didn't have time to think or speak. Tugging Grandma Nani behind me, I bolted toward Jason, hitting his hip with my shoulder and all the force of my new stronger body. He fell just as something burned into my side, but I didn't go down.

The man on the parking structure screamed, dropping his weapon and clutching his hand moments before another shot hit his leg, and he fell back from the ledge. He was bleeding up there someplace, but I couldn't see him.

My eyesight wavered. Was it over?

"What the hell?" Adam ran to Jason and helped him up. "You hit?"

Jason shook his head. "Kilani must've had a new vision. She knocked me out of the way…"

They both turned toward me, frowning. Jason was all right. I'd done it. My vision saved his life. And for the first time in mine, I risked everything for someone else.

I looked down at my hand covering my side. Blood seeped between my fingers. *Oh shit.*

My legs trembled and I sank to the pavement.

Chapter Twenty-Nine

JASON

"No!" I left the bags on the ground and ran to her side, lifting her shirt to inspect the wound. "No, no, no."

"Adam, bring me my duffel."

He put it down beside me and unzipped it. I pulled out a clean T-shirt and pressed it to the bullet hole. Kilani's eyes fluttered open as she winced.

"Sorry. We need to slow the bleeding until we can get you to the hospital."

"Jason, no." Her voice was breathy, weak. "You can do this. We both know I can't go to the hospital. They'll take a blood draw first thing."

"I'm not going to lose you." Rage tightened like a knot around my heart until my entire chest burned. No goddamn way. She would *not* bleed out from a bullet wound. I was taking her to the fucking hospital. "I can't tell if the bullet nicked an artery or an organ. You need to go to the ER where we can open the wound and keep the area sterile in case you need surgery."

"You know we can't risk it, Jason." Adam's hand was heavy on my shoulder. "She's a werewolf now. They'd want her blood type and God knows what else. We can't let the lab get any samples of her DNA, and they're not going to let you use an operating room without it."

"I don't give a crap about DNA. I'm not sitting on the sidelines this time and watching her fade away like Malcolm did. This doesn't have to be a mortal wound."

"Time to get out of here. Now." I recognized Sasha's voice without looking up. "The police are already responding to the report of gunshots." She stopped beside me. "How bad is it?"

"She's still conscious, but she won't be for long if I can't figure out where the bleeding is coming from." I put Kilani's hand over the shirt that covered her wound. "Keep pressure on it for me. This is going to hurt."

She nodded and I lifted her into my arms. Her teeth dug into her lower lip, but she didn't make a sound. I kissed her forehead. "Stay strong for me. I'm not letting you go."

Her grandmother took her other hand as Nadya and Chloe ran up.

"Get her in Chloe's Jeep. It's already running." Nadya had a death grip on the keys and met my eyes. She was a strong empath, and probably the only one here who recognized the depth of my anguish.

The Pack would have to kill me to keep me from taking my mate to the hospital and saving her life.

"Your office is closed right now, right?" Nadya asked.

"We could take you there, and you could save her without the risk of the emergency room getting her blood samples, right?"

"I'm the doctor here, and I'm telling all of you, she's going to the hospital. I can't probe a wound and repair any damage without her being sedated."

"I think I know a way."

We all looked at Gareth's godmother. Chloe's long silver hair was pulled back in a braid, her face a mask of calm. "No time to explain; get her in the Jeep." She glanced at Gareth. "Osa, you need to come with us."

Gareth and I exchanged doubtful expressions, but we hustled to the Jeep as the distant sirens grew louder. He popped the latch on the front seat for me so I could climb in back while still cradling Kilani in my arms.

Nadya helped Nani into the backseat beside us and told Gareth she'd meet us at my medical office while Chloe got in the passenger side.

This was growing into a huge clusterfuck of epic proportions.

Although my office was technically closed right now, hired security still watched the building. They'd probably notice me carrying in a woman with a bullet wound, not to mention a gang from my Pack following behind.

But I didn't say anything. The medical center was right next door through an atrium connecting our buildings. Somehow, I'd get her over there, and she'd be able to get the attention she needed to survive.

With Chloe riding shotgun, Gareth backed the Jeep out of the space and gunned the engine. We made it out to the main street as the line of black-and-whites passed by, headed for the airport with lights blazing.

Kilani blinked, staring up at me. Sweat beaded on her forehead and upper lip, physical evidence of pain, but she didn't voice any. "Jason."

I leaned down closer to her, the wind whipping through my hair. "You're going to be all right."

"I know." She nodded. "I have the best doctor in the world."

My gut twisted, my vision blurring. "You need a real surgeon."

Her breath hitched. So did my heart. She opened her eyes again. "Didn't you have a surgical rotation in med school?"

"Yes. Years ago." I shook my head. "Please, Kilani. I can't do this. I won't risk your life."

Her gaze held mine. In spite of the pain from her injury, her voice stayed level and even, that same no-nonsense nurse who helped me start my father's heart again. "When my vision flashed, I saw the green car. I didn't stop to think about the consequences because in that moment, I knew no matter what happened, you'd never let me go."

"All I wanted was for you to be safe." I shook my head. "There had to be another way."

"If you got shot, I would've lost you. I don't know how to repair a gunshot wound." Her eyes narrowed. "We can argue about this later. We both know if the bullet hit an artery I'd already be dead by now. You can fix this."

"And if I open this wound, find the bullet, and repair the damage, you could get a staph infection and the result would be the same."

"I trust you. Your Pack trusts you…" A weak smile curved on her lips. "Trust yourself."

Gareth pulled into the parking structure under the medical office building and glanced back at me. "Got a plan to get her inside?"

None of this was ever part of my plan. "Yeah, through the emergency room door of the hospital."

Nani placed a hand on my knee. Looking at her was like seeing a reflection of my mate in the future. I wanted that future with her more than anything in the world.

"Jason, the ancestors are watching over her, and if my mynah bird believes in you, I do, too."

"Enough," I growled. "It's really easy for you all to toss your trust at me, but this isn't a game. She could die. We can heal this injury with the proper care. My office isn't equipped for surgery. I don't have anesthesia, I don't have resuscitation equipment or recovery, or…"

Chloe twisted around in her seat. "Maybe not, but Gareth is a dream walker. He can hold Kilani's spirit and keep her safe. She will not cross over."

Gareth frowned. "I've never tried to reach anyone other than Nadya, and she's my mate. This might be completely different. I don't know how to make it work on command."

Chloe waved him off. "Dream walkers are healers, Osa. This is part of your soul, and now it's awakened inside of you. You do not need an instruction manual to do what the Great Spirit put you on earth to do."

Nani squeezed my knee. "We waste time fighting. Let's help my granddaughter."

I clutched Kilani a little tighter. "We can't save her with hocus pocus. She needs a surgical team." I stood up in the back of the Jeep. This was a jump I could make in my sleep, but I didn't want to jar her. "Get out of my way."

My mate touched my cheek with a cool hand. "You didn't believe in mates, either. Remember?" Her words slowed, her eyelids drifting closed. "...scientifically impossible...to recognize...your soul mate with a single touch." She opened her eyes and whispered, "Do this for me. Trust yourself."

A guttural sob choked my throat as I lifted her closer, brushing my lips to hers. "Please. If I lose you..."

"I'm not going anywhere..."

"I can't do this." The bowels of bitterness in my soul wheezed out of my mouth. "I'm afraid."

"I know." She kissed me. "But you're not alone. Not anymore."

Her eyes closed again. "Kilani?" No response. "You need to stay awake." Nothing.

My pulse rate skyrocketed, but gradually the fear in my gut twisted into anger and I grabbed it with both hands. "We have to stop the bleeding, so get the hell out of the Jeep. Now."

Everyone scrambled out, and Gareth helped me with Kilani to keep her as still as possible. Chloe yanked a blanket from the back and tucked it over Kilani, hiding the bloody wound from the security cameras. We took the elevator from the parking structure. Hopefully we wouldn't run into a security guard.

Once we were safe in my office, I laid her down on a paper-covered exam table and rushed around grabbing a disposable scalpel and a retractor from the sealed sterilized tools. These would have to do. I scrubbed my hands and pulled on a new pair of latex gloves.

"Where's Gareth?"

Chloe pointed to the door. "He's in the next room. He has to meditate or sleep to be able to find her spirit."

"So how do I know he's got her?"

"Faith."

"You've got to be shitting me."

Chloe shook her head slowly. "Science can only go so far."

Nani sat in the corner, her eyes closed, lips moving silently. No doubt chatting with her ancestors.

When did my life become every doctor's worst goddamn nightmare? I ground my teeth and rolled the table closer. "It looks like you're going to need to assist me. Wash your hands, and grab a pair of latex gloves by the sink."

Chloe followed my directions while I lifted the blanket. I unfastened Kilani's jeans, tugging them lower so I could get a better view of her injury. I grabbed a few clean towels and laid them around the wound, framing my surgical work area.

And the more I focused, the more the fear faded. I pushed aside worries that my anesthesiologist was sleeping in the next room holding Kilani's spirit in his dreams, that her Hawaiian ancestors were monitoring her vitals instead of high-tech machines, and that the woman on the table was the other half of my soul.

I was a healer. This was my calling. And death wasn't taking this woman away from me.

Not today.

Chapter Thirty

KILANI

Jason's voice was distant, random words poking through the fog in my mind. The pain faded along with the rest of the world. It was dark here, so I guessed I wasn't dead. No one guiding me toward the light. Yet.

But I also wasn't conscious.

Gravity didn't seem to exist in this in-between space. I hopped, unsure if my feet ever really touched the ground. Did the ground even exist here? I spun around in the void. Was I lost? I gave Jason my word I wouldn't leave him.

What if I couldn't find my way back?

Finally a blue spark caught my eye. I walked closer, my pace increasing as I recognized the shape. My *honu* had come to guide me.

Where?

I tried to speak, to tell him I couldn't go. I needed to stay with Jason. His wise eyes held mine, calming my jumbled thoughts. Slowly he turned, waiting for me to accompany him. I hesitated. What if he was trying to take me to Jason? His shell brightened, illuminating the darkness around me until another orange light flickered in the distance.

I pointed at the dancing brightness, and my *honu* swam forward, toward it. Worrying my lower lip, I remained rooted to my spot in the vast wasteland of this purgatory.

"Kilani? Are you out here?"

Unlike Jason's voice, this one wasn't in another world. This one was close. And I recognized it.

"Gareth?"

"Yes. I've got a fire going. Can you come closer?"

Heat, light, and a familiar face sounded like heaven.

"I can't." I wrapped my arms around my middle. Was it getting colder?

"I'll come to you."

"I have to be strong. I can't just float away." I swallowed a ball of emotion, unsure if I was talking to Gareth or myself. "Jason needs me."

"Yes, he does." Gareth was suddenly beside me.

"Why are you here?"

The corners of his stern mouth softened, almost a smile. "I'm going to keep you here, safe, until Jason gets your body repaired."

"Wait, this is actually you?" I frowned. "Impossible."

He shrugged. "I have no idea how it works, but I can walk through the shadows. Chloe calls it dream walking. When Nadya was sick, I almost lost her a couple of times, but I met her here and kept her on this side of the veil."

My worry eased up a few notches. The cold did not. "Did

you say you had a fire?"

He nodded. "Follow me."

I did, and close behind, my sea turtle shadowed me. Not that a turtle could protect me from whatever lurked in the darkness, but I accepted the comfort he brought.

We sat by the fire, and I put my palms out toward the flame. "It's warm." I shook my head. "How is any of this possible?"

"Hell if I know." He reached back, and another log appeared. He stoked the fire, staring at the sparks. "Jason and I haven't always been close, but he's a strong person. Good man."

I nodded, pulling my knees into my chest and wrapping my arms around them. "Yeah. I didn't want to like him at first. I thought he was just another doctor with a god complex, but he surprised me."

"I think you surprised him, too." Gareth finally smiled. It looked good on him. "As each of us found our mates, he still thought it was all bullshit. I wish I had been there when he touched you for the first time."

I thought back to that night and chuckled. "Actually, *I* touched *him*. He'd been in that damned fight club again. I'd never seen a doctor take such bad care of his hands before. I lifted his hand for a closer look and he freaked out. He jumped back so fast he almost fell over. I had no clue what had him so spooked."

Gareth chuckled. "Sometimes fate has a really twisted sense of humor."

"If something happens and I don't wake up, I need you to tell him something for me."

Gareth sobered, his shoulders tensing. "You're going to

be fine. Jason's a little insecure after Malcolm's death, and Nadya's and his dad's close calls made it worse, but there's no way he'll let you go."

"As I used to remind him, he's not god. He doesn't get to decide." Before Gareth could respond, I went on. "If I don't make it back, please tell him that the day you grabbed me from the hospital to help him with his father, I thought he was amazing. I didn't want it to show because I'd had my fill of being treated like shit by doctors. But...I just want him to know...that I'm so thankful fate brought us together." I blinked back a wave of tears and shook my head. "Love has always made me vulnerable, but his love...makes me strong."

Gareth nodded and poked at the fire again before meeting my eyes. "I remember that day with Wyatt on the floor, Jason fighting to get his heart beating again, and you got in there and took charge. You didn't cut Jason any slack. You were this tiny lady with a huge-ass spirit. You need that now. Dig deep and use it."

"You're right." I stood up. "What I told you before? Never mind." I grinned. "I'm going to tell him myself."

Gareth got to his feet, towering over me, and took my hand. "You are going to fit right in with our Pack." He squeezed my hand. "You're not going to stay in these shadows. There's a great life ahead of you." He smiled, nudging my shoulder. "Now tilt your head back, and let your wolf howl."

Chapter Thirty-One

JASON

"**M**y brow, Chloe."

She dabbed the towel on my forehead, drying the sweat before it could get in my eyes and keeping my hands sterile while I worked. Thankfully, Chloe had been a fast learner so far, and the blood didn't seem to faze her, either. I never would've guessed Gareth's godmother would be so calm under pressure.

The bullet had hit Kilani's pelvis, but after I plucked it out, I didn't find any bone fragments. We got lucky. She lost a lot of blood, but as long as we could keep her from getting any infections, she'd heal up just fine.

I cleaned up the wound, stitching her tendons, muscle, and finally closing her skin. Without having surgical staples, and my constant pauses to check her pulse, it took forever to hand stich everything. Not having her vitals displayed throughout the procedure was making me insane. I needed to be sure she was all right.

And then I heard something. I froze, frowning.

Chloe cleared her throat. "Need me to get something?"

I tilted my head. "You don't hear that?"

"Hear what?"

Then it came again, followed by laughter that warmed me from head to toe. It was Kilani. She was howling. My pulse raced, but nothing could wipe the smile from my face.

"Are you okay? Are we finished?"

"Better than okay." I winked at my surgical assistant. "Just about done." I tied off the final outer stitches. "Scissors."

She took the needle and handed me the scissors. I clipped the ends of the knot and gave them back. "So how do I wake her?"

Chloe set the tools down and raised a brow. "Any way you'd like."

"What about Gareth?"

"He'll walk back to himself after she leaves the dream world."

I stroked Kilani's hair back from her face. Her color was already improving. Good sign. I bent closer, my lips brushing hers. At first nothing happened. I started to pull back when her dark eyelashes fluttered and her beautiful eyes met mine.

"You did it."

I laughed and whispered, "*We* did it."

Nani came up beside me while Chloe slipped out the door. She kissed Kilani's forehead. "Welcome back, mynah bird."

"I saw our *honu*."

"Good." Nani patted her hand. "I asked our ancestors to

help you find the dream walker."

I sent everyone out while Kilani dozed in and out of consciousness. Her pulse and respiration were strong and steady. I cleaned up the exam room, bagging all the towels, surgical tools, and any other evidence that I'd performed a minor surgery.

Satisfied that her blood would never be discovered, I tied off the bag and sat down beside her bed. I took her hand, watching her chest rise and fall, and my vision blurred with tears. She was going to be fine.

Kilani opened her eyes and smiled. "Did I fall asleep?"

I started to smile. "You were shot a couple of hours ago. I think you've earned a nap."

She lifted her head. "Get a mirror. I want to see your handiwork."

"Don't get excited. I did the best I could with what I had to work with in here, but you're going to have a scar." I grabbed the mirror out of the drawer and tilted it so she could see the stiches.

She inspected the joined skin, running her finger around the edges. Finally she relaxed and smiled up at me. "I'm impressed." Kilani cocked her finger at me. "Come here."

I bent down, and she kissed me, her tongue brushing my lips. I opened to her, tasting her, drinking her in. My mate was alive, strong, and mine. When she rested her head back, her gaze roamed over my face.

"I love you."

I wanted to pull her into my arms and never let her go, but I also didn't want to hurt her, and her stitches would be tender.

"I love you, too." I caressed her cheek. "You probably

saved my life today, but it was too risky."

"I think the right answer is 'thank you.'" She raised a brow. "And you can't be upset with me for doing the exact same thing you were ready to do for me. I'm never going to be a shrinking violet hiding behind my man." Her eyes sparkled. "I'm too much wolf for that."

I rolled my eyes, kissing and loving her more than I ever realized I could. "I wouldn't want you any other way."

"Did you hear me howl?"

"I did." I chuckled. "How is that even possible?"

She shrugged. "I don't think Gareth even knows, but wherever we were, he built a fire and kept me talking. I got scared once and gave him a message to tell you if I didn't make it back, but he told me to stay with him and stay strong." She grinned. "And we howled."

"You didn't feel any pain while I was digging around in your hip?"

"Nope. I was someplace else."

"That's amazing." I straightened and inspected her wound one more time. "I'm going to write a prescription for antibiotics. Do you need a pain killer too?"

Kilani shifted and slowly sat up. She winced but shook her head. "Nah. I think I'll be fine with some Advil."

"Okay." I rolled the table to the side and turned to find her standing. Her hands were still holding onto the exam table on either side, but she was upright. "How's your hip feel?"

"Sore, but I'm not as light-headed as I thought I'd be."

"We do heal a little faster than humans." I moved in front of her, cupping her cheek. "Thank you for saving me. I'm not talking about the shooter." I searched her questioning eyes. "I was lost when you came into my life. You reminded me who I really am. You brought me home."

Her eyes welled with tears. "And you gave me one."

I held her in my arms, resting my head on hers, when someone knocked on the door. I sighed, loosening my hold on her. "Guess we can't hide out in here any longer."

She nodded and put her hand back on the exam table for balance while I went to the door.

Adam filled the doorway. "We need to talk."

"Give me a second first." I walked around him, straight to Gareth. Without bothering with the Pack greeting, I hugged the hell out of him.

He was stiff at first, but his hands finally gripped me in return. When I stepped back, he looked a little shell-shocked.

"Thanks for keeping Kilani safe while she was unconscious."

"Glad I could help." His gaze shifted to the door and back to me. "Is she going to be all right?"

"She'll have a scar, but she should be fine." I cleared my throat, struggling to keep my voice even. "She told me she got scared that she…wouldn't make it back. But you got her to stay." I shook my head. "I heard her howl."

Gareth pulled me into a tight embrace, surprising the shit out of me. Against my ear, he whispered, "She loves you. She wasn't going anywhere."

We separated, nodding, and I went back to the exam room.

Adam and Sasha were inside with Kilani.

"Close the door."

I frowned but did as Adam asked. "What's up?"

"Sorry to pull you right back into this, but Aren and Sasha went up to the top of the parking structure to grab Damian and…"

"He was gone?"

Adam nodded, glancing at Kilani. "I think you're safe for now." He met my eyes again. "But we should probably keep her grandmother with us until we're sure Nero has the message that Kilani is Pack now."

"How exactly are you going to do that?" I crossed my arms. "Damian is obviously not dead. What other message are they going to hear?"

"I'm meeting with Sebastian tonight."

"Aw hell, Adam." I dropped my hands in frustration. "He's probably the one who led us into that death trap today. He told us Damian would be waiting in Honolulu so we'd have our guard down in Reno. You can't trust that guy."

Sasha came a little closer. "I'd be the first to agree with you, Jason, but I only fired one shot. Damian was hit by two."

I frowned. "What?"

"Adam wanted him alive, so I took out Damian's leg." She paused. "Someone else hit him in the hand right before I squeezed the trigger."

"You think Sebastian shot his own brother? That's a little more than just being sure his mission wasn't a success."

"When I lived inside Nero, rumors floated around about Damian being jealous of Sebastian. Their father made no secret that Sebastian was his heir and his right hand. I'd say Damian took the assignment to impress their father. Since Sebastian failed to bring Lana in, he's no longer Severino's golden child."

I tilted my head, cracking some of the tension out of my neck. "So maybe he didn't know that Damian changed his plan."

"That's my best guess." She shrugged. "And by the

time he found out, he decided it was worth the risk to keep Damian from making a second shot and killing his target."

"You should meet him at my place. Keep Lana and the twins at the ranch. Have the meeting at my house."

Kilani took my hand, her fingers lacing with mine. "He's right, Adam."

My Alpha stared at Kilani. We all waited, and finally he nodded. "Okay. If your hunch is right that my kids are related to Severino, then we should keep them far away from Sebastian. I'll have the others stay at the ranch to protect Lana and the twins."

Adam stepped back, giving me a little breathing room, but his intensity didn't falter. "Sasha, tell Sebastian we're meeting tonight, seven p.m., at Jason's place."

Kilani insisted on resting on the couch instead of the bed. She wanted to see Sebastian. I suspected she might be hoping for a vision to make it clear whether he double-crossed us or not, but I didn't ask. Even if Sasha was right, and Sebastian shot his brother, he did it to save himself, not us. I had no illusions that he had any loyalty toward us.

I could have lost my mate today. And I wanted retribution. It was tough to think about anything else. It'd be easier if I could beat the crap out of someone, but I'd promised Kilani and myself that my nights in that boxing ring were over.

Staring out the window, I clenched my fists tight. Why weren't they here yet?

"Watching the driveway isn't going to make Adam get

here any faster."

"Yeah, I know." I crossed to her and sat in the chair. "Need any more Advil? How are you feeling?"

"I'm sore but not bad enough for a painkiller."

"You took the antibiotic?"

"Yes, Doctor." She smiled, and some of the agitation left my shoulders. She glanced at the door. "I think they're coming up the street."

Adam's Jeep. Aren and Sasha should've been right behind them, but it was impossible to hear Aren's Lotus engine over Cheney's roar. Back in high school when Adam restored his Jeep and named it, I never dreamed he'd keep it all these years.

I opened the front door. Adam, Aren, and Sasha came in and pulled up a couple more chairs. Adam sat next to Kilani. "How are you doing?"

"Much better than I was a few hours ago."

I patted Adam's shoulder. "Want something to drink?"

"Nah, I'm good."

Suddenly the room went silent. I never heard a car, but I smelled a jaguar. Adam stood, and I maneuvered myself in front of him to answer the door. Pack instincts to protect the Alpha were impossible to ignore.

I took a breath and turned the knob. Sebastian lowered his hand, no longer needing to knock.

"May I come in?"

I fought the urge to punch first and ask questions later, and stepped back to allow him in. Adam and Aren approached and I fell in on Adam's other side.

Sebastian raised a brow. "Perhaps someone can tell me the purpose of our meeting?"

Adam glanced at Kilani and back to the jaguar. "Kilani is Pack now. We need you to take the message back to Nero. Unless your father wants to deal with the entire Wolf Pack, he needs to call off the order to eliminate her."

"I am glad to see she survived."

"Why is that exactly?" Everyone turned my way. "Sasha hit Damian's leg, but someone fired a bullet into his hand. She thinks it was you. Why was it so important that Damian failed on his mission?"

Sebastian crossed his arms with a smug smirk. "It's none of your concern."

"Oh, but I think it is. I think Damian is Lana's fraternal twin. That would make you her half brother. Am I getting close?" His nostrils flared but he kept his expression blank. "And if you're Lana's brother, that makes your father, the head of goddamned Nero, related to my Alpha's twins."

Adam crossed his arms over his chest. "That makes it very much my concern."

Sebastian glared at me. "You idiot. You have no idea what you've done." He crossed the room into my personal space. "I never knew I had a sister. Until I dug into those breeding experiment records, I didn't know my father participated in his own breeding research. I thought Damian was a bastard son from a side relationship."

He ground his teeth. "I still haven't discovered why he's hiding that information, so I am allowing him to believe that his secret is still safe. If he discovers that we know, there will be nothing to stop him from collecting his grandchildren and experimenting on them like he did my brother."

All the air sucked from the room. Adam walked away, raking his hair back from his forehead. "*My* blood, *Pack* blood, is mixed with Nero." His cold gaze locked onto Sebastian. "Madeleine may be a jaguar, but she is still *Pack*. I will tear Severino limb from limb if he comes anywhere near my family."

Sebastian's voice lowered to a feral growl. "She is *my* family, too."

Adam rushed forward, but Aren caught him before he got to Sebastian. "You stay away from my family, you cold-blooded son of a bitch!"

Sebastian rolled his shoulders back, unfazed. "Where be these enemies? Capulet! Montague! See, what a scourge is laid upon your hate, That heaven finds means to kill your joys with love!"

"Spare me your poetic bullshit." Adam ripped free of Aren's grasp, but he didn't attack again.

"It's *Romeo and Juliet*, Wolf." He shook his head and glanced at me. "I realize I have many sins, but know this. All of you. Nothing is stronger than blood. And blood is what I protect."

"What happens when your 'blood' orders you to take Adam's children?"

Sebastian took a step in my direction. "That's why it was so important that my brother didn't complete this mission. After I failed to bring in Lana and Sasha, my father suspects my loyalties are in question. He killed Grace…"

He paused and cleared his throat. "To punish me. And when he gave the order to eliminate Grace's roommate, he called on Damian. Not me. If my brother had succeeded, I have no doubt my father would groom Damian for my position."

"So like I said, this had nothing to do with saving Kilani

and everything to do with saving your own ass."

"Of course." The corner of Sebastian's mouth curved into a half smile. "Would you expect anything different?" He went to the door and stopped, turning back to Adam. "If my brother gains access to the higher security documents, he *will* discover the breeding experiment. I'm trying to keep that knowledge from him because I protect my blood, which includes your mate and your children, but make no mistake, Wolf...I am not your friend or your ally."

He slammed the door behind him.

We stared at one another for a second. Adam shook his head. "This is all kinds of fucked up. This means we'll never be rid of Nero, we'll never be safe until Severino is dead." He sighed and met my eyes. "Thanks for pinning Sebastian down, Jason. We're safer knowing than not."

"How did Lana take it?"

"As well as could be expected. I think she was hoping it wouldn't be true."

"Remind her that she didn't get to pick her family." I clasped my hands together, resting my elbows on my knees. "Being related to Antonio Severino doesn't change who she is or who her children are."

When the others left, I shook my head. "This is going to be tough on Lana. She grew up in foster care. No one wants to finally find their parents and discover their dad is a sick, twisted, evil bastard."

"She deserves to know. If he comes calling, she needs to be ready."

I sent up a prayer that that day would never come.

Chapter Thirty-Two

"Well, I lost my job." I tossed my cell into my purse. "They filled my position while we were gone."

Jason placed two plates piled high with eggs and bacon on the bar and came around to take the stool next to me. "I have some news. too."

"Oh yeah?" I popped a forkful of fluffy scrambled eggs in my mouth.

"My nurse, Becky, is pregnant."

"Okay."

Even the bacon was perfect. How did I get so lucky to fall in love with a handsome, smart werewolf who could cook?

"She's a few months along now, carrying twins. She just got put on bed rest." He grinned at me.

I placed my fork on the edge of my plate and raised a

brow. "So you might need a nurse?"

"Exactly." He took a drink of orange juice. "But she'd have to be a forward thinker, you know, someone who can get what I need before I ask for it."

I smiled. "Hmmm."

"And she needs to be short…possibly Hawaiian… Her name should probably start with a *K*…"

I laughed and slid off the stool without a hint of pain. The antibiotics ran out a couple of days before, and other than some bruising and a little scar, no one would've guessed I'd been shot two weeks ago.

"Well, I'll keep my ear to the ground while I'm job hunting. Maybe I'll find your perfect nurse." I walked toward the bedroom, swaying my hips in my baggy sweatpants.

He raced up behind me and swept me off my feet, carrying me to the bed. I laughed, screaming as we wrestled on the mattress. Finally, I let him pin me underneath him. "So are you trying to ask me to work for you?"

"*With* me." He kissed my lips. "Will you come work with me?"

I pretended to give it some thought. "Well, I am available…Yes."

He kissed me in earnest then and let me roll him over. Straddling his waist, I pulled my sweatshirt over my head and tossed it across the room. He ran his hand up my legs as he stared at me with hungry eyes. "I love you."

I laid over him, taking his lower lip in my teeth. "You better."

He laughed and rolled me under him again. "If we didn't have the twins' birthday party today, I'd be sure you never left this room."

Since my injury healed, we had lots of catching up to do. Noisy catching up. I glanced at the digital clock by the bed. "Maybe if we're fast."

Jason got up, taking me with him. "I have a better idea."

I wrapped my arms around his neck. "Oh yeah?"

He carried me into the bathroom and turned on the shower. "Plus, we'll be conserving water."

We were only fifteen minutes late to Malcolm and Madeleine's party at the ranch. These twins were like no other one-year-olds I'd ever seen. Not only were they running, but they spoke in sentences. Jason told me it had something to do with the shorter gestational period. Apparently women in the Pack gave birth to full-term babies after four months, instead of nine, and the babies matured at a rapid rate until they leveled out just before kindergarten.

Malcolm scrambled ahead of his sister and tackled Jason around the knees. "Jason."

"Hey, buddy." Jason swooped him up, eliciting a bout of giggles. "Happy birthday."

Madeleine stopped in front of me and stared up. "You're Jason's."

He slid his free arm around my waist. "Madeleine, this is Kilani. She's my mate."

The little girl held her hands up to me in the universal symbol of pick-me-up-now. I lifted her into my arms and she grinned. "You're pretty."

"Thank you." I laughed. "You're beautiful, too."

Madeleine poked her brother. "We can't tell her."

Malcolm shook his head. "Nope, because it's a secret."

"A secret?" I glanced up at Jason. "Do you know about this secret?"

He raised a brow and shrugged. "What secret?"

I nudged him. "You're a horrible liar."

I set Madeleine down, and Nadya came around the corner. Her eyes lit up as she pulled me into a hug. "You look great. How are you feeling?"

"Much better. Thanks. So are you in on this secret?"

Nadya shot a playful look at the little ones. "Did you two tell her?"

Jason put Malcolm down beside his sister as they both shook their heads. "No, because it's secret and that means don't tell."

They spun around and raced away before I could question them further. I turned to Nadya again. "Has my grandmother gotten here yet?"

She nodded. "Yeah, she and Chloe are out back. They chased Adam away from the barbecue grill."

I took Jason's hand. "We should go see if they need any help."

"I think we both know the answer."

"True, but we can at least offer."

Nadya gave Jason a quick hug. "Great to see you both."

She followed after the twins, and I started to go, but Jason tugged me back to him. I stared up into his eyes. "Is everything okay?"

"Yeah. I just wanted one more minute to have you to myself." He kissed me long and slow. I savored every caress of his lips until my whole body warmed.

He rested his forehead on mine and I smiled. "What was

that for?"

"Because I love you." There was a sparkle in his eyes as he straightened to his full height and took my hand. "Come on."

We walked through the house, waving hello to Lana and Sasha in the kitchen chopping up condiments for the burgers. Live music played in the back by the barn. This Wolf Pack went all-out for a first birthday party.

I stopped, blinking as the scene changed and a flash of the future took over. Wyatt, Jason's dad, stood with him, they smiled, lifting their glasses. Where was I? I struggled to catch the details. I was dancing. With Jared. Where?

And it was gone.

Jason sighed beside me. "Tough to surprise a psychic."

"What?" I looked up at him. "How did you know I had a vision?"

"You blink hard when they come on."

"I do?"

He nodded and squeezed my hand. "I pay attention."

"Not bad for a doctor."

He chuckled. "So is the cat out of the bag?"

I shrugged. "If the big surprise is me dancing with your brother."

"What?" He raised his eyebrows. "Should I be jealous?"

I elbowed him, shaking my head. We went out back and my breath caught. Beside the three-tiered birthday cake and banner was another banner that read, *Welcome to the Pack, Kilani.*

Logan stopped strumming his guitar and leaned into the microphone. "Can we get everyone out here?"

Jason reached into the pocket of his jeans and withdrew

a gray velvet box. My heart leapt into my throat.

"Kilani, everybody here can testify that I never believed in mates. I thought it was impossible for fate to choose your destined soul mate. But I'm here today in front of my family and my Pack to say, I was dead wrong. And I am the luckiest man on earth that fate chose you for me." He opened the box. "Welcome to the Pack."

It still caught me off guard sometimes to be publically acknowledged as his mate. I hoped it would wear off eventually. Those days of being rejected were behind me, but some days my new life with Jason still seemed like a dream.

Inside the box was a silver bracelet. Each square alternated with a carving of my *honu* and a wolf. Perfect. Just like my mate.

Tears blurred my vision as I stared into his eyes. "It's beautiful."

He took it out and fastened it around my wrist. "I'm glad you like it because"—he pulled another gray box from his other pocket with a twinkle in his eyes—"it matches this."

He opened the box and a ring sparkled up at me. The band of the ring matched the bracelet with my *honu* on one side of the diamond and a wolf on the other.

"Kilani, will you marry me?"

I resisted the urge to pinch myself. Emotion choked my throat as I scanned the crowd and found my grandmother's eyes. She wiped a tear from her cheek and smiled at me.

I looked up at Jason and nodded. "Yes. I would love to marry you."

Howls erupted as Jason pulled me into his arms. He whispered against my lips, "Surprised?"

"Very." I laughed, nodding and kissing him. "Tough to

surprise a psychic."

"So I've heard." Jason took my hand, sliding the diamond ring onto my finger. "I love you."

"I love you, too."

His parents stood together holding hands, just as I'd seen in my vision at their house. His father met my eyes and came toward me, without a cane, without help, and embraced me. Tears sprang to my eyes all over again as I clung to him.

He held me tight and whispered, "Welcome to the family."

I never knew my father, no name was listed on my birth certificate, but I couldn't imagine a better man than the one holding me and offering me a place in his family.

He let me go and smiled. "I hope you'll grow to call me Dad."

I wiped my eyes and rose on my toes to kiss his cheek. "I've never had a dad."

"You do now."

Sarah came up beside us. "And another mom, too, if you can stand it."

I laughed and embraced her. "Thanks so much for opening your family to me."

The rest of the Pack descended on us, overwhelming me with love and acceptance that I never expected. After burgers and chips, and cake and ice cream, Logan lifted up his acoustic guitar again. He had a band, but they didn't know he was a werewolf, so he kept them away from Pack events.

Jared approached and offered his hand. "Could I have a dance with my new sister?"

I winked at Jason and took his brother's hand. "I'd love to."

As we danced, Jared grinned. "I can honestly say I have

never seen my brother so happy."

"He makes me pretty happy, too."

He chuckled and dipped me. "He'd better."

Jason walked toward us. "Speak of the devil." He tapped Jared's shoulder. "Can I cut in?"

"You hate dancing." Jared raised a brow.

Jason's eyes met mine. "I was just missing the right partner."

"Thanks for the dance…sis." Jared kissed my cheek.

Jason spun me into his arms. "This isn't the last surprise."

"No?"

He shook his head. As the song ended, Jared got up, holding a picture with a drape over it. I glanced up at Jason. "You *wanted* Jared to dance with me. You were distracting me so you could get that."

"I'm just glad your vision wasn't of this part of the surprise." He took the draped square from his brother. "You inspired me."

He tugged the sheet off to reveal a charcoal drawing of me and my grandmother sitting at the pond on Maui with our feet in the water.

"This is what you've been working on in the garage while I was recuperating on the couch."

He nodded, and I focused on the art again. In our downcast eyes, he'd somehow captured every facet of my strained but healing relationship with my grandmother. And in the reflection of the pond, in the subtle ripples of the water, my *honu* stared back at me. The longer I examined Jason's work, I realized there were wolves hidden in the ripples too. A Pack.

My Pack.

I gazed up at my mate, my lover, my friend, and struggled

for words. He'd given me the one gift that could never be bought or bartered for.

Ohana was finally mine. Family.

"I don't know what to say."

His lips curved into a crooked smile. "Maybe you should just kiss me."

So I did.

Acknowledgments

Thanks to the entire Entangled Publishing team for all your support for the Moon series! It takes a village, and I feel lucky to be a part of this one! Thanks to my fabulous editor and publisher, Liz Pelletier, for helping me polish this book, and to my amazing beta readers, Denise Fluhr and Heather Cox, for all your feedback along the way!

And to my fantastic agent, Laurie McLean, thanks for your support and guidance. You always make me feel like anything is possible. You're the best!

Big thanks to my Night Angels Street Team. Your love for the Wolf Pack inspires me, and your support for my books means the world to me.

And finally, thanks to my wonderful husband, Ken, who listens to me talk about characters and ideas and believes in me through thick and thin.

You're my hero!

About the Author

Lisa Kessler is an Amazon Best Selling and award winning author of dark paranormal fiction. Her debut novel, Night Walker, won a San Diego Book Award for Best Published Fantasy-Sci-fi-Horror as well as the Romance Through the Ages Award for Best Paranormal and Best First Book. Her short stories have been published in print anthologies and magazines, and her vampire story, Immortal Beloved, was a finalist for a Bram Stoker award. When she's not writing, Lisa is a professional vocalist, performing with the San Diego Opera as well as other musical theater companies in San Diego. You can learn more at http://Lisa-Kessler.com She loves hearing from readers - LdyDisney@aol.com

Discover the **Moon** *series...*

MOONLIGHT

HUNTER'S MOON

BLOOD MOON

Discover the **Night** *series...*

NIGHT WALKER

NIGHT THIEF

NIGHT DEMON

NIGHT CHILD

Also by Lisa Kessler

BEG ME TO SLAY